OVER THE EDGE

EDGE OPS
BOOK 1

TONYA BURROWS

CONTENT WARNING

Over the Edge contains mature themes and situations that may be distressing to some readers. This includes a brief on-page sexual assault involving unwanted physical contact while the character is helpless. The scene appears at the very end of Chapter 24.

The scene is not graphic, but it is intentionally upsetting and portrayed with emotional realism.

If that's something you need to avoid right now, I completely understand. Please take care of yourself—you matter more than any story.

-Tonya

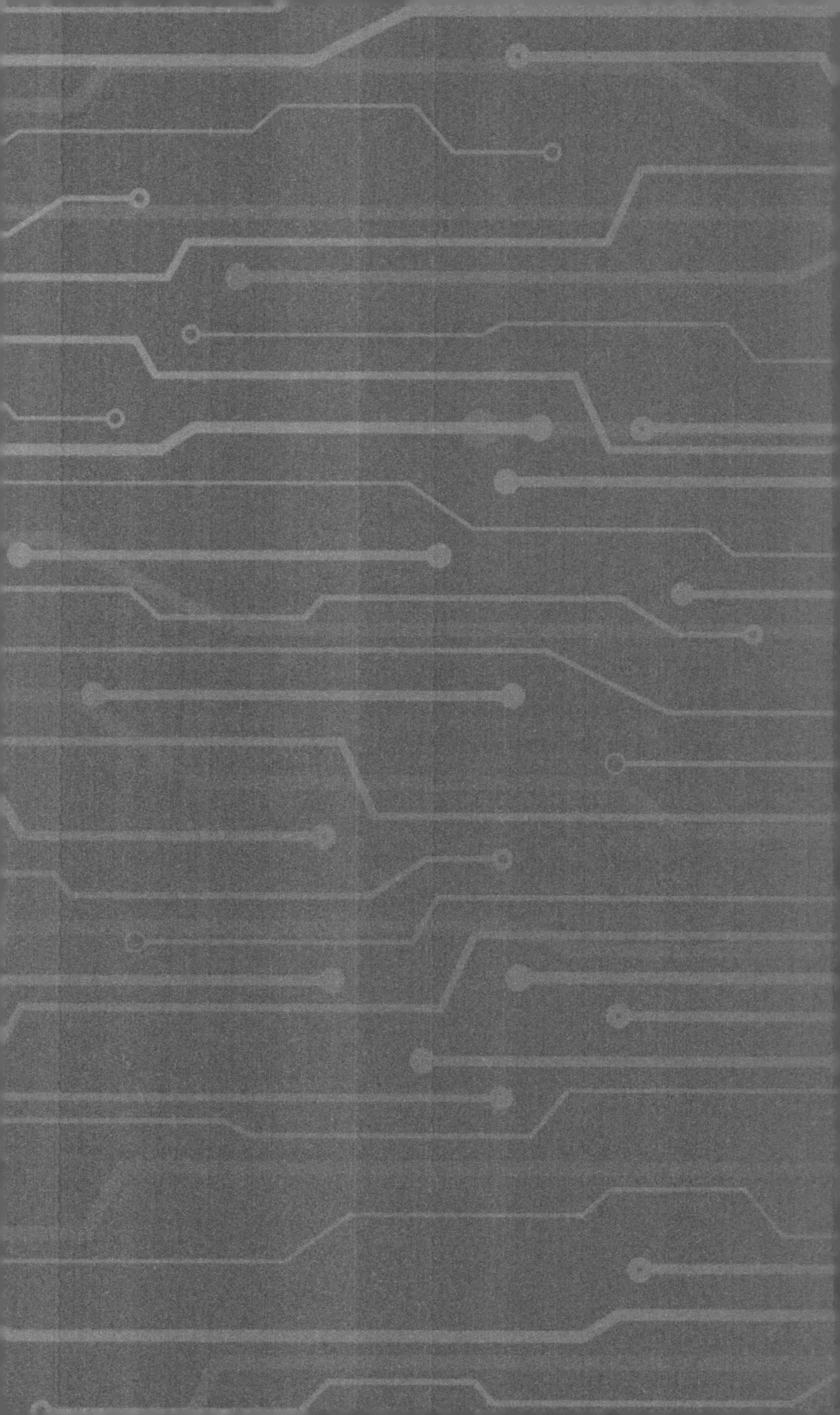

CHAPTER 1
LYRIC

By the end of my first day on the job, there were three things I knew for certain.

One: Monte Carlo was overrated. It was glossy but superficial, and the casino was no different from any other in the world.

Two: I looked damned good in my dress. The midnight blue silk clung in all the right places. The plunging neckline and the slit to my thigh showed just enough skin to be interesting without being scandalous. I turned heads as I moved through the hotel lobby. Or, rather, *Elisa Deveraux* did. And while I generally preferred to fade into the background, Elisa loved the spotlight.

And three: Flynn Shepherd was the kind of man who made you want to commit murder. Preferably with something blunt and heavy. Arrogant, overconfident, and too damn attractive for anyone's good, least of all mine.

But I'll come back to him.

My earpiece crackled with static.

"Siren, your target's shifting positions," Kate Garner said. Also known as Lil Bit or Bitty, she served as the team's overwatch specialist, responsible for communications and cybersecurity. She was the cool, calming voice in our ears when the shit hit the fan. "I repeat, Broker is moving to the bar. You're clear to engage."

I didn't reply, but adjusted my trajectory, allowing my hips to sway with deliberate sensuality as I crossed into Nico Moreau's line of sight. As I moved into position, I mentally reeled through everything I knew about him. Arms dealer. Black market broker. He didn't suffer fools and would put a bullet in my head if he caught even a whisper of my true purpose.

The art of the honey trap was something my predecessor had apparently mastered.

The bitterness in that thought gave me pause. Was it wrong to be jealous of a dead woman?

When I accepted this job in the wake of Maya's death a month ago, I knew the comparisons between us were inevitable. And the team had every right to be wary of me as the unproven outsider. But I hadn't expected those comparisons to haunt every briefing, to linger in every sidelong glance. To them—especially team leader Ethan Voss—I wasn't Lyric Renard, one of the best undercover assets the CIA had ever deployed, with a knack for disappearing into identities and reappearing with secrets no one else could get. Never mind that I'd run five solo extractions, walked out of war zones in heels and blood, and embedded three aliases so deep they'd landed on my own agency's watchlists.

My resume was solid. My qualifications for this op were the best Edge Ops was going to get on such short notice.

But none of it mattered to a team still grieving the woman I'd replaced.

A woman they all loved and lost.

A woman I'd never even met.

A woman I had no hope in hell of living up to.

Amaya Thomas.

"Champagne, please," I said to the bartender, positioning myself three stools away from Moreau. Close enough to be noticed, far enough to avoid looking like I was baiting him.

Even though I absolutely was.

Hook.

Line.

As I waited, I sensed rather than saw him approach my left side. The scent hit me first. Expensive cologne with notes of sandalwood and amber.

"Have a drink with me," a voice said, smooth as aged cognac. He didn't wait for my answer and told the bartender, "Perrier-Jouët Belle Epoque for the lady and another Macallan 25 for me."

And sinker.

Gotcha, asshole.

My lips curved into a small smile, but I waited several long seconds before I shifted to face him.

Up close, he radiated a threat the dossier hadn't captured. He was handsome in that polished, European way. Olive skin, silver-streaked dark hair swept back from sharp features, and eyes so intensely blue they seemed artificial.

"I haven't accepted your offer yet, monsieur," I said, my accent flawlessly Parisian.

Moreau's smile was indulgent. "Elisa Deveraux doesn't strike me as a woman who turns down the finer things in life."

I wasn't surprised Moreau already knew my name. Maya had established an initial contact before her death, and I'd greased those wheels a bit more before arriving in Monaco, using one of my other aliases to seed my new cover identity through the right channels. If Moreau hadn't researched me before I walked in, I'd have been insulted.

"You have me at a disadvantage." I accepted the champagne, letting my fingertips brush against his as I took the flute. "You know my name, but I don't believe I know yours."

"Nico Moreau." He extended his hand, and when I placed mine in it, he turned my hand over and pressed his lips to my wrist just above my pulse point. The touch lingered an uncomfortable moment too long, his eyes holding mine.

I wondered if he could feel my skin crawling.

"Ah, Monsieur Moreau! So lovely to finally make your acquaintance in person."

"The pleasure is mine, Mademoiselle Deveraux. I've been looking forward to our meeting. But I must say, you're not what I expected."

I subtly pulled my hand from his, lifted my glass to

my lips, and took a delicate sip of the cool, crisp champagne.

Wow. No wonder this stuff was $2,000 for a bottle. It was exquisite. "Oh? And what exactly were you expecting?"

"Most of the people who take an interest in my auctions are older men with too much money and too little conscience. You're..." His eyes drifted to my breasts before returning to my face. "Refreshing. You've piqued my curiosity. Few women in your position seek military-grade technology. What possessed you to liquidate your family's art collection and invest in emerging weapons technology?"

I took another sip of champagne. "Business is business, Monsieur Moreau. Art appreciates slowly. Technology—the right technology—yields immediate returns, as you're very aware of."

His eyes glinted with approval. "And what returns are you looking for, exactly? You're already quite wealthy."

"Security."

He didn't respond right away, just studied me with an intensity meant to make me uneasy. But I was ready for it and held his gaze. He'd built an empire by reading people, so I couldn't flinch, couldn't let him see anything more than exactly what I wanted him to see.

"Security," he repeated, tasting the word like it was a sip of the very expensive champagne in my glass. "That's rarely a problem for someone born with your advantages."

In my ear, Kate said, "His security chief is running another background check on you right now."

I smiled. "With the current state of the world, no one is safe, Monsieur Moreau." I ran a finger along the rim of my glass. "Not even those born with so-called advantages. Money can only protect you so far. What I need is something more... substantial."

I turned slightly, giving him my profile as I surveyed the casino floor. While he admired the line of my neck, I watched his security. Three men, all with the unmistakable bulge of shoulder holsters beneath their jackets.

Moreau said nothing for several minutes. He just watched me like a cat watches a mouse, and I let him. Finally, he threw back his scotch and stood. "Perhaps we could continue this conversation somewhere more private."

"Background check complete," Kate's voice came through. "You're clean. He's taking the bait."

I raised an eyebrow. "We've only just met, Monsieur."

"Let's not play coy. You flew to Monte Carlo specifically to meet me." His certainty was absolute, his tone leaving no room for denial. "If security's the issue, my suite is discreet, private, and very well protected. And the view of the harbor is spectacular. We can discuss your... investment opportunities there."

"You're very confident."

"Confidence is the currency of our world, Ms. Deveraux." He signaled for the check. "That, and knowing which risks are worth taking."

I allowed a moment of consideration to pass as he

signed for our drinks, then nodded once. "I'm intrigued enough to hear what you have to offer."

Moreau stood, buttoning his jacket before offering his arm. I slipped my hand through it, though I would've rather stuck my hand in a blender. Everything about this man repulsed me, and it took every ounce of training to maintain the mask of Elisa Deveraux, intrigued potential buyer, rather than Lyric Renard, undercover operative fighting the urge to snap his arm.

"Be careful," Kate warned in my ear. "His suite will have countermeasures. We're blind once you're inside."

We walked through the casino to the bank of private elevators. He released my arm to press the button, but as the doors opened, his hand dropped to the small of my back, guiding me inside. I allowed the contact, using it to my advantage. The closer he kept me, the easier it would be to place the tracker.

The elevator ride to the penthouse level was silent. Moreau's security detail—one man, broad-shouldered with a scar bisecting his left eyebrow—stood at parade rest in the corner, his gaze fixed on the middle distance but missing nothing.

"Do you have the merchandise here?" I asked.

Moreau's eyes flickered to me, his lips curving into a thin smile. "I never bring merchandise to initial meetings."

"I hope you have something to show me other than the view from your suite, as I have the same view from mine."

He let the silence stretch for a beat too long. "I assure you, Ms. Deveraux, you won't be disappointed."

Oh, gag me. If he planned to unzip more than a drone case, I'd have him on the ground before he could blink. Stiletto to the carotid, mission be damned.

Well, probably not. But the fantasy got me through the elevator ride.

As the doors slid open, he stepped aside, gesturing with a flourish. "I don't usually conduct business from my personal quarters." His voice was smooth, his smile almost flirtatious, but his eyes were cold. "Consider this an exception."

"I'm flattered." I let a touch of genuine Lyric crack through Elisa's silk. Just enough steel to let him know he didn't intimidate me.

The suite we stepped into was more palace than penthouse. The Diamond Suite Princess Grace—named for royalty and priced at an outrageous fifty thousand euros a night—boasted a private terrace and infinity pool with panoramic views of the Mediterranean, a dining room that could seat twelve, and rare artwork handpicked by the royal family. It was elegance, weaponized.

Floor-to-ceiling windows framed the terrace and the ink-black sea beyond, yachts glittering like scattered stars across the water.

In Moreau's case, I was sure he had.

A man waited by the elevator, stone-faced and coiled for action. Ex-military. Special forces, by the way he tracked me without moving. He nodded once.

"Everything is prepared, sir," he said in crisp, accented English.

"Thank you, Vidal. We're not to be disturbed."

I kept my smile in place, but the knot in my gut pulled tighter at the thought of being alone with him. This man had killed at least three women that I knew of, and probably a lot more that nobody knew of.

And now I was shut in his suite with him, with no extraction plan and no backup.

But that was the job.

And I was damn good at this job.

"Drink?" Moreau peeled away from me with that languid confidence, crossing the suite to a marble-topped sideboard that gleamed beneath the warm spill of chandelier light. "There's champagne, wine, brandy." He held up a Baccarat decanter. "Cognac?"

"Whatever you're having would be lovely."

"Please, sit. Make yourself comfortable." He gestured to the plush sofas in a soft dove-gray. The gold-veined table between them was laid out with fruit, cigars, and a chilled bottle of champagne like seduction was just another service offered with the suite. There was also a ruggedized black case that looked out of place among the elegant decor.

It wasn't Sentinel. It was too small. But maybe it was a prototype or something similar. Either way, I had a pretty good feeling it had come from wherever Moreau was storing his goods for the auction this weekend.

While Moreau's back was turned, I slipped my hand into my clutch, fingers closing around the micro-sensor tracker. It was no larger than a grain of sand, but powerful enough to transmit through concrete and steel. All I had to do was plant the tracker, get out alive, and let the team follow the signal to wherever

Moreau was keeping the Sentinel Mk-IV drone system.

Moreau turned back, a crystal snifter extended.

Dammit. I was too slow.

I let the tracker fall into my clutch and accepted the drink with a smile, our fingers brushing.

"To new ventures," he said, raising his glass.

"To new ventures." I clinked my glass against his and took a small sip, tasting notes of vanilla and oak, rich and complex. The cognac would've been heavenly under different circumstances.

I settled onto the sofa, crossing my legs slowly. The slit in my dress parted to reveal a calculated glimpse of thigh. Moreau's eyes followed the movement before he took the seat across from me.

"So." He swirled his cognac, studying the amber liquid as if it held secrets. "You're interested in drone technology."

"I'm interested in power," I corrected, maintaining eye contact as I took another sip. "Power equals security. These drones are simply a means to that end."

His smile sharpened with approval. "A refreshingly honest answer."

"I find honesty expedites business." I leaned forward, dropping my voice. "The Sentinel system. I've heard whispers that it's... revolutionary."

Moreau chuckled. "You have excellent sources, Ms. Deveraux. Most people don't even know it exists."

"I'm not most people." I gestured at the black case on the table. "And is that a preview of what you're offering?"

His gaze flickered to the case, then back to me. "Merely a demonstration model. A taste of what the Sentinel system can achieve."

"May I?" I reached for the case, but Moreau's hand shot out, capturing my wrist. His grip was too tight, but I refused to give him the satisfaction of seeing me wince.

"Patience, Ms. Deveraux." His thumb traced slow circles against my pulse point. "First, I need to be certain you're a serious buyer."

"I didn't come all this way for a cocktail and conversation." I eased my wrist from his grip. "My resources are considerable, as I'm sure your research has confirmed. I'm prepared to offer five million euros as a down payment, which can be immediately transferred to any account of your choice. Consider it a demonstration of my commitment."

"Money is only part of the equation." Moreau leaned back, studying me with those predator's eyes. "I need to know your intentions."

I laughed softly. "I thought arms dealers preferred not to ask such questions."

"Most don't." He moved to sit next to me, too close, our shoulders brushing. His fingers trailed over my shoulder. "But, as I said downstairs, you're not like most of my clientele. I'm intrigued by you, Ms. Deveraux. A beautiful woman with seemingly unlimited resources suddenly appearing in my world with an interest in my most coveted technology?" He tilted his head slightly. "One might wonder if there's more to your story."

I maintained my composure, letting a hint of impatience cross my features. "I assure you, my story is quite straightforward. I have wealth that needs protecting in a world that is growing increasingly hostile toward people of our… social class."

"Ah, the pitchforks are coming for the wealthy," Moreau said with a knowing smile. "Is that what keeps you up at night?"

"What keeps me up is the knowledge that wealth alone isn't enough anymore. The rules are changing. Political winds shift overnight. What was protected yesterday is vulnerable today." I gestured toward the case. "I need capabilities, not just capital."

His expression shifted, a hint of respect flickering across his features. He reached for the case, fingers hovering over the latches. "The Sentinel system represents the next evolution in targeted operations. Undetectable by conventional radar. Facial recognition at five thousand feet. Payloads customized to mission parameters."

The lid swung open, revealing a velvet-lined interior. A miniature drone nestled inside, no larger than a hummingbird. Its metallic surface gleamed with an iridescent sheen under the chandelier light.

"Beautiful, isn't it?" Moreau's voice dropped to a near whisper as he lifted the tiny device. "Imagine targeting a single individual in a crowd of thousands. No collateral damage. No witnesses. No second chances. One of these is deadly. But a swarm…" His eyes gleamed in a way that made my skin crawl. "A swarm can take down governments."

My pulse quickened. This wasn't just a technological marvel. It was a nightmare made of metal and circuitry. The tiny device looked innocuous, but could reshape global politics from the shadows.

No wonder Edge refused to abort this op, even after the operative who built this cover died.

I leaned closer, making sure my neckline gaped open, giving him a view of my lacy bra. I didn't have to fake my interest. "How many in a swarm?"

"The standard deployment is twelve, but the system can coordinate up to fifty individual units simultaneously." Moreau's eyes lingered on my chest. "Each one capable of delivering a customized payload: toxins, explosives, or..." he paused for effect, "...something more elegant."

"Such as?"

"Imagine a microfilament thinner than a human hair, but stronger than titanium. One that slices through carotid arteries with surgical precision. Death appears natural. A stroke, perhaps. Or a heart attack." His fingers brushed my neck, following the path of my carotid artery. "No one would ever know."

I suppressed a shudder, maintaining my façade of fascination. "And the range?"

"Twenty kilometers, with complete autonomy. Once programmed, they don't need remote operation. They find their target, execute, and return." He placed the miniature drone back in its case. "Or self-destruct, leaving no evidence."

"May I hold it?" I made my voice breathless, as if all this talk of death and destruction was turning me on.

"Another time," he said, closing the case with a decisive click. "This is merely a prototype. The full system is... elsewhere."

Perfect. I moistened my lips, deliberately drawing his attention. His eyes tracked the movement, as I'd intended.

"You've gone to considerable trouble to meet me, Ms. Deveraux," he said, moving closer. His thigh pressed against mine, warm through the thin silk of my dress. "I wonder what else you might be willing to do to secure this technology."

I let my lashes lower, a coy smile playing at my lips. "I'm willing to negotiate, of course."

His hand settled on my knee, fingers sliding beneath the slit of my dress. "The auction isn't until Saturday. Perhaps we could spend the intervening days... getting to know each other better."

"Perhaps." I leaned toward him slightly, even as I fought the urge to break his fingers one by one. "But first, I need to see the merchandise."

"Then would you be interested in a private showing on my yacht tonight?"

That wasn't part of the plan. I was supposed to plant the tracker now, but if the real goods were on the yacht...

I opened my mouth to reply—

The terrace doors exploded inward.

CHAPTER 2
LYRIC

I froze, hand hovering over the weapon strapped to my thigh, pulse spiking as a man strode into the room like he had every right to be there. My first thought: security. My second: assassin. My third?

Damn, he was hot.

Not ideal, brain. Not the time.

"Ms. Deveraux," he said. "I don't appreciate you disappearing on me."

Moreau's guards materialized from everywhere like shadows, but the stranger wasn't intimidated. His focus was entirely on me. Like he knew me. The real me.

But that was impossible.

I'd never seen him before in my life. He was tall and heavily muscled, with scruffy dark hair and eyes the color of the cognac I hadn't touched. He carried himself like a soldier and wore a well-tailored suit designed to disappear.

Moreau turned to me. "You know this man?"

Nope. But I had my suspicions that Ethan Voss was behind this.

I rose smoothly, setting my untouched glass aside and adopting the irritated expression of an heiress whose plans had been interrupted. "My head of security, apparently under the misapprehension that I need constant supervision. I believe I made it clear I didn't require your services this evening, Mr. Mercer."

It was the first name that came to mind. Mr. Mercer had been my piano teacher as a kid, but this guy definitely didn't look like him.

A piano teacher wouldn't have the lazy, predatory confidence of a man who knew exactly how much space he took up and dared anyone to challenge him for it.

A piano teacher wouldn't have a body built for violence.

And a piano teacher certainly wouldn't make heat curl low in my stomach.

Oh, perfect.

Now my libido decides to come out of hibernation and take notice of a guy?

Annoying. So annoying.

I stared at the man. *Don't ruin this. Just go with it. Please, for the love of God, play along.*

The stranger moved further into the room. "Your father pays me to disagree with you when necessary, Ms. Deveraux."

"*This* man is your head of security?" Moreau waved off his guards and closed the case containing the drone schematics. He passed it to Vidal, who carried it into the other room and put it into a lockbox.

Goddammit.

Now I'd have to find something else to put the tracker on.

Raising my chin, I pinned my supposed head of security with a withering glare. "The man is a hammer in search of a nail. My father insisted after the Dubai incident. I didn't think it was necessary, but... here we are."

A beat of silence.

Then two.

Dubai wasn't in my dossier. It was a lie, but hopefully one delivered with enough conviction that Moreau would believe it.

Moreau's eyes flicked to the intruder, then to me, then back to the intruder. "I see. How did you get past my guards?"

"I'm paid not to be seen," the man—'Mercer'—drawled, his voice a rough rasp that did absolutely nothing to help my libido situation. "And your guards are better at looking intimidating than actually securing the perimeter."

Moreau did not like that. A frown tried to wrinkle his brow, but Botox kept it smooth, so instead he just looked constipated.

"Mr. Mercer is excellent at his job," I added, "but terrible at understanding boundaries."

The man's mouth curved in a quicksilver smile. "Boundaries are luxuries for people who don't have enemies, Ms. Deveraux."

He stepped closer, and I caught his scent. It wasn't expensive cologne like Moreau wore. It was soap and leather and clean sweat and so very… male. His hand came to rest at the small of my back. The touch was warm through the silk of my gown, just as proprietary as Moreau's had been, but it didn't give me the same chill.

"You need to come with me, ma'am."

I opened my mouth to protest, and his fingers pressed against my spine. A warning? A signal? I couldn't be sure.

"Now."

The look in his amber eyes held me frozen, a message there I couldn't quite decipher but understood was important.

I took a moment to pull myself together, making sure my Elisa persona was firmly in place before facing Moreau again.

"Perhaps we can continue our discussion tomorrow," I suggested, allowing regret to color my tone. "I find your proposal intriguing."

Moreau studied us both for a long, uncomfortable time before inclining his head. "Of course. I have a private cabana at the beach club. Join me for a light lunch? One o'clock."

"Sounds lovely," I said, offering my hand.

Instead of shaking it, Moreau pressed his lips to my knuckles, lingering a few seconds longer than necessary. "Until tomorrow, then." When he straightened, his eyes were on my supposed head of security instead of me. "Mr. Mercer, I trust you'll take good care of our mutual interest."

The stranger's fingers flexed against my spine.

"That's what I'm paid for." He guided me toward the elevator with firm pressure on my back. Every instinct screamed to stay and plant the tracker, but Moreau's suspicions were already aroused. One wrong move could blow my cover entirely.

"A pleasure meeting you, Ms. Deveraux," Moreau called after us. "I look forward to continuing our negotiations."

The threat beneath his words was unmistakable. He'd be investigating "the Dubai incident" before our lunch. I had less than twenty-four hours to patch the hole in my cover story.

The elevator ride down to the lobby was excruciating.

The moment the doors slid shut, I stepped out of the stranger's reach. Tension knotted the muscles in my neck and shoulders, and a headache throbbed in warning at the back of my skull. I wanted answers, but didn't dare speak yet. Cameras were watching, and Moreau would absolutely comb through every frame. I had to stay in character. Cool. Controlled. Unbothered.

Meanwhile, the so-called bodyguard beside me stood with infuriating ease, his hands folded in front of him like he hadn't just steamrolled into my op and detonated weeks of prep work with a single dramatic entrance. His face was a mask of professional indifference, but there was something in his eyes, wild and sharp-edged.

I hated how aware of him I was.

When the elevator dinged, he moved again, his hand returning possessively to the small of my back like it belonged there, infuriatingly warm through the silk of my dress. I wanted to elbow him in the ribs. I also wanted to lean back into that touch.

God, was I so starved for sex that this was all it took? Sure, it had been almost a year since I'd seen any action beyond my vibrator, but come on. One attractive guy with boundary issues, and my body was suddenly all in?

Pathetic.

Focus, Lyric.

We stepped into the gilded lobby of the Hôtel de Paris Monte-Carlo, and by tacit agreement, we headed outside. I couldn't risk saying the things I needed to say in the hotel. I hadn't finished checking my suite for bugs, and I didn't dare risk anyone eavesdropping.

The night was balmy, kissed with the salt-sweet breeze off the sea and perfumed by manicured gardens that wrapped around the square in lush, deliberate excess.

We passed the famous fountain in front of the hotel, its marble nymphs frozen mid-dance beneath a spray of sparkling water. Lights shimmered across the surface like scattered diamonds. Tourists lingered near the edges, taking selfies, laughing too loudly. A Bugatti idled nearby, a woman in couture climbing out with a laugh like broken glass. Monte Carlo at midnight was all pageantry.

My "bodyguard" didn't say a word as we moved down the steps and left the façade behind. I could feel his gaze even though he stayed a step behind and to the right, exactly where a bodyguard should be. But that wasn't what he was, and we both knew it.

We turned down a quiet side street where boutique storefronts were shuttered and cobblestones replaced the polished marble. The buzz of the square faded, replaced by the softer sound of our footsteps and the distant echo of a Vespa engine somewhere near the harbor.

The air here was cooler, realer, and I felt like I could finally breathe again. But I couldn't enjoy it.

I let the cork pop on my fury, and I dropped Elisa's accent entirely. My real voice cracked through the night like a whip as I spun on him. "Who the hell are you?"

He grinned. It was a slow, lazy pull of his lips that was absolutely nothing like Moreau's practiced smile. This was genuine amusement, like he found my anger entertaining. Like I was a kitten hissing at a wolf.

Yeah, well. This kitten had claws, and she was dying for a chance to use them.

"Flynn Shepherd," he said, extending his hand like we were meeting at a damn cocktail party. "But the team calls me Outlaw."

Outlaw. I'd seen that codename attached to other Edge missions. He was an independent contractor they brought in when they needed extra muscle. A lone wolf type.

No one had mentioned he'd be joining this op.

"Outlaw," I repeated, ignoring his outstretched hand. "Yeah, you look the part."

"And you are the lovely, deadly Siren. You also look the part." If he was annoyed that I didn't shake his hand, he didn't show it. He simply hooked his thumbs in his pockets and rocked back on his heels with a devil-may-care grin. "I'm your partner."

"I don't have a partner."

"You do now." His smile widened, showcasing a dimple in his cheek and setting off a weird fluttery feeling in my belly. I hated it. The smile. The sensation. Hated that I suddenly noticed the way his shirt stretched over broad shoulders and lean muscle. Hated that I wondered what he'd look like without the suit.

Seriously. What was *wrong* with me?

I should be furious. No, I *was* furious. He'd nearly blown my cover and wrecked the mission, all while waltzing in like a knight in pressed Italian armor when I did not need saving.

I should've punched him.

"The Grim Reaper sent me," he added, an infuriating twinkle in his eyes.

Of course he fucking did.

CHAPTER 3
FLYNN

This woman was not what I expected. I knew she'd been CIA before coming to Edge Ops, but most of the spooks I'd encountered were cold automatons, overconfident blowhards, or bland chameleons without a personality to call their own.

Lyric Renard was none of those things. She was fire wrapped in silk.

I followed her into her suite and leaned against the door frame, watching as she shed the Elisa Deveraux persona as if she were peeling off a second skin.

And damn if I wasn't a little impressed.

Without a word, she picked up a scanner and started sweeping the room for bugs. I could tell her I'd already done it before tracking her to Moreau's suite, but where was the fun in that?

Besides, I was enjoying the view as she bent to run the scanner along the baseboards.

That dress really was something else.

"Stop staring at my ass, Shepherd." She straightened and set the scanner aside.

I grinned. "Just admiring your technique."

She shot me a look that could've given Satan himself frostbite and tapped her earpiece. "Kate, get me a meeting with Ethan. Now."

Yeah, I was definitely going to enjoy needling her. Call me a masochist, but there was something wildly entertaining about a woman who looked at me like I was the grime she scraped off the bottom of her designer shoe. Most women found me charming. Lyric wanted me dead, or at least gravely wounded. Kinda liked that about her.

Kate's voice crackled in both our ears. "He's busy. You can debrief with me."

Lyric exhaled sharply through her nose. "No. I want to know why the hell Shepherd is here, and I want to hear it from Ethan himself."

I leaned in the doorway, arms crossed, watching the subtle twitch of her eyebrow, the clench of her jaw, the flex of her slender fingers—tells most people would miss, but I'd built a career on spotting. She was barely holding it together. The hotel's buttery lighting glinted off the platinum in her hair, making the strands shimmer like champagne. I had the stupid, sudden urge to reach out and see if it felt as cool and silky as it looked. Probably would've lost a hand. She looked like she wanted to put a bullet in me. I found that more appealing than I probably should have.

This woman was wound tight. Whether it was her

nature, the solo-operator mindset, or just the fury of being blindsided, I couldn't say. Probably all three.

Made a guy wonder what it'd take to make her come undone.

And just how fun it might be to help her do it.

After a long beat of silence, Kate's voice came back, resigned. "I'll patch him in."

A few seconds later, the suite's massive flat-screen flickered to life, and Ethan's face appeared. The last time I saw the man, he'd looked like a recruitment poster for the military. Clean-shaven, square-jawed, all sharp edges. But not tonight.

Jesus, he looked like hell. His beard had grown in wild and wiry, and his hair brushed his collar. Bruises and cuts dotted what I could see of his face under the beard, like he'd gone three rounds with a champion fighter and only barely walked away. Which was saying something, because I knew from experience that Ethan Voss could throw a punch hard enough to knock a guy flat.

Edge's last mission in California had been a cluster-fuck and half the team landed in the hospital. Ethan gave me the bare bones when he called in his favor, and I didn't ask for more. I don't do teams anymore. The only reason I was here was because I owed Ethan. And, yeah, maybe because part of me was curious about the woman trying to fill Maya's shoes.

"Report," Ethan said.

Lyric stopped pacing, squared her shoulders, and lifted her chin. She clearly wanted to rip into him for dropping me into her mission unannounced, but she held it back. Gave her report like a pro. "Moreau took the bait. He's interested in Elisa for more than a payday. He invited me to his yacht."

Ethan nodded. "Good."

"But I wasn't able to go or place a tracker on him." Her eyes cut toward me. "I was interrupted."

I grinned at her.

Ethan eyed us warily. After a beat, he said, "Not ideal, but not a deal breaker. We'll adjust."

Lyric crossed her arms. Every inch of her said *annoyed*. "I was interrupted by my 'security detail.' Moreau has run a background check on Elisa. That was expected. We had planned for it. But now he'll be digging into Mr. Mercer, my supposed head of security, and an 'incident' in Dubai."

Ethan didn't blink. "Kate will handle that."

"Already on it," Kate confirmed off-screen, her voice coming from both the TV and my earpiece. "Flynn will be Colt Mercer, head of Elisa's security. I'll send you his dossier."

I couldn't resist. "Please tell me he's from Texas so I can unironically wear a cowboy hat."

"Well, you *are* originally from Texas, right?" Kate asked.

"Yes, ma'am. Killeen." But my dad's Army career had us hopping around bases so often that I didn't really have a hometown. I'd left the Texas accent behind a long time ago, but I could call it back when needed. And, right now, it was pissing Lyric off, so I laid it on extra thick.

"There you go. The best lies are grounded in the truth." If I wasn't mistaken, there was a smile in Kate's voice. "Colt Mercer is now a Texan."

"Yeehaw."

Lyric growled. She was about two seconds away from hurling something heavy at my head. "We're not here to play cowboy, Shepherd."

"Shame. I've got a collection of boots and spurs that would really sell the image." I didn't really. Everything I owned fit into one rucksack. But I wanted to see her reaction.

She didn't disappoint.

"Are you always this obnoxious, or are you making a special effort for me?"

"Princess, you bring out the best in me," I drawled, enjoying the way her jaw tightened at the endearment.

Ethan cleared his throat. "If you two are done, we have an operation to run."

Lyric dismissed me entirely, focusing on Ethan. "You sent me in with an unknown variable. Mind explaining why this Shepherd character crashed my op?"

"You're welcome, by the way."

She spun back to me, eyes blazing. "I didn't need saving."

"Yeah, you did, sweetheart."

"Don't call me sweetheart. Or princess. Or… anything!"

"Now, I gotta call you something since we'll be working together."

"To you, I'm Siren," she bit out.

Siren. Her operational codename. It suited her.

"Okay, Siren." I all but purred it, turning the name into a caress. Then I shook my head. "Nope. Doesn't work for me, princess."

Her scowl deepened. "Grim, I don't need a babysitter."

"He's not a babysitter," Ethan said, running a hand through his disheveled hair. "He's an asset."

"An ass, maybe," she muttered.

I chuckled. "That's just hurtful, princess."

Ethan gave a sigh full of I-don't-have-time-for-this. "Flynn, what did you do?"

"Why do you automatically assume I did something?"

"Because I know you."

He got me there. "Yeah, fine. I made a scene." I shrugged. "Moreau had her alone in his suite, and we had no comms. I didn't want to find her floating in the Mediterranean tomorrow morning, so I played overprotective bodyguard, swooped in with a territorial display, and extracted her before things got messy."

"And I had no idea who he was!" She whirled on me again, shoving a finger at my chest. "I had Moreau eating out of my hand. I was two minutes away from a private tour of his fucking yacht. I could've been on my way to Sentinel now."

My stomach soured at the thought of her on Moreau's yacht, and my smile dropped away. "Jesus, E. Don't tell me she doesn't know about Moreau's extracurricular activities."

"Of course I know. I may have been dumped into this mission, but I do my homework," Lyric snapped. "I know exactly what Moreau does to women who interest him."

She was so close I could see the gold flecks in her green eyes. Her perfume—citrus and something seductively spicy—wound around me, and for a second, I lost my train of thought.

I had to take a step back to clear my head. "Then you know putting yourself on that yacht alone would've been suicide. The last three women—"

"Went missing," she finished. "I'm aware. But unlike them, I'm trained for this. I had it handled."

"You think he would've let you walk off that yacht after showing you his toys?" I leaned forward, dropping the teasing tone. "Moreau doesn't share his secrets with people who can leave."

Something flickered across her face—doubt, maybe —but she masked it quickly. "I can handle myself."

"I don't doubt that for a second, Siren." And I didn't. The way she moved, the way she calculated— everything about her screamed competence. But competence didn't always save you from a bullet. "But Moreau's got a body count that would make a cartel boss nervous."

She sighed, her shoulders dropping a fraction. "I know his file."

"The file doesn't tell you everything." I rubbed my jaw, remembering. "In Singapore, I saw what was left of a woman who crossed him. She was an MI6 agent. Good one, too. He kept her alive for three days before dropping what was left of her in the harbor."

"Well, I'm not going to cross him. I'm going to smile, flirt, and steal his tech."

"And I'm going to make sure you get out alive afterward." I held her gaze, all teasing gone. "Whether you like it or not."

"Flynn's presence isn't up for debate," Ethan cut in, his tone all badass black ops commander. "You need backup, and with half the team on medical leave, he was the only option."

"Wow, E. You make me sound like a last resort," I drawled, placing a hand over my chest in mock offense. "I'm hurt."

Ethan just glowered at me. The guy carried tension like it was tactical gear. Was it any wonder riling him up had become a personal pastime?

Lyric's shoulders pulled tighter. "I prepped for a solo op. Now you're changing the parameters mid-mission with no warning."

"Parameters change," Ethan said flatly. "You adapt. That's part of the job."

"But—"

"Adapt, Renard," he said again, cutting her off. "You need someone to watch your six, and Flynn is one of the best. Ex-Ranger. I'm not losing another operative."

She laughed, but there was no humor in it. "I had it under control."

I tilted my head. "You sure about that?"

She spun on me, full of fury. "Oh, I don't know, *Shepherd,* did you see me stumbling through that conversation? Did I look like I needed someone to come in and play knight in shining armor?"

I held up my hands. "Just doin' what I'm told, darlin'." I let the drawl roll in heavier this time, just to poke her further. Tipped an invisible hat, too, for good measure.

She made a noise—low, furious, a hiss of sheer exasperation—and turned back to the screen. "I'm not working with him. Send someone else."

Ethan's expression didn't change. "Flynn also has experience with Moreau. He's tracked his operations across three continents."

That got her attention. She glanced at me, reassessing. "You've worked on Moreau before?"

"Tangentially," I admitted. "Crossed paths with him in Marrakech two years ago. Again in Singapore last summer. Man's got a type when it comes to business associates. Ruthless, paranoid, and willing to kill their own mothers for the right price."

"And what about his personal type?" she asked, and I could practically see those tactical wheels in her head turning. "What does he like in his women?"

"He has two. Vulnerable, needy, and alone. You can imagine what he does to those women. He tends not to keep them long."

"The other?"

"Beautiful, dangerous, and slightly out of reach." I let my eyes drift over her, making no effort to hide my appreciation. "You nailed it."

She inhaled through her nose, slow and controlled. She was trying real hard not to explode as she returned her attention to the screen. "I work alone."

"Not on this team you don't," Ethan said and shot

me a penetrating look. "That goes for both of you. While you're working for me, no lone wolf shit. Understood?"

"Spoilsport," I muttered, earning another glare from Lyric.

"When you meet Moreau for lunch tomorrow," Ethan continued, "Flynn will be with you. No exceptions, no arguments."

The look on Lyric's face suggested she had plenty of both, but she swallowed them back. Interesting. She might fight me tooth and nail, but she followed orders when they came from the boss. "And when Moreau digs into him?"

"Let him," I said, stretching lazily. "I can sell whatever story we need."

She studied me then, and I felt like she could see all the way down to the stuff I didn't want anyone seeing.

Well, fuck. I didn't like that one bit.

"Fine," she bit out. "But for the record, I don't like this."

"Noted," Ethan said dryly. "Keep playing your part. If you can't get a tracker on him, plant it on Vidal. Flynn, you stay close. If Moreau tries anything, shut it down."

"Easy enough," I said.

Ethan's eyes cut back to Lyric. "And, Renard?"

She stiffened. "Sir?"

"Keep your emotions in check."

Her face didn't move, but I saw the flinch in her eyes.

That hit a nerve.

I scowled at Ethan. He could be such an ass sometimes. Okay, most times.

"Understood," she said.

The screen went black.

Lyric stormed toward the bar, yanking open the mini-fridge with enough force to rattle the glasses on top. She pulled out a miniature bottle of vodka and downed it like a shot.

"Drinking on the job?" I asked, eyebrow raised.

"I'm off the clock until tomorrow." She tossed the empty bottle in the trash. "And I need something to help me tolerate your presence."

I chuckled, pushing off from the wall to wander around the suite. It was nice—not as opulent as Moreau's, but still dripping with luxury. "You know, most women find me charming."

"Most women haven't had their operations hijacked by you."

"Just following orders."

She scoffed. "Men like you don't follow orders."

"Men like me?"

"Lone wolves. Contractors." She waved a dismissive hand. "Men who think rules are suggestions, and loyalty is negotiable."

"Well, I make an exception for Ethan." I let out a low whistle. "And he really doesn't trust you, does he?"

"He thinks I'm not good enough. I'll never be as good as—" She caught herself and kicked off her shoes, sending them skittering across the marble floor. One landed upright, and the other toppled onto its side. "Doesn't matter."

"Oh, it definitely matters. You *want* them to trust you."

"You don't?"

I shrugged. "Trust gets people killed."

She faced me fully. "And yet here you are. Playing watchdog for a team you have no interest in belonging to."

I smiled. Damn. I liked this woman and her quicksilver tongue.

"I'm here because Ethan asked. It's that simple. But you?" I stepped a little closer, testing her. "You, I can't figure out. Why are you fighting like hell to prove something to people who won't even let you in the door?"

Her eyes narrowed. "That amuses you?"

"Hell, yeah, it does. Because I already know how this ends, Siren. You keep trying to be one of them, and one day, you realize you never were."

A flicker of vulnerability crossed her face, there and gone so fast I almost thought I imagined it. She turned away, grabbed another mini bottle of vodka, and poured a splash into a glass with juice. When she turned back, her icy shields were back in place, like they had never cracked.

"You don't know me."

No. I didn't.

But I wanted to.

And that was a problem.

I should've walked away. Should've booked a flight out of there and let this be Ethan's problem.

But I didn't.

Instead, I prowled closer and leaned in like I was going to kiss her. Her eyes flared with undeniable interest, even as she tried to smother it.

Trouble.

This woman was absolute trouble.

And damn if I didn't already want to see how much.

I smiled. "No, I don't. Not yet."

"Not ever." She took a long, slow drink of her cocktail, then set the glass down with a decisive click and got in my face. I smelled the vodka and juice and that delectable perfume of hers. Up close, I could see the faint freckles dusting her nose, the slight smudge of mascara beneath her left eye. She was even more stunning at this distance, and my cock stirred to life with an interested twitch.

Down, boy. Worst possible time for optimism.

"Let's get one thing straight," she said, each word a precise knife cut. "We are not partners. We are not friends. I didn't ask for you. I don't need you. And if you get in my way—"

"Let me guess, you'll kill me?"

"You don't matter enough to waste the bullet." She picked up her glass again and carried it toward the suite's bedroom. "Get out. Moreau may think you're my bodyguard, but that's just for show. I don't need you up my ass all night."

With that, she shut the double doors in my face.

Firmly.

"Oh, Siren," I called, just loud enough for her to hear. "If I were up your ass, you'd know it."

Silence.

Then a sharp intake of breath. A muttered curse.

Followed by the snick of the lock.

I laughed.

Yeah. I was definitely going to enjoy this.

CHAPTER 4
LYRIC

I hadn't slept. Not really. I'd closed my eyes, tried to drift off, but every time I did, my brain replayed the night in excruciating detail. Flynn crashing my mission. Flynn smirking like he owned the damn world. Flynn calling me princess with that teasing light in his amber eyes.

And, worst of all, Flynn starring in a dream that left me waking up hot, flustered, and even more pissed off than before.

Ugh.

I rolled onto my back and stared at the ceiling of my suite, willing myself to shake it off.

My body was an idiot. There was no other explanation. Some awful, primal part of me must've short-circuited at the worst possible moment, because I sure as hell had no other reason to be dreaming about Flynn Shepherd pinning me against a wall with those rough hands, that stupid mouth, that mischievous look in his eyes—

Nope. Not thinking about it. Absolutely not.

I shoved the covers off and got up, already vibrating with frustration. This was his fault. If he hadn't waltzed into my op with that lazy, smarmy attitude, none of this would be happening. And now, instead of focusing on the meeting with Moreau, I was wasting time scrubbing unwanted images out of my head.

God. Why was I so hung up on a man I just met? A man who'd nearly blown my cover and seemed to take perverse pleasure in getting under my skin? A man who made me want to both punch him in the face and...

No.

Fine. If my brain refused to cooperate, I'd focus on something I could control.

Elisa Deveraux.

I started with my makeup, contouring and blending away any trace of the restless night before. A hint of blush, a subtle smoky eye, a rich shade of lipstick, not too bold, not too soft. Just enough to make Elisa Deveraux look like she woke up effortlessly stunning. My hair came next, swept into a sleek, elegant chignon that screamed wealth and control. Every detail mattered. Every piece of the illusion had to be seamless.

Now I needed an outfit.

Men were easier to manipulate when they were distracted, and nothing scrambled their brains faster than a great pair of tits. I had a nice set, and I wasn't above using them when the job called for it. I opted for a tailored jumpsuit in a dark, rich hunter green that complemented my skin. The wide legs allowed for easy movement—important if I needed to make a quick exit, or worse, fight my way out—and the plunging V-neck was deep enough to draw the male eye without risking a nip slip. Diamond studs went into my ears. A delicate diamond watch circled my wrist. A whisper of sexy jasmine and sweet vanilla perfume. Subtle, intoxicating.

By the time I was done, I barely recognized myself.

Good. That was the point.

I smoothed a hand over my jumpsuit, picked up a wide-brimmed hat, and stepped out of the suite…

Flynn was waiting for me, leaning against the opposite wall, maddeningly at ease, owning the space like the hallway had been designed for him to lounge in. He hadn't shaved, and the faint stubble dusting his sharp jawline made him look even more rakishly unbothered.

The lazy curve of his mouth sent a ripple of heat through me. And, just like that, all the time I'd spent slipping into Elisa's skin evaporated. I was Lyric again, irritated and off-balance.

I hated that.

His gaze dragged over my outfit, and he chuckled. "Fancy."

A slow, unwanted awareness spread low in my stomach. He looked at me like he wanted to lick me head to toe.

I huffed and shoved the hat onto my head, turning to make sure my suite's door locked behind me. "Why are you here?"

"Good morning to you, too, sweetheart."

My eye twitched. "Don't call me that."

With my back to him, I couldn't see him, but I heard that infuriating grin in his voice when he said, "Figured we should grab coffee and strategize before your big date with Moreau."

I shouldered past him. "It isn't a date. It's a meeting."

"Whatever helps you sleep at night, princess."

Keeping my expression smooth as glass, I stopped mid-step and turned. "Call me that again," I said, honey sweet. "I dare you."

Flynn's grin only widened, his amber eyes crinkling as he pushed off the wall. He closed the distance between us in two easy strides that managed to be both unhurried and predatory. "Careful with those dares, princess. I'm not known for backing down."

I forced myself to hold his gaze, refusing to back down despite the heat crawling up my neck. "You think I am?"

The corner of his mouth quirked up, and his eyes—those damnable eyes—dropped to my lips for a fraction of a second before meeting mine again. My breath caught. Just for a second. Just long enough to hate myself for it.

"No. That's what makes you interesting."

He towered over me, close enough that I caught that scent again—woodsy and warm and masculine. It wasn't cologne, and it wasn't overpowering. Just... there. And I had to resist the urge to inhale deeply.

For a heartbeat, I thought he might close that last bit of distance between us, and a treacherous part of me wanted him to.

The ding of the elevator shattered the moment, and I stepped back too quickly. His eyes sparked; a predator who'd just seen prey twitch. But it was either retreat or throw myself at him and climb him like a tree, and I wasn't about to hand him that kind of victory.

Not when he was enjoying this way too damn much.

I forced a slow breath through my nose, smoothing my jumpsuit as if I could press out the heat still lingering on my skin. Calm. Collected. Unaffected. That was the goal. Even if my heart was still beating like I'd barely made it out of something dangerous.

I strode toward the elevator. "I need coffee before I deal with all of… this." I gestured vaguely in Flynn's direction without looking at him.

His laugh was full of wicked amusement. "All of my animal magnetism?"

I punched the elevator button. The doors slid open instantly, and I stepped inside without responding.

Flynn followed. Of course he did. I felt him behind me, close enough to mess with my focus.

The doors slid shut again, trapping us inside.

I stared straight ahead, willing myself to think about anything else.

Not the way his scent lingered, woodsy, warm, and masculine.

Not the way my skin suddenly felt too tight.

Flynn shifted closer, his arm brushing my shoulder. "Admit it, Siren." His voice was low, far too smug, and far too close to my ear. "You had dirty thoughts last night, too."

The doors opened.

I stepped out.

I didn't look back as I marched across the opulent

lobby to the cafe. Flynn's footsteps behind me were unhurried, confident, and only fueled my irritation. I could practically feel his smirk burning into my back.

The hotel's café was a sun-drenched space with marble-topped tables. A handful of early risers—wealthy tourists and business people—lounged with their espressos and newspapers. Perfect for our cover. I chose a table near the window, angling myself to keep sight lines on both the entrance and the terrace beyond.

Flynn slid into the chair across from me like he had every right to be there.

The waiter hurried over as soon as we sat down.

"Black coffee," I said, pulling off the hat and setting it on the empty seat beside me.

"Caramel macchiato," Flynn added, completely unashamed. "Extra drizzle and whipped cream."

I blinked at him. "You don't seem like a caramel drizzle kind of guy."

He shrugged. "And you don't seem like the fun kind of girl."

"I'm plenty of fun."

His grin widened. "Now that I'd like to see."

"I bet you would," I said, keeping my voice cool even as heat crawled under my skin. I leaned back in my chair and crossed my legs, using the motion to create distance between us. "We need to get our story straight before Moreau."

Flynn tracked the movement, those sharp eyes missing nothing. "Our story is straight. You're the bored heiress looking for thrills. I'm your latest plaything."

"You're my security consultant," I corrected, though the word *plaything* conjured images I immediately shoved out of my head. "That's the cover we agreed on."

"Security consultant by day, plaything by night." His voice dipped lower. "Rich women like Elisa Deveraux don't hire men like me just for their professional expertise."

My fists clenched, but before I could say a word, the waiter returned with my black coffee and Flynn's sugar-laden monstrosity. I watched, slightly horrified, as he took a long sip, leaving a faint trace of whipped cream on his upper lip.

He caught me staring and deliberately licked it away. "Something on your mind, princess?"

"You enjoy being annoying, don't you?"

"I'm not annoying. I'm a delightful ray of sunshine." He leaned back in his chair, stretching those long legs under the table. His foot brushed mine.

Accidentally? I couldn't tell.

I shifted away, ignoring the warmth that rippled through me at the brief contact. "Our covers have a strictly professional relationship only."

Flynn's eyes sparkled with mischief. "You think Moreau will buy that? A man like him watches people, studies them. He'll see right through us if there's any..." He paused, searching for the word. "Chemistry."

"There's no chemistry."

"No chemistry? Sweetheart, the periodic table's jealous of us." Flynn leaned forward, dropping his voice to a rumble that vibrated straight through me.

"Every person in this room can feel it. Moreau will, too."

I set my cup down with a sharp clink. "I am not pretending to be your lover."

"Who said anything about pretending?"

"God. You are so—"

"Charming? Funny? Irresistibly sexy—"

I cut him off with a slicing gesture through the air. "Insufferable. I was going to say insufferable."

He grinned. "Admit it, the other stuff crossed your mind first."

I took a long sip of coffee to ground myself. The bitter heat burned down my throat. When I set the cup down again, I'd wrangled my emotions and expression back in check. "Look, we need to focus. Moreau is dangerous. If we slip up, we're both dead."

"Yeah, I'm aware," Flynn said, and the teasing note vanished from his voice. "He doesn't just bring random people into his inner circle. He's paranoid. Calculating. If he's reaching out to Elisa Deveraux, it's because he wants something specific. My guess? He wants more than a business partnership, if you get my meaning."

"I know what I'm doing. If he wants sex, and it gets me closer to accomplishing the mission, he can have it. This isn't my first rodeo."

Flynn went still. The light in his amber eyes extinguished. One second, they were dancing with mischief; the next, they were cold.

"Not happening." His voice was flat, devoid of inflection.

"Never said it was, Siren. But Moreau's known for

testing his business partners in creative ways. I told you what happened to the MI6 agent in Singapore."

A chill slid down my spine. This wasn't playful Flynn. This was the operative behind the charming mask. The dangerous man who'd earned his place *in* Edge Ops, however temporary it was.

I exhaled slowly. "Okay, and?" I asked, as if he'd just given me a weather report.

Flynn's jaw tightened. "And Moreau doesn't like competition. Think about it. You show up alone? He holds all the cards. But if you have someone? If you walk in with a man who already has his hands on you—"

His gaze flicked downward, and I realized he'd reached for my hand. And I'd let him.

I pulled it away. His gaze lifted to meet mine again.

"If he sees Elisa with a man who very obviously loves her and would take a bullet to protect her, he's going to take it as a challenge."

My stomach tightened. "You're saying this makes me a prize?"

Flynn's gaze didn't waver from mine. "Yes."

My throat felt dry. I took a slow sip of coffee to ease the tightness. I didn't know what kind of answer I expected—something cocky, maybe. Teasing.

Not this.

"And in this scenario, you'd be what, exactly?"

Flynn didn't smile. "I'll be the thing he wants to take from you."

CHAPTER 5
LYRIC

The words bounced around in my head all morning. I couldn't say what about them bothered me so much, but they sent a chill through me when Flynn spoke them, and the unease only grew as I stepped onto the terrace of the private beach club.

I was in Moreau's territory.

Flynn walked beside me, loose-limbed and at ease, a man who had nothing to prove. I kept my stride measured, my expression cool beneath the shade of my wide-brimmed hat. Elisa Deveraux walked like she owned the world, and today, I had to make Moreau believe it.

We were led to a low table set beneath the shade of a pergola, the Mediterranean stretching endlessly behind it. The space was intimate by design, meant to make his guests feel both privileged and trapped.

Moreau wasn't there yet. It was another power play, making sure we knew his time was more valuable than ours. I settled into the cushioned chair and studied the postcard-perfect view as a server poured champagne into delicate flutes.

Flynn sat beside me, his arm resting along the back of my chair, his body angled toward mine. Protective. Possessive. The role came naturally to him, and that irritated me more than it should have.

"Relax, princess," he murmured next to my ear. "You look like you're about to snap someone's neck. We're supposed to be enjoying ourselves."

I forced my shoulders to soften, letting Elisa's performative boredom settle over my features as I reached for my glass. "I'm perfectly relaxed."

"Your jaw says otherwise."

Before I could respond, footsteps approached across the marble terrace. I didn't turn—Elisa wouldn't be eager—but I felt Flynn's subtle shift beside me, his body coiling.

Moreau had arrived.

Dressed in tailored linen, he moved toward us with the casual confidence of a predator who didn't need to rush.

"Ah, Elisa," he greeted smoothly, reaching for my hand and lifting it to his lips. The kiss lingered uncomfortably long. A test to see if I'd flinch.

I didn't.

I let him hold my hand, my fingers neither tightening nor retreating. Indifference was its own kind of power.

Moreau's gaze flicked to Flynn as he lowered my hand. "And you brought Mr. Mercer."

"I rarely go anywhere without him." I trailed my nails down Flynn's forearm—and, yes, I was secretly thrilled to see the goosebumps my touch raised on his skin.

So Mr. Charming was just as affected by me as I was by him. Good to know.

I sent him an indulgent smile. "He has his uses."

Flynn's gaze heated as his fingers brushed the nape of my neck beneath my hair. Electricity zipped down my spine, and my nipples tightened against the soft fabric of my jumpsuit.

Oh, shit.

We were playing a dangerous game, and Moreau was watching it all, clocking every reaction.

"Well." Moreau's smile froze as he settled into the chair across from us. "This is a change from yesterday."

"Yes," I said, injecting a bit of breathlessness into my laugh. "I wasn't happy with him yesterday. He can be… possessive. It's annoying, but we worked it out."

"So I see. I had hoped for a more intimate conversation. Without your new…" He looked at Flynn the way most people looked at cockroaches. "Security guard, is it?"

"Among other things." Flynn smiled, all teeth. "Elisa and I are something of a package deal these days."

Moreau leaned back, his eyes narrowing. "Package deals can be… renegotiated."

"Not this one." Flynn's fingers traced another slow, idle pattern against my shoulder, his featherlight touch lighting up my every nerve ending like fucking sparklers.

And judging by the mischief in his eyes, he knew exactly how he was affecting me.

I resisted the urge to elbow him in the ribs.

"The Sentinel drone system," I said, and turned back to Moreau, redirecting the conversation. "Let's discuss what I came for."

Moreau signaled to a server for more champagne. "The drone system is going up for auction. You're welcome to come bid on it, of course."

I lifted a brow. "Everything has a price."

Moreau hummed. "What price are you offering?"

"Double what you could make on it at auction. Up front. No complications."

"Why?"

I sat back, exhaling as if contemplating whether I even wanted to bother explaining. "As I told you last night, security. I don't trust men with guns. They're flawed. Bought. Bribed. Human. I want security that can't be turned against me."

Moreau looked at Flynn. "That doesn't bode well for your continued employment, Mr. Mercer."

Flynn made a quiet sound, something between a scoff and an amused laugh. "Some things you just can't replace with machines."

God, he was arrogant.

I ignored him and kept my focus on Moreau. "I'm not interested in playing warlord. I want something better: A future where power isn't decided by whose army is bigger, but by whose security is untouchable."

Moreau tilted his head, watching me the way a spider watches a fly twisting in its web. "You expect me to believe you'd put a billion-dollar drone system in a glass case and let it gather dust as a deterrent?"

"I expect you to believe I'm smart enough to use it properly."

"Ah, Elisa, I like you. You're bold. But I must admit, your… attachment to Mr. Mercer is distracting." Moreau's gaze flicked to Flynn's hand still resting on my shoulder, his thumb still moving in lazy circles.

"You seem tense, Moreau," Flynn said, amusement practically dripping from his words.

Moreau's smile turned glacial as he picked up his glass. "Not tense. Merely curious about the nature of your relationship. It seems… complicated."

"The best things usually are," I replied smoothly. I deliberately leaned into Flynn's touch, a calculated move that made Moreau's jaw tighten.

"I find complications tedious," Moreau said. His eyes never left mine as he took a measured sip from his glass. "In business and pleasure."

Flynn's thumb paused its maddening circle on my skin. "You deal in black market weapons tech. Seems pretty fucking complicated to me."

"On the contrary. The rules are quite simple when you're the one who makes them."

"Then you should be very interested in my offer," I countered. "It's as simple as it gets."

Moreau set his glass down with a decisive clink without taking a drink. "Simple, yes, but not the most lucrative. The world is changing, Elisa. We're on the brink of another world war, and nations are fighting to stay relevant. They would pay handsomely for an edge like Sentinel. So would the black market. And, frankly, I don't think your pockets are deep enough."

Flynn snorted, and there was a definite edge of impatience in his tone now. "So you'd rather sell it to some terrorist who thinks they can win a war with it?"

"Wars are profitable," Moreau replied.

I leaned forward again. "What I'm offering is the future, Monsieur Moreau. And the future pays more than whatever short-sighted bid you'd get from some warlord at auction. Like you said, the rules only stay simple when you're in control. How long do you think that lasts once you let this tech loose?"

"Imagine," Flynn added, "every small-time player with a grudge and enough money to spend coming for you because they think you've gotten too powerful."

Moreau exhaled a half-laugh. "I'm careful with who I invite to my auctions."

"Right," Flynn said, deadpan. "I'm sure all of them are upstanding citizens who would never betray you."

Moreau shifted in his chair.

There it was. The crack.

I moved in to exploit it. "What I'm offering is more than money. I'm offering a business partnership. You sell Sentinel to me, and I use my connections to market it as an exclusive security system to all of my friends. The demand for specialized tech goes through the roof, and every player in the market comes to you for their own private version of Sentinel. The oligarchs and oil lords, the heirs and diplomats. All the ones who matter.

You'll be the sole supplier of the world's most secure private network."

He didn't respond immediately, but I could see the wheels turning behind his eyes.

"Security," Moreau repeated, as if tasting the word. "A bold strategy, Elisa. It would potentially take years to pay off."

"I'm in it for the long game," I said. "Are you?"

A tense silence followed. The only sound was the clink of his ring as he tapped his finger against his glass.

"I'll consider it…" His smile finally returned, but it was a razor-thin line. "If you have dinner with me." His gaze cut to Flynn. "Alone."

And there it was. Just as Flynn had predicted, Moreau wanted all of Elisa—her money, her attention, her body—but Colt Mercer was in his way.

"Dinner?" Flynn drawled. "Hell of a gamble, asking a woman out in front of the guy who makes her scream his name every night."

I exhaled sharply and really hoped it came across as annoyance rather than the suppressed laugh it had been.

The look on Moreau's face was priceless. "Confidence is an admirable trait, Mr. Mercer. Though in excess, it often reads as overcompensation."

"Moreau, when a man delivers like I do, he doesn't need to compensate for a damn thing."

A muscle twitched near Moreau's temple.

I exhaled again, fighting down the smirk trying to rise, hoping I still looked vaguely irritated.

But inside?

Oh, I was absolutely enjoying this.

Moreau swirled his drink, taking his time, like he hadn't just been verbally gut-checked in front of an audience. Then, slowly, his smirk returned, and his gaze slid back to me, dismissing Flynn entirely. "So, Elisa. You've heard my counteroffer. What do you say?"

I let the moment stretch just long enough to make him sweat before I sighed. "Alright. Dinner."

Flynn tensed beside me. His hand curled into a loose fist against his thigh, his whole body going still. He was pissed, and I didn't think it was just an act. Which was ridiculous because this fake-lover, make-Moreau-jealous thing had been his plan from the start.

Moreau stood, and I followed suit. Flynn stayed seated.

"Excellent," Moreau said. "I'll send a car for you at eight."

"Looking forward to it." I turned away before I could see Flynn's reaction and strolled out of the beach club into the bright afternoon. I heard Flynn's angry footsteps approaching fast behind me.

The second we climbed into the sleek black limo waiting at the curb, Flynn let out a short, disbelieving laugh. "You have got to be kidding me."

"Relax, Shepherd. It's just dinner."

He scoffed. "You're letting that smug bastard think he's got a shot."

"That's the point," I said, throwing him an exasperated look. "He's easier to manipulate when he thinks he's winning."

Flynn shook his head, dropping back against the

seat. "Yeah? He's also gonna spend the entire night trying to figure out how to get you into his bed."

I smirked. "I know. And he'll fail."

Flynn exhaled, rubbing a hand over his jaw. "Still don't like it."

I shook my head in disbelief. "This was your plan!"

"My plan was to play your lover, so I had a reason to stay glued to your side more than a regular body-guard. But then you went and agreed to dinner alone with him!"

"Because it's what the mission requires." I pulled off my hat and shook out my hair, suddenly feeling claus-trophobic in the confines of the limo. "You think I want to spend an evening with that slimy bastard? This is my job, Flynn. I do what needs to be done. Besides, I've handled worse than him before."

"Have you?" Flynn's gaze searched my face. "Because the way you tensed up when he kissed your hand back there suggests otherwise."

Heat crawled up my neck. "I didn't tense up."

"Like hell you didn't." He caught my hand—the one Moreau had kissed—and rubbed his thumb over the spot. "Look, I get it. You want to prove yourself. But this isn't about proving anything. It's about staying alive long enough to complete the mission."

"I can handle one dinner," I said, softer now. "Besides, what choice do we have? He's not going to negotiate with both of us there, and if I can't buy Sentinel off him, then I need access to the auction."

Flynn was quiet for a long moment, his jaw working like he was chewing on words he didn't want to say.

Finally, he exhaled, and a faint smile touched his lips. "At least I got to bruise his ego."

"You certainly did," I said with a quiet laugh, leaning back in the seat and stretching out my legs. "Though, for the record, you're never getting me to scream your name."

His head turned sharply, his gaze locking onto mine, and just like that, the air inside the limo shifted. Thickened.

That faint smile spread into a slow, seductive grin. "That a challenge, princess?"

I rolled my eyes. "Not in the slightest."

Flynn leaned close enough that I could feel the heat of him and breathe in the scent of leather and soap. "Could've fooled me."

My breath hitched, and for a second—just a second—I thought about closing the distance between our lips. I wanted to prove him wrong. But I also wanted to prove him right.

His hand slid to my jaw, thumb brushing the curve of my cheek, and then his mouth claimed mine, slow at first, like he expected me to pull away.

I didn't.

I curled my hands against his shirt. I meant to push him away. I really did. But instead, I just held on, and then I was pulling him closer.

Flynn's lips moved against mine with a confidence that made my head spin. This wasn't the teasing, playful Flynn from earlier. This was something hungrier, more dangerous. His tongue swept across my lower lip, and I opened for him without thinking, a soft sound escaping my throat that I immediately wanted to take back.

But God, he tasted good. Like caramel and coffee and something uniquely him that made me want to crawl into his lap and forget about missions and covers and everything else.

His other hand found my waist, fingers splaying wide against the silk of my jumpsuit, and I could feel the heat of his palm burning through the fabric. My pulse hammered against my throat as he angled his head, taking the kiss deeper.

We were supposed to be fake lovers, but there was nothing fake about the way my body responded to him, the way every nerve ending lit up like a live wire. It had been so very long since I'd felt heat like this, wild and reckless, from just a kiss.

Had I ever?

No.

Not like this.

He groaned, low and rough, a sound of triumph and frustration all at once. He shifted, pulling me closer so I straddled his lap, the kiss turning fierce and impatient, reckless and consuming, just like everything else between us. I couldn't tell where his breath ended and mine began. His grip on me tightened like he was staking a claim, and somewhere in the back of my mind I knew this was a bad idea—a really, really bad idea—but it didn't stop me from grinding down on the hard ridge of his cock.

I thought I heard myself moan. Or maybe it was him.

Then the limo jerked to a halt.

Oh, God. What was I doing?

I wrenched back, eyes wide and lips tingling with the ghost of his mouth. My heart was a riot inside my chest.

Flynn's amber eyes were dark, pupils blown wide, and his hair was mussed where my fingers had tangled in it. When had I done that?

He sat there, sprawled in the seat, his legs spread, his very obvious erection straining against his slacks.

He grinned. "Told you, princess."

I glared at him and swiped my hand over my mouth, trying to erase the taste of him. "I didn't scream your name."

His laugh was low, rough, and supremely satisfied. "You will."

My insides went all fluttery, and heat crawled up the back of my neck. I turned away, reaching for the door handle. "Keep dreaming, Shepherd."

CHAPTER 6
FLYNN

Lyric didn't go into the hotel.

She didn't explain, simply climbed out of the limo and started walking. I didn't argue. I didn't say a word. I adjusted my still half-hard cock to avoid getting arrested for indecent exposure, then followed her, telling myself I wasn't already in too deep.

Eventually, we ended up on the narrow, winding streets of Le Rocher.

The afternoon sunlight slanted between the ancient buildings, casting long shadows across the cobble-stones. Monaco's old town was a stark contrast to the glittering casinos and modern yachts that dominated the harbor view. Here, centuries-old buildings pressed in close, their weathered facades telling stories that predated the principality's reputation for excess and glamour. Silk-scarved tourists posed for selfies, shop-keepers called out in French, and the scent of salt and sugar drifted through the air.

And Lyric moved as if she were on a mission.

I kept a careful distance, close enough to protect her if needed, far enough not to crowd her space. Whatever was driving her away from the hotel clearly needed room to breathe.

Finally, she stopped in front of a stand offering everything from coffee to gelato, and stared at the faded awning fluttering in the breeze.

She looked almost… lost.

I stopped beside her. "You walked all the way up here for gelato?"

She shook her head. "I need to not be Elisa Deveraux for five damn minutes." She approached the stand, ordering a pistachio gelato in flawless French.

When the vendor looked to me in question, I ordered an espresso, also in pretty damn flawless French.

"What?" I felt her eyes on me as I pulled a few euros from my pocket to pay. "You really think Grim would send someone in who doesn't speak the local language?"

"No." She took her gelato from the vendor. "But men like you usually—I just didn't expect…" She trailed off, eyes dropping to my mouth for a fraction of a second before looking away.

I accepted the change and my espresso, then held out a hand, indicating she should lead the way. "Didn't expect a brain behind all my devastating good looks?"

"Something like that." A reluctant smile tugged at her lips. "Though I wouldn't go as far as 'devastating.'"

"You wound me, princess." I watched as she licked a perfect stripe up the side of her gelato cone. The sight shouldn't have been distracting. I shouldn't have been tracking the movement of her tongue with such intensity. Definitely shouldn't be picturing her doing the same to my cock.

I took a sip of my espresso, letting the bitter heat burn away thoughts I had no business entertaining. "Well, I didn't expect you were a pistachio kind of woman. Figured you'd go for something more dramatic. Blood orange."

"I like pistachio."

"Is that Lyric talking, or Elisa?"

She hesitated. "I don't know. That's the problem."

We kept walking, and I let the silence stretch while she processed that.

"How many aliases have you had?" I asked finally.

She exhaled hard. "Too many."

"And do they all like pistachio gelato?"

She shot me a sideways glance. "Do all of yours like espresso?"

"There's only one of me, sweetheart."

She huffed a breath that might have been a laugh.

We ended up at a stone overlook behind the palace, where the cliff dropped straight to the sea and cannons stood guard, relics from a prettier, bloodier time. The hike up the hill had done little to dampen her restless energy. She paced. I leaned against the wall and finished my espresso while she wore a groove in the pavement.

She stopped suddenly and turned toward me. "I think I envy you."

Not what I'd expected her to say. "Because of my devastating good looks?"

"Anyone ever mention ycu have an over-inflated ego?"

"It's not ego when it's true."

She gave a soft snort.

I set my empty cup on the stone wall, studying her face. The afternoon sun caught in her eyes, turning them the color of sea glass. "So what do you envy?"

"The certainty. You're Flynn. Just Flynn. Colt Mercer might be the cover, but you seem to have no trouble keeping Flynn and Colt separate." She gestured vaguely with her cone. "I've been so many people that sometimes I forget which parts are actually me. I don't even remember what my real laugh sounds like." Her voice was low and sad and yanked at something in my chest I'd spent too many years trying to keep buried. "I don't know who I am when I'm not playing a role."

I pushed off the wall and stepped closer. "I know who you are. You're a woman who likes pistachio gelato."

She scoffed. "You're not letting that go, are you?"

"No. Pistachio is the worst."

"Excuse me?" She whirled to face me fully, genuine offense flashing in those sea-glass eyes. "Pistachio is sophisticated. Complex. It's not some basic vanilla or chocolate—"

"It's green ice cream that tastes like nuts."

"It's nuanced."

"It's pretentious."

"You're an ass." But she was almost smiling now,

and something tight in my chest loosened. This fire—this passion over something as ridiculous as gelato flavors—this was real. This was Lyric.

"There she is," I said softly.

Her smile faltered. "What?"

"The woman who will defend pistachio gelato to the death. That's not Elisa Deveraux talking. That's you." I reached for her chin, gently, and made her look at me. Her eyes were wide and uncertain. I wasn't the only one off-balance here.

She recovered first and stepped back on the pretense of discarding the rest of her cone.

"What about you, Shepherd?" she asked, brushing her hands together. "Got any ghosts you're hiding from?"

"Sure. A whole goddamn platoon of them. But you're right. I do know who I am."

"And who's that?"

"I'm the guy who keeps walking into shit he shouldn't because I can't seem to stop myself."

She poked a finger at my chest. "That is a terrible character trait for someone in your line of work."

"Yeah, well, at least my life's never boring."

"Personally, I wouldn't mind a bit of boring." She faced the sea, bracing her hands against ancient stone. The wind gusted, tugging her hair out of its neat twist, bringing with it the scent of the Mediterranean and a trace of that citrus and spice perfume of hers.

She breathed in deeply and lifted her face to the sky. She looked like she wanted to open her arms, throw herself over the edge, and fly away.

If she did, would I stop her?

Or join her?

I'd started freelancing after the military because I'd craved freedom. And I thought I had it. I took the jobs I wanted, turned down the ones I didn't, and answered to nobody but myself. No uniform, no chain of command, no obligations except the ones I chose.

But, watching her, I realized I was as trapped in this life as she was. Trapped by the need to keep moving, to not look back, to never get too close to anyone or anything. Trapped by the boundaries I'd drawn to keep myself alive and sane.

After a long moment, Lyric exhaled softly and turned away from the view.

Guess we weren't going over the edge today.

She wandered along the parapet, trailing her fingers along the rough surface. She eventually paused at a fountain tucked into an alcove between two buildings. It was nothing like the flashy monstrosities near the hotel and casino, with their music, lights, and perfectly timed water shows designed to impress drunk tourists.

This one was old. Simple. A sea nymph poured water from a chipped shell into a shallow pool, the stone stained green in places and worn smooth by time. The basin was filled with coins from all over the world.

It wasn't trying to be beautiful. It just… was.

I liked it better than the others.

I dug a couple of coins out of my pocket and offered her one. "Make a wish?"

She shook her head. "I stopped believing in wishes a long time ago."

"Let me guess… somewhere around the time you started carrying a weapon?"

That earned me another almost-smile. "Before. Way before."

I tossed one of the coins in.

She leaned over to watch it disappear under the rippling surface, then sent me a sidelong glance. "Don't tell me you believe in wishes."

"I believe in hedging my bets." I held out the other coin for her. "Can't hurt, right?"

She hesitated before slowly taking it from my hand. "What did you wish for?"

"Breaks the rules if I tell you."

"I thought you weren't much for rules."

"Some are worth following."

She turned back to the fountain. The afternoon light glinted off her hair, turning it to white gold, and I wondered if that pale, silvery blonde was her natural color. It suited Elisa, but now that I knew her, I didn't think it fit Lyric. If I had to guess, she was more fire than frost—something like strawberry blonde or copper, the kind of color that caught sunlight and burned with it.

"You know what I'd wish for?" She flipped the coin and caught it between her fingers. "One day where I don't have to calculate every word, every gesture. One day where I could just… be."

"What would that look like?" I asked, genuinely curious. "A day of being you."

She closed her eyes, still clutching the coin. "I'd wake up late. No alarm. I'd wear clothes that feel good, not ones picked to create an impression. I'd eat whatever I wanted without worrying about maintaining a cover identity's diet preferences." She opened her eyes, looking almost embarrassed. "It sounds pathetic when I say it out loud."

"Doesn't sound pathetic to me." I moved beside her, close enough to feel her warmth but not touching. "Sounds human."

She flipped the coin again, letting it dance across her knuckles. A small, impressive trick that revealed more training than she probably intended to show.

"I'm not supposed to be human in this job, Shepherd. I'm supposed to be whatever they need me to be."

I watched her face as she said it—the way her guard dropped for a second, revealing something honest and hungry underneath. It wasn't Elisa talking now. This was all Lyric.

"So take it," I said.

Her eyes snapped to mine. "What?"

"Take your day. Right here, right now." I gestured to the ancient stone around us, the sprawling blue horizon. "Nobody's watching. No targets, no mission parameters. Just you and me and whatever the hell you want to do with the next few hours."

She studied me as if I were a puzzle with missing pieces. "We have three days to find the drones before the auction, and Moreau could move them at any time. I don't have the luxury—"

"There's always a reason not to," I cut in. "Always another mission, another target. Another excuse to keep the armor on." I touched her hand where she still held that coin. "But you know what happens if you never take it off? It starts to rust shut."

She didn't pull away. "Speaking from experience?"

"Maybe." I shrugged. "Or maybe I just want you to drop the armor so I can get you naked."

A laugh escaped her—startled, genuine. The sound caught her by surprise, her eyes widening slightly like she'd discovered something long-lost.

"There it is," I said softly. "Your real laugh."

She stared at me for a long moment, then flipped the coin into the fountain without looking. The splash was barely audible. "You're dangerous, Flynn Shepherd."

"So I've been told."

She turned back to the view, but something had shifted. The rigid line of her shoulders softened, and when she exhaled, it felt like she was releasing more than air.

"Four hours," she said finally. "That's all I can spare."

"That's all I'm asking."

Her gaze met mine, still guarded. "What exactly did you have in mind?"

"We're in Monaco, princess. What do you want to do?"

She seemed startled by the question, as if no one had asked her that in years. Maybe they hadn't.

"I want to see the aquarium," she said finally.

I grinned and gallantly held out an arm. "Your wish is my command."

CHAPTER 7
FLYNN

THE MUSÉE OCÉANOGRAPHIQUE DE MONACO PERCHED ON the very edge of a cliff face, rising from the rock like a palace built for Neptune himself. Inside, the air was cool and blue-tinted, the murmur of tourists fading behind us as we wandered deeper into the labyrinth of tanks.

"You know, of all the things I expected you to choose, this wasn't on the list." I said, watching her profile as she stared, transfixed, at a tank of jellyfish pulsing pink and blue against the dark water.

"What did you expect? Shopping? Gambling?" She didn't look at me, but her lips curved slightly. "That's what Elisa would choose."

I moved closer, drawn to the way the aquarium light played across her face. "And what makes Lyric choose jellyfish?"

"They're beautiful," she said, "but deadly. No brain, no heart, just instinct and poison."

"Sounds like my ex," I quipped.

That earned me another real laugh. Two in one day —I was on a roll.

She tracked one particularly graceful specimen with her eyes. "They're survivors. They've outlasted dinosaurs, but they're existence is so simple. So pure. They just… are. No pretending to be something they're not."

I couldn't help myself. I had to touch her. She looked ethereal in this light, like something out of mythology. I reached out and trailed my fingers over the curve of her cheek, curling my hand around the back of her neck and pulling her against me.

Jesus, this was a bad idea.

Just like the kiss in the limo had been.

But she didn't pull away.

Instead, she melted into me, one hand sliding up my chest to curl around my collar. Her eyes closed briefly, almost a surrender, and when they opened again, I saw something I hadn't before—a flash of genuine desire, unguarded and raw.

"Careful," I murmured.

"I'm always careful," she whispered, but there was nothing careful about the way her body arched toward mine or how her fingers tightened around my collar.

I backed her against the glass. Her breath hitched, that small sound hitting me harder than any explosion ever had.

"No," I said, "you're not. Not right now."

Something fierce and hungry flashed in her eyes. "I don't want to be careful. Not for these four hours."

She kissed me this time, nothing like the calculated seduction she played out for Moreau.

This kiss was real. Messy. Desperate. Her lips were demanding, teeth grazing my lower lip, her body pressing against mine like she was trying to climb inside my skin. When my hand slid to her waist, drawing her closer, she made a sound in the back of her throat that nearly undid me.

Warning bells clanged in my head, but I ignored them and tangled my other hand in her hair, messing up what remained of Elisa's perfect style. I wanted to see what Lyric looked like with her hair wild, her makeup smudged, and her carefully constructed walls down.

Her hands were everywhere, sliding under my jacket, nails scraping lightly against my back, tugging at my shirt. When she slipped one hand between us and traced the waistband of my pants, I caught her wrist.

"Not here," I rasped against her mouth, even as every cell in my body screamed at me to shut up and let her continue.

Her pupils were blown wide, leaving only a thin ring of green around the black. Her lips, swollen from our kiss, curved into a smile that was pure temptation. "You started it back in the limo."

"And I plan to finish it. Just not in front of the jellyfish."

"Afraid you'll get performance anxiety?" She traced a nail over the bulge at my fly, and I swear I felt the touch all the way down my spine.

I bit back a groan. "More concerned about traumatizing the school group about to round that corner."

On cue, the excited chatter of children filtered through the aquarium.

Lyric stepped back, though her fingers remained tangled with mine. I watched her, fascinated, as she made no move to fix her disheveled appearance. For these four hours, she wasn't trying to be perfect.

"And," I added in a growl against her ear as the kids oohed and ahhed over the jellyfish, "when I finally get you naked, I want more than a quick fuck against a wall. I want time. Space." I grazed her earlobe with my teeth and felt her shiver. "Privacy."

Her lips parted, eyes still dark with desire, but there was uncertainty there, too, like she wasn't sure if this was part of the act or something more dangerous.

It was definitely something more dangerous.

And if I had any sense in my head, I'd slam on the brakes now.

"I thought you were a man who took what he wanted," she whispered.

"I am." I brushed my thumb across her lower lip. "And what I want is to take you apart slowly. Thoroughly. Not rushed between exhibits with tourists walking by."

Her breath caught, and she looked almost fragile. Then the mask slipped back into place, though not completely. This was still Lyric, not Elisa.

"Don't make promises you can't keep, Shepherd."

I laughed darkly. "Sweetheart, I never do."

She glanced at the dainty gold watch on her wrist, then up at me with a smirk that promised trouble. "You only have three hours left."

"Not enough." I caught her hand and pulled her toward the exit. "But I'll make it count."

CHAPTER 8
LYRIC

He took me to his hotel room. It wasn't as fancy as my suite at Hotel de Paris Monte-Carlo, tucked in a small, boutique establishment a few streets away from the glitz and glamour of the main harbor. The room was small but clean, with two queen-sized beds and a balcony that overlooked a narrow street lined with laundry strung between buildings. It felt real in a way that the opulence of the casino district didn't.

And it was closer to the aquarium.

As soon as the door shut, I shoved him against the wall, my fingers in his hair, my mouth on his. He tasted like espresso and bad decisions, and I didn't care. I didn't care that we were teammates, or that he was the one person I wasn't supposed to want.

All I knew was that I needed this. Needed *him*.

The kiss was molten. I poured myself into it, forgetting everything but the pressure of his mouth and the hard lines of his body against mine. I pushed his shirt over his shoulders, fingers greedy on his skin.

His breath hitched, and I reveled in the feeling of power. That I could make a man like Flynn Shepherd —cocky, dangerous, always one step ahead—react like that.

His hands slid down my back, cupping my ass and lifting me against him in one smooth motion. My legs wrapped around his waist instinctively, the hard ridge of his arousal pressing exactly where I needed it.

"Bedroom," I managed to gasp between kisses.

"Lyric—" he started, but I silenced him with another kiss.

I didn't want to talk. Talking meant thinking, and thinking meant remembering all the reasons this was a terrible idea.

I wiggled the straps of my jumpsuit off my shoulders, hating that I chose this fucking impossible outfit this morning instead of the easy access of a skirt or dress.

Flynn's laugh rumbled against my collarbone, his teeth grazing the sensitive skin there. "Impatient, princess?" His hands found the zipper at my back, dragging it down with torturous slowness.

"Three hours," I reminded him, voice breathless as I caught his lower lip between my teeth. "Clock's ticking, so shut up and help me out of this thing."

The jumpsuit peeled away, the silky fabric sliding down to pool at my waist. I wasn't wearing a bra, and my nipples tightened under his gaze. The hunger in his eyes made liquid heat pool between my thighs.

"Christ," he muttered, one calloused thumb brushing over a hardened peak. "You're—"

"Don't talk, Shepherd. There are better things you could be doing with your mouth right now."

"Your wish is my command, princess." Flynn shifted our positions, and my back hit the wall hard enough to rattle the generic art hanging there. His mouth replaced his thumb, hot and wet against my breast. Stars burst behind my eyelids as his tongue circled my nipple, teeth grazing just enough to send electricity racing down my spine. His hands gripped my thighs, holding me steady as I rocked against him, desperate for friction.

I tugged at his hair, urging him back up to my lips, suddenly desperate to taste him again. His mouth was hot, hungry against mine, as if he'd been starving for sex as long as I had.

Ha. Who was I kidding? Flynn Shepherd probably never went hungry for sex. But at that moment, I didn't care. Not when his hands were everywhere, leaving trails of fire across my skin.

I fumbled with his belt, cursing when my fingers slipped on the buckle.

Flynn chuckled against my mouth and reached down to help me. His belt gave way with a satisfying clink of metal, and I wasted no time slipping my hand beneath the waistband of his boxer briefs.

"Fuck," he hissed when my fingers wrapped around him, hot and hard and ready. I stroked him once, twice, savoring the way his breath caught, the way his eyes darkened to molten amber. His pulse throbbed against my palm, and I wanted more—wanted to feel him inside me, wanted to forget everything but this moment.

A knock shattered the illusion.

We froze, both of us breathing hard, my hand still wrapped around him, his mouth hovering over my nipple. For one insane moment, I contemplated telling him to ignore it.

Another knock, more insistent this time. "Outlaw? You in there?"

Mr. Grim Reaper himself. Ethan.

Reality crashed back like a bucket of ice water.

Oh, shit. My boss was on the other side of that door, and I was standing here half-naked in a hotel room I had no business being in.

"You've gotta be kidding me," Flynn muttered against my skin. "What the hell is he doing here? I thought he was in Seattle."

"He doesn't trust me." I unwrapped my legs from his waist, stumbling slightly as my feet hit the floor. My legs felt like gelatin, and I hadn't even orgasmed.

God, if Flynn and I ever made it to bed, he was going to ruin me.

Ethan pounded on the door again. "Open up. I hear you in there."

Flynn tucked in his shirt and ran a hand through his mussed hair. "Yeah," he called back, voice surprisingly steady. "Give me a minute."

My hands trembled as I yanked the jumpsuit back up, fumbling with the zipper. I could become anyone in seconds, slide into a persona like a second skin, but right now I couldn't even get back into my own clothes.

"Here, let me." Flynn took me by the shoulders,

gently turned me around, and tugged the zipper up. I held my breath, aware of everything—his touch, his nearness, the weight of everything that might have been. The desire to finish what we'd started was an ache beneath my skin, and I almost couldn't stand it.

Once zipped, he spun me back to face him. His shirt was half open, his belt undone, his hair a mess. He looked like sex incarnate, like everything I'd been denying myself for far too long.

He searched my face, eyes still dark with heat and something that looked dangerously like longing.

"Later," he promised, voice rough. "We'll finish this."

I nodded, not trusting myself to speak. My body hummed with frustration, with desire that had nowhere to go. I smoothed my hands over my jumpsuit, trying to erase the evidence of what had just happened, but my skin still burned where his mouth had been.

"Your hair," Flynn whispered, hands moving to fix the mess we'd made of my perfectly styled blonde locks.

I reached up to help, fingers still unsteady. "Does it look obvious?"

"Everything about you looks obvious right now." His eyes darkened again as they swept over me. "Your lips are swollen, your cheeks are flushed, your nipples are hard." His voice dropped to a seductive rumble. "And I bet if I dip my fingers between your legs, your sweet pussy will be soaked."

"Ugh, stop." I pushed him away before I climbed

him like a tree right here. "You're making it worse. Ethan can't see me like this."

He chuckled and jerked his chin toward a nearby closed door. "Bathroom's there. I'll distract him."

I ducked into the bathroom, catching sight of myself in the mirror. He was right. I looked exactly like what I was: a woman who'd just been thoroughly kissed and interrupted right before getting thoroughly fucked.

I smoothed down my hair and splashed cold water on my face, willing my pulse to slow. I couldn't face Ethan like this. He already looked at me like I was a poor substitute for Maya, an imposter in her clothes. If he saw me now, disheveled and desperate, he'd have even more reason to doubt my competence.

"Get it together," I muttered to my reflection. The woman staring back at me looked wild-eyed and flushed. Not Elisa Deveraux. Not Agent Renard. Just Lyric, caught with her hand in the cookie jar—or more accurately, down Flynn Shepherd's pants.

My lipstick was destroyed, smeared beyond salvaging. I wiped it away with a tissue, wincing as I heard Flynn opening the door, his voice impressively casual as he greeted Ethan.

"About time." Ethan's voice filtered through the bathroom door. "What the hell were you doing in here?"

"Sleeping. Jet lag's a bitch."

I could almost picture Flynn's casual shrug, the way he'd run his hand through his already-mussed hair to sell the lie.

"Yeah?" Nolan 'Maverick' Riley said with a laugh, his Irish lilt turning the single word into a dare. "Who with?"

"Ah, I see you brought the whole Scooby gang," Flynn drawled.

I groaned. Great. The whole team was here.

I took a deep breath and stared at my reflection again. Four hours. That's all I'd asked for—four hours to just be myself. And I'd barely gotten one before reality came crashing back.

I smoothed my hands over my jumpsuit one last time. It was back in place, though I couldn't help noticing that my nipples were still prominently visible through the fabric.

Nothing I could do about that now.

I schooled my features into professional indifference. Time to be Agent Renard again. Not Lyric. Not the woman who'd been moaning against Flynn Shepherd's mouth two minutes ago.

When I stepped out of the bathroom, six pairs of eyes swiveled toward me. So not the whole team. Just most of it. Ethan and Nolan, plus Ethan's too-serious second-in-command, Trent 'Vigil' Dalton, the brilliant but grumpy hacker, Osamu 'Ozzy' Sato, and medic Alistair 'Preacher' Shaw. The only ones missing were Kate, plus Leo 'Sly' Santiago, and Rafe 'Sparky' Castellanos, who were on medical leave, still recovering from the mission that killed Maya.

But the guys here didn't exactly look mission-ready, either. Nolan's eye sported multiple shades of purple fading to a sickly yellow at the edges, and a line of stitches marched along the hard edge of Trent's jaw. Ozzy and Preacher had the least visible marks, but Oz's wiry frame was more gaunt than usual, and Alistair's normally warm eyes were shadowed with exhaustion.

"Renard." Ethan's tone was flat, his gaze moving between Flynn and me. "What are you doing here?"

I lifted my chin slightly. "Debriefing." The double entendre hit me a second too late, and I caught Flynn's smirk from the corner of my eye. Dammit.

"That's what we're calling it now?" Nolan burst out laughing. "You have lipstick on your face, Outlaw."

Flynn wiped at his mouth with the back of his hand, examining the smear of color with exaggerated interest. "Huh. Would you look at that?"

Ethan didn't look amused. His face was always hard, but now it was so stony it would fit right in on Mount Rushmore. The man embodied his operational code name like no one I'd ever met. He was 'grim' in every sense of the word. "I don't give a damn what you two do on your own time, but this isn't your own time. This is an op, and I need everyone focused."

"We're focused," I said, maybe a bit too quickly.

Ethan's eyes narrowed. "Are you? Because right now you look like two teenagers caught making out in daddy's car."

"With all due respect, I've completed every assignment, secured every objective you've given me since I joined this team. My personal life doesn't impact my performance or—"

"It does when your 'personal life' is another member of my team during a critical mission." Ethan's jaw tightened. "Maya would never—"

Something in me snapped. Maybe it was the frustration of being interrupted. Or maybe I was just sick of the comparisons. "I'm not Maya."

Ethan's expression darkened. "Believe me, I'm well aware."

The hurt sliced through me, but I refused to let it show. I'd spent too many years perfecting my mask to let it crack now. "I understand your concern, but I assure you, we are both professionals. The mission comes first."

Flynn moved to stand beside me. "There was no need to drag the team halfway around the world. We had things handled here."

While I appreciated the support, the proprietary hand he set on my back undermined my claim to professionalism. I stepped away from his touch, putting distance between us that I instantly regretted. The warmth of his hand left a phantom imprint on my back, and I fought the urge to lean into it again.

"Maya always meant it to be a team operation," Ethan said.

"But she died, and your team went through a meat grinder. I'm surprised Nolan can even see out of that eye." Flynn jerked his chin toward the pilot, who grinned.

"Takes more than a black eye to ground me," Nolan said, winking with his good one. "Besides, what else was I gonna do? Sit at home watching reruns while you lot have all the fun?"

Flynn ignored him and nodded to Ethan. "And you look like you haven't slept in weeks. You brought me in to help Lyric because your team was in no shape to run point. And, honestly, from what I've seen, she never needed the help to begin with. She could've successfully run this op solo."

He didn't say it like a compliment. He just laid it out as if my competence were a fact, not an opinion. Like he didn't just approve of my abilities, he trusted them.

And that shouldn't have made me feel anything.

But warmth bloomed in the center of my chest, entirely at odds with the cold professionalism I was trying to project. My pulse tripped. My breath caught. And for one traitorous second, I wanted to lean back into him, to bask in his belief in me.

Which was dangerous. So dangerous. Because it meant I cared what he thought. Maybe more than I should, and if I let my guard down any more, I'd probably trip over my own ovaries.

Ethan's jaw tightened. "The team's had time to recover."

"Two weeks isn't recovery," I said quietly. "It's a band-aid over a bullet hole."

"And y'all are still bleeding," Flynn added softly. "Especially you, E."

I didn't think the man's expression could get any harder. I was wrong.

"We're done with this conversation," Ethan said, his

voice arctic. He turned on his heel and strode for the door. "Briefing. My room. Ten minutes."

The door slammed behind him.

For a second, no one moved. Then Ozzy followed him out without a word, nose still buried in his phone.

Trent cleared his throat. "Alright, here's how it's going to work." He glanced between Flynn and me, then at the bed. "Lyric stays at her suite at the Hotel de Paris, but Flynn, you won't be sleeping there with her. We've got another room down the hall. Oz and I will take that one with Ethan. Nolan and Alistair, you're in here with Flynn."

Nolan picked up the duffle bag he'd dropped when he walked in and eyed the two beds. "I call dibs on the one that hasn't been christened yet." He tossed his bag onto the bed farthest from the door, his grin widening. "Unless you two already tried both?"

Heat crawled up my neck. "We didn't try either."

"Unfortunately," Flynn muttered.

Nolan's laugh was quick and delighted as he flopped back on the bed. "Interrupted at the good part, were you? That's tragic."

"Reckon that means I'm on the floor." Alistair dropped his medical bag off his shoulder with a heavy thud. His accent was Southern, but not sweet—more mountain steel than molasses. A far cry from Nolan's Irish lilt, which practically winked at you between syllables.

There was something about Alistair's voice that made you want to trust him, made you believe every word he said. And suddenly I understood why the team called him Preacher.

"Nah," Nolan smirked and rolled, patting the mattress beside him suggestively. "C'mon, Ali. Plenty of room. If you're nice, I'll even let you be the big spoon."

Alistair gave him a flat, unamused stare. "I'd rather spoon with a porcupine."

"Ouch."

"A *rabid* porcupine."

"Well, mate, you're missing out. I've been told I'm an excellent cuddler."

"By whom? The ugly blow-up doll you keep in your locker at HQ?"

Nolan gasped and pressed a hand to his chest in mock offense. "Take that back! Helga has feelings!"

I watched their banter with a strange sense of displacement. It felt practiced, comfortable—the kind that came from men who had faced death together and survived to joke about it. These men were a unit. A family. And I was the outsider.

Trent grunted and shook his head. "All right, you two. Got it out of your system?"

"For now," Nolan decided after a beat.

"Good. Get your shit together and let's go. Ethan's not in the mood for delays."

Nolan's smile vanished. He hopped off the bed and followed Trent out, leaving Alistair lingering in the doorway.

He watched us a beat, then said quietly, "Flynn's not wrong."

Flynn lifted an eyebrow. "About what?"

"The bleeding," he replied. "Ethan's holding it together by sheer force of will right now. Maya's death gutted him, and work's the only thing keeping him upright."

"I know," Flynn said, softer than I'd ever heard him. I looked at him sharply. There was a lot of weight in those two words. History. Maybe even regret. He'd said he was only a freelancer, but had he fought side-by-side with Ethan before?

Alistair nodded like he'd expected that. "Yeah, I know you do." Then he turned to me. "Don't take it personally, Lyric. Ethan's not trying to be cruel. He's just... running on empty and doesn't know how to stop without falling apart. And unfortunately, right now, you're the easiest target for his anger."

He didn't wait for a response. Just gave a faint smile and stepped into the hall, closing the door behind him with a soft click.

I stared at the closed door. When I first signed on, I wanted to be part of this team. For someone who spent most of her life alone, wearing identities like coats, the idea of belonging, of being known, had been seductive.

But now…

I realized I never would be. Not really. Not to them.

"Hey," Flynn said, his voice breaking through my thoughts. "You okay?"

I blinked, pushing down the unwelcome tightness in my throat. "Fine."

"Liar." His fingers brushed my cheek, tilting my face toward his. "You're thinking too loud."

I stepped back, suddenly unable to handle his

gentleness. I wanted the cocky version of Flynn back. The one who smirked and teased and didn't look at me like he *saw* me.

Because I knew how to handle *him*. This version, with worry in his eyes and softness in his touch? I didn't know what to do with that.

So I took the coward's way out and spun toward the door. "We should go. Grim's waiting."

CHAPTER 9
LYRIC

The debrief had been mercifully short.

Ethan didn't ask what I was doing in Flynn's hotel room. He didn't need to—he wasn't stupid, and his glare had spoken volumes. But to my surprise, he didn't pull me from the op. Didn't cancel the meeting with Moreau. In fact, he agreed it was our best shot at securing an invite to the auction.

A win, technically.

Except now I had a handler.

The team had set up in Flynn's hotel, taking over several adjoining rooms to form a command center. Now, Ethan wanted check-ins after every contact and updates before and after every meeting. Real-time surveillance from the tracker Ozzy embedded in my watch. I was supposed to improvise like a good little spy, but not *too* much. Blend in, seduce, manipulate— but only within parameters he'd approved in advance.

Like I was a marionette.

I didn't know if he was reacting to Maya's death or

punishing me for not being her, but either way, it was clear Ethan didn't trust me. Not completely.

And that made two of us. I've worked with men balancing on the razor's edge of burnout before, and it never ended well.

I took a long, steadying breath, but it didn't settle the knot twisting in my gut.

Ethan wanted Elisa Deveraux—Maya's polished creation, all smooth edges and effortless seduction. And I could be her. God, I'd become her so convincingly, even I wasn't always sure where she ended and I began. But Elisa wasn't a person. She was a performance. A product of grief and necessity and carefully calibrated control.

And tonight, I had to sell that performance to a man who dealt in death like it was currency.

There wouldn't be backup. No safety net. No one waiting in the wings if I flinched at the wrong moment or said the wrong thing. Just me, Moreau, and whatever price he decided I was worth.

So I braced myself.

And became her.

The dress I chose for dinner was a black silk sheath with Elisa's signature plunging neckline and a slit that reached up to my thigh. I pulled it on like armor, smoothing the fabric as I studied my reflection in the mirror. The woman looking back at me was composed, polished, every inch the kind of woman a man like Moreau would want to own.

I caught movement in the mirror and lifted my gaze to meet Flynn's. He lounged in the doorway, arms crossed, eyes stormy. He had been uncharacteristically quiet since we left the team, watching me like he was one wrong breath away from detonating.

"You don't have to do this," he said finally, voice low and rough.

I reached for my earrings, sliding the delicate diamonds into place without breaking eye contact in the mirror. "Yes, I do."

His gaze swept over me, but for once it wasn't cocky or appreciative. It was angry. *Possessive.* "Moreau's a predator. You know that, right?"

"Of course I do."

Flynn growled under his breath. "Then maybe don't dress like you're inviting him to take a bite."

"Bait needs to be appetizing."

He pushed off the doorframe and closed the distance between us in two strides, the heat of him like a bonfire. "You're playing a dangerous game with someone who doesn't follow the rules."

"That's the job."

"No," he bit out. "The job is getting Sentinel out of his hands. It's not..." He cut himself off, but I already knew what he was going to say.

It's not letting him touch me. Not letting him *own* me.

My lips tightened. "If that's what it takes to get the invite, I'll do it."

His eyes went molten. "The hell you will."

I turned to face him fully, temper flaring. "Excuse me?"

"If he puts his hands on you," Flynn said, low and lethal, "I'll break every bone in his body."

My heart kicked hard against my ribs. "You don't get to decide that."

He didn't back down and crowded me against the vanity. I hated him for using his bigger size against me. I hated myself more for the heat pooling in my core at the possessive gleam in his eyes.

"I'm your backup on this op." His voice dropped to that dangerous register that made my skin tingle. "Your safety is my responsibility."

"My safety, not my virtue." I tried to maintain a professional detachment, but my voice came out breathier than I'd intended. "I can handle Moreau."

Flynn's fingers brushed my bare shoulder, featherlight but searing. "I don't want him laying a hand on you, Lyric. If he tries, I'll put him in the ground."

Heat surged through me. "You don't own me."

"No," he said, eyes blazing. "But I want to. God help me, I fucking want to."

The words landed between us like a match dropped on gasoline. My breath caught. My blood roared. Every nerve ending went white-hot with fury—and something far, far worse.

Need.

I curled my hands into fists at my sides to keep from touching him. "You don't get to go all caveman on me just because we almost fucked. I have a job to do, and I'll do whatever needs to be done to make sure this op is successful."

"So you plan to fuck him?"

My stomach curdled at the thought. Before this afternoon, I'd known it was a possibility—hell, a probability that I'd have to go to bed with Moreau to secure an invitation to his auction. Now with the memory of Flynn's lips still fresh in my mind, the idea of Moreau's hands and mouth on my skin made me sick.

I pressed my palms against his chest, not quite pushing him away but establishing distance. His heart hammered beneath my fingers. "No, I don't plan to fuck him. But I don't plan to let him hand Sentinel to someone who'll use it to kill innocent people either, so if I have to take him to bed, I will. It's the job."

Flynn's jaw worked. For a split-second, I thought he might kiss me again, might crowd me back against the vanity and finish what we'd started in his hotel room. Part of me wanted him to, wanted the decision taken out of my hands.

Instead, he stepped back, leaving me cold where his heat had been.

I stayed frozen, breath shallow, pulse still thrumming from the contact.

The air between us crackled—not just with want and fury, but something raw and dangerous I didn't dare name. I hated that he'd gotten under my skin. Hated the way my heart still slammed against my ribs, the way my hands still tingled where they'd touched him.

And most of all, I hated that when he pulled away, some reckless part of me wanted to close the distance again.

But I didn't move.

Because if I let him matter—if I let *this* matter—I'd lose the edge I needed to survive what came next.

So I did what I always did. I put on the mask.

I turned back to the mirror and reached for my lipstick.

He didn't answer, but I could feel him watching me as I applied the red, my favorite shade. The one that always looked like war paint.

"You don't have to prove anything to them," he said quietly. "Not to Ethan. Not to anyone."

I capped the lipstick with a click and forced a bright smile into my voice. "Thanks for the pep talk, but I've got this."

I grabbed my clutch, my confidence, and what was left of my composure, and walked toward the door.

Flynn didn't try to stop me.

And I didn't turn back.

Because if I looked at him now, I wouldn't go.

And failure wasn't an option.

CHAPTER 10
LYRIC

THE RESTAURANT WAS THE KIND OF PLACE WHERE SECRETS were bought and sold over five-course meals. The private dining room oozed opulence—low candlelight, crystal stemware, a sweeping view of the Monaco skyline glittering beyond floor-to-ceiling windows. A setting designed to flatter a woman into forgetting her place in the social hierarchy.

I wasn't flattered.

And I was sick of men thinking they owned me. Moreau. Ethan. Even Flynn.

Especially Flynn.

His voice still echoed in my head—*"I want to. God help me, I fucking want to."*

He had no right to that possessiveness. No claim on my decisions. I wasn't a damsel in distress. I was the damsel who *caused* distress.

Moreau was already seated when I arrived, lounging with the lazy arrogance of a man who had never heard the word *no* and wouldn't recognize it if it slapped him. His suit was midnight blue and molded to him like a second skin. The cut of the fabric, the glint of the watch beneath his cuff, the way he swirled his wine glass—it was all curated. A masterclass in power projection.

Power he expected me to acknowledge.

I didn't.

Instead, I stepped into the room like I owned it, let the maître d' pull out my chair, and sat without waiting for Moreau's approval.

"Elisa," he purred. "You look stunning."

I smiled. "I know."

His chuckle was low, indulgent, like I'd performed for him. "And I see you left your guard dog behind."

"Colt Mercer isn't my guard dog," I replied, setting my clutch on the table. "He is a highly trained security specialist and my lover. He wasn't happy about being left behind."

Moreau's eyes sharpened, his amusement suddenly edged with something darker. "Ah. So that's the arrangement."

"There is no arrangement. Just mutual satisfaction."

"I see. Well, maybe *we* can come to a mutually satisfying arrangement tonight."

Gross. Inwardly, I gagged. Outwardly, I kept my pleasant smile firmly in place. "Maybe we can."

"Excellent. This calls for wine." He lifted a finger, and the waiter appeared as if conjured, setting down two glasses of wine.

"1995 Château Margaux," Moreau said, watching with a hungry glint in his eyes as I brought the glass to my lips. "I also took the liberty of ordering dinner for you. Châteaubriand with black truffle jus and pommes Anna. I hope you don't mind."

It was another power play. Everything with him was, every gesture calculated to shrink the space I occupied. To make me feel small. Controlled. Owned.

Unlike Flynn.

Flynn's possessiveness earlier, as infuriating as it was, had come from someplace raw and honest. He didn't need me to stroke his ego just to feel like a man. Moreau, on the other hand, craved it.

"Perfect," I lied, letting the wine roll across my tongue. Ask me, it wasn't worth the seven-hundred-dollar price tag. I'd had better ten-dollar bottles.

He ran a finger around the rim of his glass, his gaze sweeping over me, assessing like a collector studies a rare artifact for flaws. "Tell me, *chérie*. What is it you truly want from Sentinel?"

I tilted my head just enough to catch the light in my earrings. "I already told you. Security. Control. The same thing every man in that auction room wants."

"Ah, but you are not a man. And your kind typically prefers softer methods. Subtler games." He reached across the table and captured my hand, his thumb tracing the pulse point at my wrist. "Are you playing games with me, Elisa?"

I allowed it, maintaining the cool, unaffected facade of Elisa while calculating how many fingers I could break before his guards, tucked discreetly away in the shadows, made it to the table.

At least three.

Our dinners arrived, and Moreau released my hand, sitting back to shake out his napkin. He took his time cutting into his filet before speaking again. "You intrigue me, Elisa. You come from money, but you move like someone who's had to fight for power." His gaze dropped to my hands. "I imagine you don't enjoy being underestimated."

"I don't mind," I said lightly, spearing a potato with my fork. "Underestimation is an advantage."

He hummed, clearly pleased. Whether it was with the dinner or our verbal sparing match was anyone's guess. "A woman who understands the game. Rare."

"A woman who wins the game," I corrected, lifting my glass again.

He smirked. "We shall see."

The rest of dinner passed in a delicate dance of probing questions disguised as small talk. Moreau asked about my background, my family connections, my education. I fed him the fiction Ozzy had crafted—a Swiss boarding school, a fortune inherited from my father's shipping empire, investments in defense technology that had turned a modest inheritance into a formidable portfolio. Each lie was cushioned with enough truth to make it digestible, each answer calculated to make me desirable as both an auction participant and a conquest.

He nodded approvingly at all the right moments, but I could see the calculations happening behind his eyes.

He didn't believe me. Not entirely.

Good. I didn't want him to trust me too easily. Men like Moreau respected resistance… to a point.

When the plates were cleared, he reached into his jacket and pulled out a small velvet box, setting it on the table with a slow, deliberate push.

"Another liberty," he said, his smile lazy.

I didn't immediately reach for it, and he tapped a finger against the top.

"Go on."

I exhaled through my nose, then flicked open the lid. Inside, nestled against black silk, was a diamond bracelet—delicate at first glance, but edged with marquise-cut stones that gleamed like tiny blades.

"It reminded me of you," he said. "Elegant. Sharp."

I closed the lid and pushed it back across the table. "I don't want diamonds. I want Sentinel."

Moreau's smile tightened at the corners. "You're direct. I like that." He pushed the box back toward me. "But I insist. Consider it a gesture of goodwill. A symbol of what could be… if we reach an understanding."

His eyes never left mine as he reopened the box, lifted the bracelet, and held it suspended between us. "May I?"

It was the first time he'd asked permission for anything, and we both knew it wasn't actually a request. I extended my wrist, letting him clasp the cold diamonds around it. They caught the light and threw prisms across the tablecloth when I turned my arm.

"Beautiful," he murmured, his fingers lingering on my skin too long. Then he leaned back in his chair and picked up his wine glass, swirling the blood-red liquid. "Tell me, Elisa. How far are you willing to go to secure Sentinel?"

I took a careful sip of wine to buy myself a half-second. This was the moment—the fulcrum point where my next words could either secure an invitation or get me killed.

I set the glass down with care and smoothed my hand over the linen napkin in my lap. This was the part where Elisa Deveraux would purr, would lean in, would offer just enough suggestion to keep him biting.

But I couldn't make myself do it.

Moreau was a handsome man by all conventional beauty standards, but those eyes were empty. A shark's eyes. He tweaked a primal part of me that warned of danger—not the delicious, reckless danger Flynn represented, but the kind that made my skin crawl.

Flynn was right about one thing: Moreau was a predator. And predators watched for weakness. If I let him see how much he rattled me, I wouldn't leave this restaurant with an invitation.

I'd walk out with a target on my back.

So I swallowed my revulsion and leaned forward. "That depends."

His gaze dropped to my breasts, his eyes half-lidded. "On?"

"On whether you're offering a business transaction, or something else entirely."

Moreau's lip curled. He leaned forward, and his cologne invaded my space. His hand slid beneath the table, settling with possessive weight on my thigh.

"Why choose? Some deals are best sealed in both board-rooms and bedrooms."

Once before Monte Carlo, before Flynn, I would've done it, no hesitation. Sex was just another mask, after all. Another currency.

But now I couldn't stop comparing.

Flynn's touch igniting something in me I thought I'd cauterized years ago. Moreau's hands, smooth and manicured, landing on my skin like ice.

Flynn's eyes, hungry but honest, versus this predator's calculating gaze.

Flynn's possessiveness, raw and instinctive, versus Moreau's ownership.

Moreau's hand slid up my thigh, and the bit of dinner I'd had curdled in my stomach. I kept my expression smooth, my posture relaxed. But inside, I was screaming like a spider was on my leg instead of his hand.

He leaned in and kissed me. I knew it was coming, and yet I couldn't suppress the involuntary stiffening of my body. His lips were cold and practiced, moving against mine with the prowess of a man who'd learned technique but never passion.

And once again, Flynn invaded my thoughts.

Flynn, whose kisses were wild and unpracticed and real. Whose touch never once felt like a transaction.

Flynn, who didn't need to prove anything to anyone because he already knew what he was.

Everything in me revolted, a visceral rejection I couldn't hide. I jerked back too quickly, too sharply.

A mistake.

Moreau pulled back with the kind of satisfaction that made my stomach churn. "Ah," he murmured. "There it is."

I locked my jaw.

He reached into his jacket once more. This time, he pulled out a gold-embossed invitation and placed it between us with a casual flick of his fingers.

"You'll have to wait for the auction, I'm afraid," he said lightly. "A shame. I was hoping we could come to an… earlier arrangement."

I slid the envelope into my clutch without breaking eye contact. My wrist itched under the weight of the bracelet, but I didn't take it off. "Then I'll see you at the auction."

Vidal approached and leaned down, murmuring something in Moreau's ear.

"Take care of it." Moreau didn't look at me again when he added, "And escort her out."

I stood slowly, offering my most gracious smile, and let the guard lead me toward the exit. This night hadn't been a complete disaster—I had managed to secure an invite to the auction—but I kicked myself for reacting the way I had to the kiss. I should've slid my tongue into his mouth, climbed into his lap, and used the opportunity to plant the tracker.

Instead, in the moment of truth, I'd flinched. Recoiled like an amateur.

C'mon, Lyric. You're better than that.

Yes, I was. And I was going to plant the damn tracker.

At the last turn in the corridor, I opened my clutch

and slowed, pretending to search for something. Vidal slowed, too, but his attention was on his phone now, brows drawn in a tight scowl as he typed one-handed.

He was distracted.

Which was the best opportunity I was going to get.

I stepped too close, bumping his arm with my shoulder as I reached for something inside my clutch. The phone slipped from his grip, clattering to the floor at the same time my lipstick, compact, and a handful of credit cards spilled from my bag.

"Oh, how clumsy of me," I said smoothly, already kneeling.

Vidal let out a sharp sigh and crouched, too, reaching for his phone.

But I got to it first and pressed the tiny tracker against the case, where it would hopefully blend into the matte black finish. Ozzy assured me it would be undetectable unless someone were explicitly looking for it. They couldn't scan for it either. The tech was too new, too advanced.

"Forgive me," I murmured as I handed it back with a sheepish smile. "I wasn't watching where I was going."

He didn't respond, just gave me a long, flat look and slipped his phone back into his pocket as he straightened to his full height.

I rose more slowly, tucking the last of my things back into my clutch and smoothing my hair.

"Mr. Moreau has arranged transportation for you," Vidal said, his accent clipping the words into harsh consonants. He gestured toward a sleek black Mercedes idling at the curb.

I smiled. "That won't be necessary. I have my own car."

Vidal's expression didn't change. "Mr. Moreau insists."

Of course.

I kept my smile plastered on my face until I reached the hotel, maintaining the charade of gratitude for Moreau's "courtesy."

The moment the car pulled away, I dropped the façade, my shoulders slumping, hands trembling. I curled them into fists to hide it, fighting the urge to tear the diamond bracelet from my wrist and throw it into the sparkling fountain.

I had to get inside and out of this dress.

Because whatever Moreau had told his man to *handle*… I had a feeling it wasn't good.

CHAPTER 11
FLYNN

Waiting's the one thing I've never been good at.

I paced the suite, whiskey glass in hand, trying to outrun the images of Lyric with Moreau. Dinner. Wine. His hands on her. His mouth.

Fuck.

I'd already checked her tracker three times. Sent Ozzy a dozen texts until he basically told me to fuck off. Verified the extraction plan with Ethan. And then again with Trent.

It wasn't enough.

Nothing would be enough until she walked through that door.

I downed the rest of my drink and set the glass on the sideboard harder than necessary. The tumbler cracked, sending a thin line up the crystal. It matched the one running through me—that slow, spider-web fracture that had been spreading since I watched her walk out that door.

The suite felt too small, too confined. I ran a hand

through my hair, checked my watch for the hundredth time, and glanced at the door again.

When the lock finally clicked, every muscle in my body went taut.

Lyric stepped inside, and I knew immediately something was wrong. Her movements were too controlled, her face too blank. The poised mask of Elisa Deveraux was firmly in place, but beneath it, I could see the edges fraying.

"Are you okay?" I kept my voice quiet, even as my pulse kicked into overdrive.

She didn't look at me right away. Just shut the door, exhaled slow and measured, and leaned back against the wood like she needed a second to steady herself.

My stomach tightened.

She pushed off the door and walked toward the bedroom, dropping her clutch on the dining table. "I lost the chance to buy the drone system outright, but I got an invitation to the auction."

That didn't answer my question.

I followed her to the bedroom. "Try again."

Lyric glanced back at me, her expression too carefully neutral. "I'm fine."

She whirled around, eyes flashing with something dangerous. "What do you want me to say, Flynn? That I had a lovely evening? That Moreau was a perfect gentleman?"

I stepped closer, studying her face. The careful composure was slipping, revealing something raw underneath. Something that made my blood run cold.

"What happened?" I asked, my voice dropping to

that deadly quiet that even my fellow Army Rangers had known to fear.

She didn't answer. Just looked away, her throat working as she swallowed.

That's when I saw it. The diamond bracelet encircling her wrist caught the light as she moved. Something ugly and primal rose inside me. I crossed the space between us in two strides and caught her wrist.

"What did he do?" I kept my voice low, but I could hear the razor edge in it.

"Nothing I couldn't handle." She tried to pull away, but I held firm.

"He gave this to you?"

"Yes. It's a tracker."

"Audio?"

"No." She drew a breath. "He doesn't trust me, but he wants me."

I turned her wrist over over with more gentleness than I felt and unclasped the bracelet. The weight of it was obscene in my palm. I tossed it onto the dresser. "That stays off when you're not with him."

She looked up at me then, something like relief flashing in her eyes. Her pulse raced beneath my fingers where they still circled her wrist. "Did he kiss you?"

"Flynn, don't. You can't—"

I cut her off with my mouth on hers. Not gentle. Not asking. A claiming kiss that was as much about erasing Moreau's touch as it was about marking her as mine. I needed to replace whatever he'd done, whatever he'd said, with something real.

She made a sound in the back of her throat—half

protest, half surrender—before her hands fisted in my shirt, nails digging into the fabric.

I pulled her closer, one hand at the small of her back, the other cradling her jaw. She arched into me, desperate and needy in a way that made my blood burn hotter. Her lips parted, and I took full advantage, deepening the kiss until we were both breathing hard. Her fingers found the buttons of my shirt, popping several in her haste to get to skin.

Jesus. Everytime we touched was hotter, and my cock was already painfully hard. I was desperate to get her under me, to pin her to the bed, and swallow her cries as I sank deep into her pussy.

This wasn't just about wanting her anymore. This was about need. Raw. Visceral. The kind that bypassed thought entirely.

"I hated it," she whispered against my mouth. "I hated his hands on me."

Something dark and possessive surged through me. I backed her toward the bed. "Then let me erase him."

Her eyes flashed with heat and anger all at once. "You don't get to decide that."

"Tell me to stop then," I challenged, my voice rough even to my own ears. "Tell me you don't want this."

She didn't. Instead, she yanked me down, her mouth crashing against mine with bruising force. There was nothing gentle about the way she kissed me—all teeth and tongue and desperation—and I matched her ferocity, backing her toward the bed until her knees hit the edge.

We fell together, a tangle of limbs and half-shed

clothing. Her dress hiked up around her thighs as I settled between them, the heat of her burning through my pants. I caught her wrists and pinned them above her head, breaking the kiss to look down at her.

"Did he touch you here?" I asked, trailing my free hand along her collarbone.

She shook her head, breath coming in short, sharp pants.

"Here?" My fingers skimmed the curve of her breast through the silk of her dress.

"No."

I lowered my head, pressing my lips to the pulse hammering in her throat. "Tell me where, princess."

"My thigh."

I growled against her throat, then slid down her body, pushing her dress higher until I found the spot. "Here?" I pressed my lips to her inner thigh, just above her knee, my stubble scraping against her soft skin.

She nodded, her breath catching.

"Then I'll start here." I nipped at her flesh, then soothed the sting with my tongue. I wouldn't leave a mark—not where anyone else could see it—but I needed to reclaim every inch Moreau had touched. Replace his cold, calculating fingers with heat. With need. With something real.

Her thighs trembled as I worked my way higher, leaving a trail of kisses and gentle bites. When I reached the edge of her panties—black silk, barely there—I looked up, caught her watching me with those green eyes gone dark with desire.

I hooked my finger around the damp fabric and pulled it aside, revealing her glistening folds. She was wet for me, all slick heat and need. I couldn't help the groan that escaped me.

"Fuck, Lyric."

Her hips shifted restlessly. "Flynn, please..."

The pleading in her voice sent a fresh surge of blood to my already painfully hard cock. I wanted to take my time with her, to worship every inch of her body until Moreau's touch was nothing but a forgotten nightmare. But the hunger in her eyes told me she needed something else right now. Something primal.

I dragged my tongue through her center in one long, slow stroke, savoring her taste. Sweet and tangy and addictive. Her back arched off the bed, a strangled cry escaping her lips. I gripped her thighs, holding her open for me as I devoured her, circling her clit with deliberate pressure before sucking it between my lips.

Her fingers tangled in my hair, pulling almost to the point of pain as I circled her clit with my tongue. I loved that edge of violence in her touch—the way she wasn't afraid to take what she wanted, to direct me where she needed me most.

"Right there," she gasped, arching into my mouth. "God, don't stop."

I had no intention of stopping. Not until she came undone beneath me, until she couldn't remember anyone's touch but mine. I slid two fingers inside her, curling them to find that sweet spot that made her hips buck against my mouth. Her walls clenched around my fingers as I pumped them in and out, matching the rhythm of my tongue against her clit.

"Flynn," she gasped, her voice breaking. "I'm close—"

A sudden, sharp ping cut through the room like a bullet.

"Fuck," I growled against her thigh, pressing my forehead there for just a moment as we both froze. My fingers were still buried inside her, her body trembling on the edge of release.

I pulled back, meeting her eyes. They were wide, pupils blown with desire and frustration. The tracker pinged again, more insistent.

"It's Moreau's security chief," she said, voice ragged. "I couldn't get the tracker on the prototype, so put it on Vidal's phone."

I cursed under my breath and reluctantly withdrew my fingers, pressing a final kiss to her inner thigh before sliding up her body. Our foreheads touched, both of us breathing hard.

"Rain check," I murmured against her lips, stealing one last kiss before pulling away.

She nodded, already shifting from lover to operative with a speed that was both impressive and maddening. "I need to change."

Pity. I liked that dress and how the silk did nothing to hide her pebbled nipples. I watched her grab a handful of black clothes from the dresser and disappear into the bathroom, then flopped back on the bed. My cock was still standing at attention and I shoved my palm against it to try to get some relief. It didn't help.

The taste of her was still on my tongue, her scent all over me.

I forced myself up and grabbed the rucksack I tossed in the corner. The faster we got this done, the faster we could get back here and finish what we started. I yanked my shirt over my head and exchanged it for a fitted black thermal, followed by tactical pants and my combat boots. I buckled on my shoulder holster, checking the SIG before sliding it home. Two extra mags went into the cargo pockets of my pants, along with a tactical knife strapped to my ankle.

"Should I call Ethan?" I called.

"No. For all we know, Vidal could be going to visit his mother." Lyric emerged from the bathroom transformed—black tactical pants and fitted long-sleeve shirt. All business. The only hint of what we'd been doing moments before was the flush still coloring her cheeks and the slightly swollen curve of her bottom lip. She'd wiped away all traces of makeup, and somehow looked even more beautiful without it.

She scooped her hair back into a ponytail. "I don't want to loop the team in until we know for sure. It could be nothing, and I don't want to give Ethan even more reason to doubt me. We check it out first, then call in the cavalry if needed."

I nodded, checking my weapon one last time. "Fair enough."

Last thing we needed was Ethan or, God forbid, the ever-grouchy Ozzy, micromanaging this op. It was bad enough they had her on a short leash as it was.

I crossed to her and tugged on her ponytail. "But if it

turns out Vidal's just grabbing a late-night snack, I'm going to be seriously pissed."

A ghost of a smile crossed her face. "You and me both."

CHAPTER 12
FLYNN

Nothing like a little midnight B and E with a beautiful woman who nearly came apart in your mouth thirty minutes ago.

Man, sometimes I really love my job.

The tracker led us to a private airfield on the outskirts of Monte Carlo, where the rich and infamous park their jets between champagne-soaked weekends of gambling and Mediterranean yacht parties. The airfield was a playground for billionaires—all sleek hangars and private terminals that never asked questions as long as the money was right.

Vidal's signal had stopped moving about fifteen minutes ago, pinging steadily from a hangar at the far end of the runway. Sleek, modern, and clearly designed to keep prying eyes out. Perfect place to stash experimental tech you're planning to sell to the highest bidder.

"What do you think?" Lyric whispered, crouched beside me in the shadows of a maintenance shed. She'd pulled a black cap down over her hair to hide the golden strands, and combined with the dark tactical gear, she looked like a shadow given form. Beautiful. Dangerous. "Two guards at the main entrance, probably more inside."

I studied the hangar through my night-vision monocular. "There's a service entrance on the east side. Minimal coverage. Probably our best bet."

She nodded, all business now, though I caught her glancing at my mouth when she thought I wasn't looking.

Yeah, princess. I'm still thinking about it, too.

The memory of her taste lingered on my tongue, and the unfinished business between us hummed in the air like an electric current, but we were both professionals. We could compartmentalize. For now.

Focus, Shepherd.

"Take point," I murmured, slipping the monocular back into my pocket. "I'll handle any security systems."

We moved in tandem through the shadows, keeping low as we skirted the perimeter fence. The service entrance was just where I'd spotted it—a small door tucked between industrial air conditioning units, barely visible unless you knew to look for it.

"Camera," Lyric murmured, pointing to a small black dome mounted above the door.

I pulled a compact signal jammer from my pocket. "Ozzy's new toy. Should give us two minutes before their system notices the loop."

She raised an eyebrow. "You stole Ozzy's prototype?"

"Borrowed," I corrected with a smirk.

"Borrowing implies he knows you have it."

"Just a temporary reallocation of resources." I activated the jammer. "Besides, he'd never let me test it otherwise."

"He's going to kill you."

"Only if he finds out." I watched the tiny light shift on the device shift from red to green. "We're good. Clock's ticking."

Lyric moved immediately, extracting a set of lock picks from her belt. She worked fast, and within seconds I heard the satisfying click of the lock disengaging. She was good—really good. Like, better-than-me good, though I'd never admit that out loud.

She eased the door open just enough for us to slip through, and we entered the darkness of the hangar's service corridor.

The air inside was cool and smelled of jet fuel and metal. Our footsteps were whisper-quiet as we moved deeper into the building. Up ahead, a slice of light spilled from beneath a door.

"Movement," Lyric breathed, freezing in place.

I nodded, drawing my SIG and keeping it low. We pressed ourselves against opposite walls as the door opened, spilling harsh fluorescent light into the corridor. A guard stepped through, radio crackling at his hip, heading in the opposite direction.

Once he was gone, we continued forward, following the corridor until it opened into the main hangar space. We paused at the threshold, taking in the scene before us.

The hangar was massive, easily large enough to house multiple private jets, but instead of aircraft, the space was filled with shipping containers arranged in a grid. Armed guards patrolled the perimeter, their movements regular and predictable.

"Holy shit," Lyric murmured as we slid into cover behind one of the containers. "How are we going to find Sentinel?"

I spotted a stack of crates nearby and shot her a quick grin. "Can you climb?" Before she could protest, I slipped away, scaling the crates to reach the catwalk that ran along the upper perimeter of the hangar. From here, I was shielded from view by the poor lighting, but had a perfect view of the entire operation below.

Lyric settled next to me with a huff. "What are you, freaking Spider-Man?"

"I'm a man of many talents."

She snorted softly and looked down at the floor below. "My God. There's so much more than just Sentinel here."

"Yeah, looks like Moreau's been collecting all the fun toys."

The sheer volume of tech assembled in the hangar was staggering. It wasn't just Sentinel MK-IV. This was a full-blown black market weapons bazaar in the making and I dreaded to think what other goodies waited in those many crates. If even one of these technologies fell into the wrong hands, the consequences would be catastrophic. All of them together? Unthinkable.

I spotted Vidal across the hangar, standing with two

Asian men in expensive suits who were definitely not security. One handed him a tablet, which he studied intently before nodding.

"Buyers," Lyric breathed. "Fuck. They're doing pre-auction viewings."

I grabbed my radio off my belt. "Time to loop in the team."

"Wait—" she started, but I'd already switched to the team's secure channel.

"Grim, this is Outlaw. Come in."

A beat of silence, then Ethan's voice came through my earpiece. He sounded calm and collected, but I knew the man better than just about anyone. He was pissed. "Outlaw. Where the fuck are you and Siren? Oz said you're not at the hotel."

"We took a joyride and ended up in Broker's storage facility."

A beat. "You're… *where*?"

Oh, yeah. He was beyond pissed. I could picture him pinching the bridge of his nose right now, that vein in his temple throbbing.

"Siren planted a tracker on Broker's security chief. He led us to a hangar at a private airfield. There's more than just Sentinel here. It's a goddamn candy store of illegal tech. Multiple containers, armed security, and potential buyers already getting tours."

"Stand by," Ethan said, his voice tight with suppressed fury.

Lyric shot me a look that could have melted steel. "I told you to wait."

I shrugged. "Better to ask forgiveness than permission."

"Not with Grim," she hissed, pressing deeper into the shadows as a guard passed nearby.

Before I could respond, Ethan's voice cut back in. "What exactly are we looking at, F?"

I scanned the facility, cataloging what I could see. "Multiple shipping containers, uniformly arranged. Military-grade security. At least eight armed guards that I can see, probably more we can't. Vidal's giving a tour to what looks like Chinese buyers."

"Chinese military intelligence," Lyric corrected. "I recognized the guy on the left from a previous job. His name is Wei Zhao. Deep cover MSS agent who specializes in weapons procurement."

I pulled out my monocular and watched the men move toward a container labeled with nothing but a barcode. "I haven't had the pleasure of tangoing with China's version of the CIA before."

"Wouldn't recommend it," Lyric said dryly.

"Can you identify what they're examining?" Ethan asked, his tone shifting from anger to focused, intense team leader.

I adjusted my position slightly, trying to get a better view without exposing myself. The Chinese agents were hovering over what looked like a glass display case, Vidal gesturing proudly at whatever lay inside.

"Negative. Too far away," I replied. "So what's the play here? We've got eyes on multiple weapon systems, but no confirmation on Sentinel's location."

A pause. Then Ethan's measured response: "Sabotage what you can and get the hell out of there. I'll send Maverick to scoop you up."

"Might get hot."

"Mav can handle it."

"Copy that," I murmured, watching as Vidal guided the Chinese agents to the next container. "We'll need twenty minutes."

"You've got fifteen," Ethan replied. "Radio with your exfil. Maverick will be waiting."

I switched off the radio and turned to Lyric. "Time to get creative."

"Wait. If we try something here, we're as good as dead." She put a hand on my arm to stop me from moving and moved closer so that her lips were directly by my ear. It sent heat straight to my cock and took me back to the the hotel room.

"Look." She pointed in the opposite direction from Vidal and the Chinese agents. The hangar doors were open, and men were loading the crates into a truck. "If we follow it, we might be able to find out the auction's location."

"It's not on the invite?"

"No. We're supposed to meet Moreau Friday at the docks."

I exhaled a breath. "So it's probably happening on a fucking island. The truck will just take us to Moreau's yacht."

"Exactly." Lyric's breath on my ear was torture.

I wanted her mouth back on mine.

Hell, I wanted her everywhere.

"They're going to hold the auction on international

waters," she whispered, "where it's beyond most countries' jurisdiction. We follow, we watch. Then we can plan a proper assault instead of improvising in a hangar full of armed guards."

I watched the men loading the truck. They were working methodically, moving crates according to some system I couldn't quite figure out. But one thing was clear—they were only taking certain containers, leaving others behind. "Grim wants us to sabotage what we can here and bail."

"And I want to complete this mission without getting shot." She shifted beside me, her shoulder brushing mine. "We might learn more than we would by blowing things up here and risking exposure."

She had a point. "Fine," I conceded. "But those containers can't make it to their destination."

"They won't." She paused. "Trust me, Flynn."

I looked at her. In those green eyes, I saw fierce determination—and something else. Vulnerability. She thought I didn't trust her, and that fact hit me like a sucker punch. We'd known each other for less than a week, and somewhere between flirting and fighting, she'd become important. Someone I wanted to protect —not because she needed it, but because I wanted to be the one she turned to when she needed help.

"I trust you," I said.

And, despite my best instincts, I meant it.

I didn't do partners or teams, except in limited circumstances that came with high rewards. In fact, Ethan Voss was one of only two men on Earth I trusted implicitly. The other was Tucker Quentin, and that was because the three of us had bled together in places that never made it onto maps. And because working for Tuc always came with very nice paydays. The guy had more money than God now and wasn't shy about sharing it with his battle buddies.

But Lyric was different. She'd slipped past my defenses with alarming ease.

I was letting her into spaces I normally kept locked down tight. And that was dangerous…

Maybe more dangerous than any weapon in this hangar.

CHAPTER 13
LYRIC

THE TRUCK LURCHED INTO MOTION, HEADLIGHTS CUTTING swaths through the darkness as it pulled away from the hangar. In the shadows, Flynn and I moved like ghosts, keeping pace along the perimeter fence.

"If we lose that truck, we lose Sentinel," I hissed, my legs pumping as we sprinted across the tarmac. The transport was picking up speed, heading for the airfield's rear gate.

"We're not losing it," Flynn growled, veering toward a row of parked vehicles. He tested the door of a sleek Mercedes.

Locked.

He moved to a BMW and cursed under his breath when it, too, wouldn't budge.

I tried the black Audi next to it, and the door swung open without resistance. I slid behind the wheel and set to work overriding the onboard computer.

"Someone's getting fired," Flynn said and jumped into the passenger seat. "You need help?"

"No."

The engine roared to life. Ten seconds. A personal best.

Flynn's face lit with fierce satisfaction. "That's my girl."

"I'm not your girl."

"You will be when I have you screaming my name later."

Cocky bastard.

But he wasn't wrong. I had every intention of finishing what we started in his hotel room.

He pulled his gun and shifted in his seat, checking our six just as something pinged off our bumper. "Aw, fuck. We've got trigger-happy company."

I checked the mirror. Two guards had noticed us and were running our way, guns up and firing.

Flynn thumped a hand on the dashboard. "Go, go, go!"

I gunned it. The Audi shot forward, tires squealing as we raced after the transport truck.

The gates were closing ahead. Automatic metal barriers sliding together like the jaws of some mechanical beast. I pressed the accelerator harder, my knuckles white against the steering wheel.

"They're going to lock us in," I muttered, calculating angles and speed. We had maybe five seconds before those gates sealed shut.

"Floor it," Flynn said, his voice steady despite the bullets pinging off our rear quarter panel.

I did. The Audi surged forward, engine screaming as we shot toward the narrowing gap. Metal scraped against metal as we squeezed through with inches to spare, the side mirror snapping clean off against the gate.

"Jesus," Flynn breathed, twisting to look back at our pursuers. "That was close."

"We're not clear yet." I kept my eyes fixed on the truck's taillights ahead. It was moving fast down the coastal road, weaving through late-night traffic with surprising agility for its size.

Flynn checked his weapon and flashed me a grin that made heat pool low in my belly. "Admit it. You're having fun.

"I'm working," I shot back, but couldn't quite keep the smile from my voice.

"Yeah, you are, and it's so fucking hot."

There was something undeniably seductive about the way he watched me work, like every calculated risk I took was foreplay. I swerved around a delivery van, gaining ground on the transport.

"Save the dirty talk for when we're not being shot at," I said, but my body disagreed, already humming with anticipation beneath my tactical gear.

"We're not being shot at right now."

The rear window exploded in a shower of glass, bullets punching into the upholstery.

"You had to jinx it," I snapped, ducking lower in my seat as I swerved hard to avoid another spray of bullets.

A sleek black SUV had materialized behind us, its high beams flooding our interior with harsh white light. The passenger leaned out the window, rifle raised.

Flynn twisted in his seat, returning fire through our

shattered rear window. "Two hostiles, heavily armed. Driver's trying to get alongside us."

"I see them." I cut across two lanes, causing a chorus of angry horns. The transport truck was still ahead, moving with surprising speed. "We need to lose our tail without losing the truck."

"Leave that to me." Flynn reached into his tactical vest and pulled out what looked like a golf ball with a blinking red light.

"What's that?"

"Another of Ozzy's toys." He opened the sunroof, wind whipping through the car. "Don't tell him I borrowed this one, either. Take the next right."

I yanked the wheel hard, tires screeching as we careened onto a narrow side street. The sedan followed, gaining ground now that we were off the main road.

"On my mark, spike the brakes," Flynn said and pulled himself through the sunroof.

"Oh my God. Don't get shot."

"Would you be sad?"

"No, I would be pissed. You—"

"Now!"

I slammed on the brakes. The Audi fishtailed, and in that moment of controlled chaos, Flynn hurled the device directly under our pursuers' car. Three seconds later, an electromagnetic pulse fried their electronics. The sedan veered wildly off course and crashed into a row of parked scooters, its engine dead.

"Go!" Flynn shouted, dropping back into his seat.

I floored it, tires screaming as we shot back toward the main road. "We're going to lose the truck."

"Not with the way you drive, Siren. Gun it."

Heat curled through me at the compliment and pushed the Audi harder, the engine protesting as we took the next turn too fast. The truck's taillights glowed ahead, distant but not gone. Not yet.

Then a flash of movement in the rearview caught my eye.

A drone.

Shit.

"I really fucking hope that's not Sentinel," Flynn muttered, already leaning out the window.

I took my eyes off the road long enough to look at the drone. "No. It's too small, but still not friendly," I muttered, swerving hard as the drone dipped lower, its red targeting light sweeping across our windshield.

Flynn twisted in his seat, tracking the drone's zigzagging approach with his SIG. He fired twice at the drone, missing both shots as it darted away. "Damn thing moves like a hummingbird on crack."

"Third time's the charm," Flynn muttered, steadying his aim. The drone swooped in again, and this time, when he fired, the bullet connected with a satisfying crack. The drone spiraled, smoke trailing from its ruptured body, before it smashed into the pavement behind us.

He whooped. "Got the little bastard!"

"Nice shot," I muttered, eyes locked on the truck ahead as we gained ground.

Flynn reloaded. "All those quarters at carnival shooting galleries finally paid off."

I cut him a sideways glance. "Please tell me that's not really where you learned to shoot."

He just grinned.

A black SUV suddenly roared out from a side street, cutting across our path with screeching tires. I wrenched the wheel hard to avoid a collision, but our bumpers clipped. The Audi fishtailed, tires fighting for purchase.

"Hold on!" I shouted, struggling to regain control as we spun. The car clipped a parked moped, sent it skidding into a flower stand, then slammed sideways into a row of metal barriers, the impact jarring my teeth. I straightened the car, but we'd damaged something vital in the crash. I couldn't get it up to speed, and smoke poured from under the hood.

Flynn leaned out the window, gun in hand. Whether or not he actually learned to shoot at the carnival, his accuracy was astonishing. I caught his reflection in the cracked side mirror—eyes hard, mouth grim. He dropped one of the shooters, but two more replaced him, hanging out the side of the SUV like they were invincible.

"Damn it, Flynn, they're not giving up!"

He ducked back inside a second before bullets slammed into the metal frame where his head had been. "Persistent bastards. I'll give them that. Can't you go any faster?"

"No." Even as the word left my mouth, the Audi coughed and shuddered to a stop. Through the spider-webbed windshield, I watched the transport truck disappear around a bend. The SUV that hit us was already reversing, preparing for another strike.

"Time to improvise," Flynn said, kicking his door open. "Out. Now."

We scrambled from the wreckage as the SUV's engine roared. Flynn grabbed my hand and pulled me into a narrow alley between two buildings just as the SUV plowed into the Audi, crushing it like it was made of tinfoil.

I scanned for the truck. It was still visible, turning at the intersection ahead. "We need another car. We can't let it reach its destination."

"There." Flynn pointed to a motorcycle parked outside a café, keys dangling in the ignition. The owner had stepped inside, helmet hanging from the handlebars.

Flynn swung his leg over first and grabbed the helmet, jamming it onto my head. I climbed on behind him, my arms circling his waist as he brought the engine to life with a throaty roar.

"Hold on tight," he called over his shoulder, gunning the throttle.

"You're fucking nuts!" I shouted as he cut across a boulevard without checking traffic.

"And you're loving it!"

Dammit, I was.

I clung to him, my thighs pressed against his, my body molded to his back as we chased after the vanishing taillights of the truck. "Get us as close as possible."

The motorcycle leapt forward, engine screaming as

Flynn pushed it to its limits. My arms tightened around his waist, feeling the solid muscle beneath his tactical gear. He handled the bike like it was an extension of himself. We shot through a red light, narrowly avoiding a taxi that blared its horn. I could feel Flynn's laughter vibrating through his back. The man was genuinely enjoying this—the chase, the danger, all of it.

We gained on the truck. I could make out details now—reinforced panels, no windows in the cargo area, military-grade tires designed to keep rolling even after being shot.

It turned sharply, barreling through an outdoor café and leaving chaos in its wake. We followed, barely dodging an overturned table as debris rained across the road. My breath came in ragged gasps. My pulse hadn't slowed in ten minutes.

I laughed. Couldn't help it. "Pull up alongside it!"

He spared a glance over his shoulder. "What's the plan?"

"Boom!" I shouted, already reaching into my tactical belt for the compact grenade I'd stashed there.

Flynn shot me a look of disbelief as he accelerated, bringing us alongside the massive vehicle. "You're carrying explosives? Since when?"

"Since always." I pulled the safety pin with my teeth, holding the spoon in place. "Get me closer to his window."

"I think I might love you," Flynn said and swerved the bike dangerously close to the truck, our knees nearly brushing the metal panels.

The driver spotted us, his eyes widening in alarm.

He jerked the wheel toward us, trying to force us off the road. Flynn anticipated the move, dropping back just enough to avoid being pancaked before accelerating again. We were neck and neck with the cab now, close enough that I could see the sweat beading on the driver's forehead, the whites of his knuckles as he gripped the wheel.

I released the spoon, counted two heartbeats, and hurled the grenade through the driver's open window.

"Go!" I screamed, thumping Flynn's shoulder.

He didn't need to be told twice. The motorcycle surged forward as he twisted the throttle to its maximum, putting distance between us and the truck. Three seconds later, a deafening boom split the night. The truck swerved violently, careening sideways before tipping onto its side with a screech of metal against asphalt.

"Nice throw." Flynn cut the bike in a tight arc, circling back toward the crash site. Smoke billowed from the cab, flames licking around the edges of the shattered windshield.

I jumped off the bike and ran over to the truck. The cargo container door was ajar, one of the hinges blown clean off by the blast. Inside, black carbon-fiber crates were stacked floor to ceiling, secured with industrial strapping that had partially broken free in the crash. I had no idea if Sentinel was on board or not, but, either way, this shit wasn't going to end up in Moreau's auction.

"We need to move," Flynn called, scanning the street. "Moreau's men can't be far behind."

I climbed into the container, my boots crunching on broken glass. I pulled "Give me sixty seconds."

Flynn hesitated. "What are you doing?"

"We can't risk any of this tech making it to the auction." I placed charges all along the interior of the truck, working quickly, muscle memory taking over. Thirty seconds in, I heard sirens in the distance.

"Siren, we've got incoming!" Flynn shouted.

I glanced over my shoulder to see headlights cutting through the smoke. Not the authorities. Not yet. The black vehicles were all Moreau's security. I set the final charge and jumped out of the truck.

"How much C4 are you carrying?" Flynn asked as he took my hand and yanked me toward the bike.

"None now."

"Yep, I'm definitely in love. You're the perfect woman. Marry me."

"You're full of shit." I rolled my eyes and swung onto the bike behind him. "Ninety-second timer," I reminded. "Move!"

Flynn twisted the throttle, and the motorcycle shot forward just as the first SUV screeched to a halt beside the overturned truck.

We tore away from the scene, engine roaring as we wove through the labyrinth of Monte Carlo's streets. Flynn took corners so tight my knee nearly scraped the pavement, but I trusted his control implicitly, my body moving with his like we'd been riding together for years.

Behind us, the night sky erupted in a blinding flash of orange and white. The concussive blast hit us seconds later, a wall of sound and pressure that rattled windows and car alarms for blocks. The motorcycle wobbled beneath us as Flynn fought to maintain control.

"Jesus Christ, Lyric," he shouted over his shoulder, laughter in his voice. "What did you use? That was no standard-issue charge!"

"Modified thermite compound," I called back, my arms tightening around his waist. "Burns hot enough to melt most circuitry. Whatever was in that truck is slag now."

A few more blocks and we ditched the bike. I hit the ground running, lungs burning, adrenaline still roaring through my veins like fire. Flynn was right there with me. We made it three blocks before ducking into an underground parking garage, disappearing into the shadows just as a set of headlights swept past the entrance.

The only sounds were our harsh breathing and the distant drip of water echoing off concrete. Every foot-step, every shift, bounced off the walls tenfold, ampli-fying everything. We ducked behind a support pillar. I tried to steady my breathing, but my hands were shak-ing. The adrenaline was ebbing and leaving a mess behind. I tried to cover it by checking my weapon.

Flynn noticed immediately. Of course he did. He caught my wrist before I could hide it. "Breathe, princess. You're crashing."

"I'm fine."

"No you're not." He pulled me toward him by my wrist, and his lips crashed down against mine, hot and desperate. The kiss was raw, consuming—all teeth and tongue and wild need. My back hit the concrete pillar as he pressed against me, his body hard and unyielding. I gasped into his mouth, my shaking hands finding purchase in his hair, pulling him closer even as my rational mind screamed to push him away.

I didn't care. Not now. Not with the taste of danger still metallic on my tongue and my blood singing from our escape.

Flynn's hands moved to my hips, pinning me against the pillar. One slid up to cradle my jaw, tilting my head back to deepen the kiss. The stubble on his chin scraped against my skin, a delicious burn that only heightened every sensation.

"God, you were amazing out there," he murmured against my lips, voice rough with desire.

His words sent a fresh surge of heat through me, a different kind of adrenaline replacing the combat high. I arched against him, suddenly desperate for more contact.

"Flynn—" My voice caught as his mouth found the sensitive spot below my ear.

Footsteps echoed through the garage. Close. Fast.

We froze, then broke apart, instincts snapping into place. I nodded toward the far wall. Flynn nodded back. No words needed. Just motion and muscle memory. We split off, moving in opposite directions, flanking positions—classic pincer. Catch them in a crossfire.

I counted three sets of footsteps—two from the ramp, one circling wide. It was hard to pin them down with the way sound bounced through the space, but that worked in our favor too.

They were fast. We were faster.

I felt everything. Every breath, every shift of air. I was alive in a way that only combat ever made me feel.

Well, combat and Flynn's mouth on me.

We paused at opposite corners. I signaled. *Three targets, armed.*

Flynn nodded and gave me a look, pointed at me, then made a fist. *You good?*

I gave a single nod, just as they closed in.

The one on the right moved first, sweeping his weapon across the space ahead of him. He didn't see me until it was too late. I surged out of the dark, grabbed his arm, and twisted hard. His wrist snapped with a sharp pop, and the gun hit the floor. He opened his mouth to shout, but I drove my knee into his gut and spun him around to use his body as a shield as I scanned for his buddies.

Flynn's fight was louder, more brutal. He didn't bother with finesse. Just force. I heard the sharp crack of impact, the wet snap of something breaking, and the thud of a body hitting the ground.

The second man barely had time to register what was happening before he adjusted his aim toward me. But Flynn was there, materializing from the shadows, a blur of controlled violence. He caught the gunman's wrist, twisted, and slammed him against the concrete wall with enough force to crack plaster. The man's weapon clattered to the ground as Flynn drove an elbow into his throat, cutting off any possible shout for backup.

My opponent wasn't done. He threw his head back, trying to catch my nose, but I shifted just enough that his skull grazed my cheek instead. I tightened my hold, forearm pressing against his windpipe as I kicked his legs out from under him. We went down together, my weight driving him face-first into the concrete.

"Stay down," I hissed, pressing my knee between his shoulder blades.

He didn't listen. They never do.

He bucked beneath me, stronger than I'd anticipated. I rolled with the motion, using his momentum against him. As he twisted, I caught his jaw with my elbow. His head snapped back, and when he fell this time, he stayed down.

Flynn's man was already unconscious, slumped against the wall. Flynn stood over him, chest heaving, eyes wild with adrenaline and something darker, hungrier. He wiped blood from his mouth with the back of his hand, then looked at me, a feral grin spreading across his face.

"I fucking love my job." Then his gaze dropped to the man at my feet, and he whistled. "Did you break his neck?"

I looked down and winced. The man's neck bulged at an unnatural angle. "Wasn't trying to. I just tapped him with my elbow."

"Remind me never to piss you off. You fight like a demon."

I scoffed but couldn't stop the tiny flicker of pride

that warmed my chest. "You've been pissing me off since the moment you crashed my op."

"Not like that, I haven't." He nudged one of the unconscious men with his boot, then bent to scoop up the guy's weapon. "We can't leave them alive. They've seen your face."

My heart thudded hard. He was right. If they talked, the whole Elisa Deveraux persona would burn.

Flynn's eyes met mine—steady, unreadable. "I'll handle it."

I didn't nod. Didn't speak. Just looked away.

Two silenced shots.

When I turned back, Flynn was already crossing the space between us. His hand curled around my arm. "You good?" he asked, voice low, rough with adrenaline.

No. But also yes. Because every nerve in my body was lit. Because I could still feel his hands on me, his mouth on me. Because I'd just killed a man and let him kill two more, and all I wanted right now was him.

I nodded.

His eyes searched mine for a beat too long before his fingers laced through mine. "Let's move."

CHAPTER 14
LYRIC

WE MADE OUR WAY BACK TO MY HOTEL ON FOOT, WINDING through alleys and side streets to avoid being seen. We didn't speak. We didn't need to.

In the elevator, we stood on opposite sides, not touching. The air between us crackled with tension that made my skin prickle and my pussy clench. Flynn's gaze burned into me, stripping me bare without laying a finger on me. I felt exposed, vulnerable, and so fucking alive.

By the time we reached the suite, my keycard trembled in my hand. The lock clicked. The door swung open.

The second it shut behind us, I lunged for him. We collided, hard, and the impact sent something crashing to the floor as his mouth crashed into mine. Not gentle, nothing sweet about it. Just the raw, desperate hunger that had been building all night

He pressed me back against the door, and I moaned

into his mouth as I felt the hard length of his cock against my stomach. He cupped my tits under my shirt, kneading the soft flesh through my bra. I arched into him, my nails digging into his shoulders, my legs instinctively spreading to give him better access.

"Fuck," he groaned against my lips. He slid his hands down to grip my thighs, lifting me effortlessly until my legs wrapped around his waist. I could feel him pressed against my soaked panties, and I rocked my hips against him, desperate for friction.

"God, Flynn." My head fell back against the door as he kissed down my neck, his teeth grazing my skin, nipping, sucking, marking me like I was his.

"Tell me you want this." His breath was hot against my ear, sending shivers down my spine.

"Yes." I rolled my hips again, grinding against the hard bulge of his cock, and sank my teeth into his shoulder. "I want this."

His control snapped.

He let me slide down his body and tore off his jacket and shirt in one fluid motion, revealing a torso carved from granite.

He was so beautiful.

I skimmed my hands over him, mapping every inch of his body—the hard planes of his chest, the ridges of his abs, the sweat-slicked skin that burned under my touch.

Flynn moved like he fucking owned me, all rough hands and raw power. He yanked my shirt over my head, his eyes going dark as he tossed it aside. His fingers traced the curve of my tits, his touch sending electric shocks straight to my core.

"Christ, Lyric," he breathed, his voice wrecked and ragged. The way he said my name—a half-growl, half-moan—made my entire body tighten with need.

He shoved me back against the wall, pinning me with one knee between my legs, and I whimpered as he rocked against me, as he mouthed down the slope of my shoulder, setting my skin on fire. My bra fell away with a flick of his fingers, freeing my breasts to his mouth and hands. The sensation was electric—his hot tongue flicking over one nipple, his thumb rubbing rough circles over the other— and I bucked against him, my nails digging into his skin.

I was so wet, so gone for him, every touch like a lightning strike that left me gasping and desperate for more.

I was lost in him, drowning in the scent, the feel, the fury of Flynn.

His knee pressed higher between my legs, and the pressure made me grind down against him, seeking more, seeking everything.

"Goddamn," Flynn growled as he shifted his weight, letting me slide down the wall until my toes barely grazed the floor. He hooked his fingers into the waistband of my panties and dragged them down, following the erotic slide of silk with his mouth and tongue until he was kneeling in front of me.

I shivered—not from cold, but from the intensity of his stare. He looked at me like I was a fucking feast and he was starving.

I bit my lip, squirming under the heat of his gaze, feeling the slickness between my thighs with every breath, every heartbeat. "You just gonna stand there?"

"I've been thinking about this pretty pussy all night. And now look at you, so fucking wet for me." He spread my thighs wider until I was dripping onto his fingers. "Have you been this wet all night, my dangerous, deadly siren?"

"All night," I gasped, my head falling back against the wall as his fingers traced through my folds, circling but never quite touching where I needed him most.

His answering smile was pure sin. "You get off on danger, princess?"

"I get off on you," I admitted, the words tumbling out before I could stop them.

Something flashed in his eyes—hunger, possession, triumph—as he lowered his mouth to my inner thigh. His stubble scraped deliciously against my sensitive skin, and the first stroke of his tongue had me arching off the wall, a strangled cry tearing from my throat. He licked into me like a man possessed, broad, flat strokes that gathered my wetness before focusing on my clit in hard, perfect strokes that had my legs trembling. So goddamn good.

My fingers tangled in his hair, torn between pulling him closer and pushing him away as pleasure built too fast, too intense. I couldn't think. Couldn't speak. My thoughts were a blur of *yes* and *now* and *please don't stop*. I was breathless, panting, riding his face with desperate, shameless abandon. Two of his thick fingers slid inside me, curling to find that perfect spot, and I cried out, my entire body shuddering.

"That's it," he growled against my clit, the vibration sending another jolt of pleasure through me. "Come for me, Lyric. Let me taste how sweet you are when you fall apart."

His fingers pumped harder, faster, his tongue relentless against my swollen bud. My vision blurred at the edges. My whole world narrowed to the heat of his mouth, the pressure of his fingers, the way he pulled me apart and put me back together all at once. I was so close—so fucking close—teetering on the edge, my muscles clenching around his fingers as the pressure built to something unbearable.

"Flynn—" His name was a broken plea on my lips as the first wave crashed over me. My back arched, my thighs clamping around his head as I shattered, coming hard against his mouth.

He didn't stop, working me through the orgasm until I was flying outside my body. And when I finally came down from it, gasping and boneless and completely undone, Flynn was there to catch me.

He laughed softly. "You want me keep tasting you?" His fingers were still deep inside me, moving in and out, and my legs trembled so violently I thought my knees would give out. "Or do you want me to fuck you raw?"

"Fuck me," I begged, grinding against his wicked mouth as he teased my clit again with his tongue. "I need you inside me."

When he finally pulled back, his lips were glistening with my wetness, his eyes dark and hungry. He rose to his feet in one fluid motion, towering over me with that feral look still burning bright. His cock was hard and straining against his pants, and I reached for him, palming his length through the fabric.

"Fuck me," he hissed, his hips jerking forward into my touch.

"That's the idea." I rose to my feet and threaded my fingers through his hair, yanking his lips down to mine. "Get over here."

A smirk played on his lips—a challenge, a dare—and then he was kissing me again, rough and wild. I tasted myself on him and fucking loved it.

I unhooked his belt, yanking it free with a snap, then fumbled at the button of his pants in frantic desperation. "Too many clothes."

He helped me, shoving his pants down his hips, and the weight of his cock slapped against his abdomen— thick, heavy, flushed with need. My mouth watered at the sight of him. I wrapped my fingers around his length, reveling in the silky hardness, the way he pulsed in my palm.

"Jesus," he groaned, his head falling back as I stroked him, my thumb gathering the moisture beading at his tip. "Your fucking hands."

I sank to my knees, looking up at him through my lashes as I ran my tongue along the underside of his shaft. His eyes went molten, his fingers tangling in my hair as I took him into my mouth.

"Lyric," he gasped, voice rough and broken. "That

mouth—fuck—"

I hummed around him, taking him deeper until he hit the back of my throat. His hips jerked forward involuntarily, and I relaxed, letting him slide even deeper, loving the way his thighs tensed and his breath hitched. Power surged through me as I watched him come undone, this dangerous man reduced to ragged breaths and desperate groans by my mouth alone.

"Stop," he finally growled, pulling me off him with gentle force. "Or this ends way too soon."

But he didn't let me finish. With a muttered curse, he pulled me to my feet and spun me around, pressing me face-first against the full length mirror hanging on the wall. His cock slid between my thighs, teasing through my slick folds without entering me.

"Condom," I managed to gasp, my nails scraping against the cool glass as he nipped at my shoulder.

"Fuck. Right." He left me long enough to find his discarded pants. Seconds later, I heard the rip of foil and the snap of latex.

Then he was back, pressing against me, his cock sliding through my folds again. He positioned himself at my entrance, teasing me with just the tip, pressing his chest against my back, his lips brushing my ear. "Tell me how you want it."

"Hard," I breathed, arching back against him. "I don't want to be able to walk tomorrow."

A growl rumbled through his chest. His hand slid down my spine, over the curve of my ass. His palm came down with a sharp crack against my ass, and I gasped, my body jerking forward from the delicious sting. Heat bloomed across my skin as he massaged the spot, soothing and inflaming in equal measure.

"Does my naughty siren like that?"

"Yes," I moaned, pressing back against him. "God, yes."

His palm cracked against my other cheek, and I bit my lip to keep from crying out, my pussy clenching around nothing, desperate to be filled.

"You're so fucking beautiful," he growled, positioning himself at my entrance. "Look at yourself."

I lifted my gaze to the mirror, catching my reflection—cheeks flushed, eyes wild, my nipples hard little nubs, my lips swollen from his kisses. Behind me, Flynn's body was all hard planes and rippling muscles, golden skin marked by my nails, his eyes burning with hunger. He looked like a predator about to devour his prey, and I looked like I couldn't wait to be consumed.

"Watch," he commanded, his voice a rough whisper against my ear. "Watch me take you."

He held my gaze in the mirror as he thrust into me in one savage stroke. The sudden fullness knocked the breath from my lungs. He was thick, stretching me in the most delicious way, and I couldn't stop the moan that escaped me.

"Christ, you're tight," he groaned, his forehead dropping to my shoulder. "So fucking perfect."

He began to move, slow at first, each thrust deliberate and deep. I braced my hands against the mirror, pushing back to meet him, taking him deeper with each stroke. The angle was exquisite, hitting spots inside me that made my vision blur.

"Harder," I demanded, arching my back to take him deeper. "I'm not going to break."

Something dark and primal flashed in his eyes. He gripped my hips, fingers digging into my flesh hard enough to bruise as he picked up the pace. The sound of skin slapping against skin filled the room, mixed with our ragged breathing and my desperate moans. Each thrust drove me higher, closer to that edge where coherent thought dissolved into pure sensation.

The sight of us together was obscene and perfect—his muscles flexing with every thrust, my body yielding to his, the place where we joined slick and glistening. I couldn't look away, mesmerized by the raw hunger in his eyes, the way his jaw clenched with each drive of his hips.

I was going to come again. I could feel it building—hot and tight and inevitable—and I wanted it, needed it more than air or sanity or anything else that wasn't Flynn.

"Look at you," Flynn growled, his voice wrecked. "Taking my cock so perfectly. Like you were made for me."

His hand slid around to find my clit, circling the sensitive bud in time with his thrusts, and I cried out, my inner walls clenching around him.

"Oh, God!"

"Not God." His other hand closed around my throat, applying just enough pressure to make my pulse pound beneath his fingers. "You say my name when I'm inside you."

"Flynn," I gasped, the word tearing from my throat as his cock hit that perfect spot inside me.

"Good girl. The growled approval sent another wave of heat crashing through me. His fingers worked faster against my clit, his thrusts becoming erratic as he chased his own release. "Come with me, Lyric. Let me feel you."

The pressure of his hand on my throat, the relentless pounding of his cock, the slick circles of his fingers on my clit—it was too much.

"Flynn!" My scream was fierce, raw, torn from me as the orgasm hit like a fucking freight train. My whole body shook with it, every nerve ending going supernova as I shattered around him.

He was right there with me, thrusting harder, faster —pumping into me like he was losing his goddamn mind. I felt him tense, felt the ripple of muscles beneath his skin as he buried himself deep.

He came undone with a ragged groan, his whole body tensing as he spilled into me, hot and thick and fucking endless. The heat of him sent another wave crashing through me, pushing me over the edge all over again.

We stayed like that—connected, trembling, stunned by the force of what had just happened between us. Then his forehead dropped to my back, his breath coming in ragged gasps against my skin.

"Goddamn. I knew it would be good between us, but... fuck, Lyric." His voice was rough, raw, like he'd been screaming for hours. "That was..." He trailed off like he couldn't find the right word.

I couldn't, either. I didn't think I could speak at all. What were words?

My legs were jelly, my mind scattered in fragments around the room. Every nerve ending still tingled, aftershocks rippling through me with each brush of his skin against mine.

My reflection stared back at me—flushed cheeks, wild eyes, lips swollen from his kisses. I looked thoroughly ravished, completely undone. The woman in the mirror was someone I barely recognized, raw, vulnerable, exposed in ways that had nothing to do with being naked.

Flynn carefully withdrew, his hands never leaving my body as he steadied me. The loss of him left me feeling oddly hollow, but I wasn't ready to examine that too closely. He disappeared briefly to deal with the condom, then returned to wrap his arms around me from behind, his chin resting on my shoulder as we gazed at our reflection.

"You okay?"

I turned to face him, still panting, and—

Reality hit like a sledgehammer.

I just fucked Flynn Shepherd.

My eyes flew wide, and I shoved him away with a sound that was half gasp, half accusation.

"Holy shit," I said, scooping up my clothes and clutching them to my naked body like they could protect me from… whatever this was.

Flynn just grinned that signature cocky smirk I'd promised myself I wouldn't fall for.

"What?" he asked, all innocent.

"What?" I couldn't even process what he'd just done to me. What we'd done together. My brain felt like it had been struck by lightning and left smoldering.

"You look surprised." He took a step toward me, all easy arrogance and simmering heat. He was still naked, and he was already hard again, his cock standing out from his body in a way that sent another jolt of desire through me.

Like he hadn't just fucked me senseless.

Like he had every intention of using it again tonight.

He was more dangerous to me than anyone else in this city—a live wire I'd just grabbed with both hands and wanted to grab again.

"Surprised?" I laughed, a little too high-pitched, a little too frantic as I backed away. "I'm not surprised. I'm… I'm insane, apparently."

That earned me a low chuckle and another step forward. "Insanity looks good on you."

"You—" My words faltered as I yanked on my shirt.

"I what?" He was close now, so close I couldn't think straight, couldn't remember why I was supposed to be mad or cautious or anything but completely feral for him.

No.

Flynn Shepherd was off-limits. He was a walking red flag. He was everything I didn't need, everything I shouldn't want.

But here I was, aching for another taste.

He tilted my chin up, forcing my eyes to meet his. "You wanted me." It wasn't a question, and we both knew it. "You begged for me."

My skin felt raw, hyperaware of every breath, every nerve still buzzing from the intensity. "I didn't think…"

"You didn't think I'd fuck you until you screamed my name?" His grin widened. "I told you I would, princess."

The memory flashed, and another jolt of need pulsed through me. I glared at him to cover the flush creeping up my neck. "You're such a dick."

He laughed, low and wicked. "Pretty sure you love my dick."

"Pretty sure I hate you." But my words were weak, unraveling at the edges as I fumbled with my clothes.

"Keep lying to yourself, princess. We both know you're not done with me."

His mouth was on mine again, brutal and sweet, relentless and coaxing all at once. I should have pushed him away, should have remembered what a bad idea he was, should have remembered why I hated that cocky grin and arrogant swagger.

Instead, I moaned into his mouth and kissed him back, hungry and desperate, letting him pull me against the heat of his hard body. He lifted me effortlessly and carried me into the bedroom.

He tossed me onto the bed, and I fell back with a gasp as he followed, effortlessly pinning my wrists above my head in one hand while he ripped open another condom package with his teeth.

"One night," I whispered, parting my legs to welcome him. "You get one night."

"If that's all I get…" He rolled on the condom, positioned his thick head at my entrance, and filled me with one vicious stroke. I arched beneath him, gasping at the delicious fullness.

"I'm going to make it count," he promised, his voice a rough growl against my ear. "I'm going to ruin you for all other men, Siren."

I didn't say it, but I was pretty sure he already had.

CHAPTER 15
FLYNN

I'D SPENT MY ENTIRE ADULT LIFE PERFECTING THE ART OF waking up alone. I'd had my share of women over the years—good women, dangerous women, beautiful women, and everything in between—but I'd never been the type to linger the morning after. Not after missions, and definitely not after sex. I was always planning my exit before I even arrived. It was my personal code, my survival instinct, the reason I was still breathing while so many others weren't.

I wasn't looking for permanence. No roots or connections that couldn't be easily severed. My life was compact by design—everything I owned fit in one duffel bag. My relationships were the same.

Clean. Uncomplicated. Disposable.

It was the way I liked it.

Until Lyric.

I blinked awake to light filtering through the terrace doors, painting the room in soft gold. My body ached in places I hadn't noticed last night. Not from the chase, not from the fight, but from her. From the way we'd torn into each other like the world was ending.

Hell.

She was still sound asleep beside me. She lay on her stomach, one arm tucked beneath her pillow, the other stretched toward me. The sheet had slipped to her waist, exposing the elegant line of her spine, the soft curve of her shoulder blades. Her hair was a tangle of platinum and gold against the white pillowcase, and there was a mark on her shoulder where I'd gotten carried away with my teeth. She looked softer in sleep, the sharp edges and walls she kept so carefully constructed during waking hours momentarily dismantled.

An unfamiliar, unsettling sensation spread through my chest.

I wanted to stay with her.

The realization hit me like a suckerpunch.

I wanted to wake up next to this woman tomorrow. And the day after that. I wanted to learn the map of those freckles, memorize the sounds she made when she came apart beneath me, discover what made her laugh, what made her cry, what made her trust—and what had made her so afraid to.

Well…

Fuck.

I'd known Lyric Renard for less than a week, and somehow she'd already gotten under my skin in ways no one else ever had. It wasn't just the sex, though Christ, that had been mind-blowing. It was everything else. The way she'd handled herself during the chase.

How she'd fought beside me like we'd been a team for years. The way she never backed down, never flinched, never hesitated.

I imagined, for the first time in my adult life, what it might be like to have something real. Something that lasted beyond a mission or a night. Something that mattered. What if, after Sentinel was secured and Moreau was neutralized, there was... after? What if there was breakfast in bed and lazy Sunday mornings? What if there were inside jokes and favorite restaurants and a side of the bed that was mine?

What if there was a life beyond the job?

The possibility felt foreign, almost ridiculous, like trying on someone else's too-tight clothes. I'd spent my entire career—my entire life—being the guy who could walk away. The one who didn't get attached. The one who never looked back. It was what made me good at my job.

But looking at her now, I couldn't imagine walking away. Not tomorrow. Not ever.

The thought should have terrified me. Instead, it felt like coming home.

Christ. When had I turned into such a sap?

She stirred, her breathing changing rhythm as she drifted toward consciousness. I watched her brow furrow slightly, her lips part on a soft exhale. Then her eyes fluttered open, unfocused at first, then sharpening as awareness returned.

I watched the walls slamming back into place, her expression shuttering closed, her body language shifting from soft to guarded in the space of a heartbeat.

The change was immediate and heartbreaking.

"Morning," I said, keeping my voice casual despite the sudden tightness in my chest.

"Morning." She pulled the sheet up to cover herself, a pointless gesture after everything we'd done last night, but telling all the same. She sat up, gaze darting around the room like she was assessing threats and exits.

I'd seen that look before. Hell, I'd worn it myself enough times. But seeing it on her face now, directed at me, felt like a knife between my ribs.

She finally exhaled hard and shoved her hair back from her face. "What time is it?"

"Just after seven."

Lyric nodded and got out of bed, keeping the sheet wrapped around her like armor. She didn't look at me as she reached for her phone on the nightstand, scrolling through notifications with more focus than the task required. "Ethan's pissed."

"Of course he is." I flopped back against my pillow and stretched my arms over my head. "I expected nothing less from Grim."

"He wants a full debrief at eight."

Jesus, the ice in her voice could freeze a guy at ten paces. This wasn't the woman who'd moaned my name last night, who'd laughed breathlessly as we collapsed in a tangle of limbs. This was Siren—professional, detached, and completely unreachable.

"Hey," I said, propping myself up on one elbow. "You okay?"

"Fine." The word was clipped, dismissive. "Just

trying to figure out what I'm going to say to him. I'll be lucky if he doesn't fire me on the spot."

"That's not what I meant."

She finally looked at me. I would've preferred to see annoyance or anger or anything else other than that carefully neutral expression. "Look, Flynn. Last night was... intense. The chase, the fight, the adrenaline. Sex was a natural release valve."

I felt my jaw tighten. "A release valve?"

"You know what I mean."

"No." I swung my legs over the bed and stood, not bothering with modesty. "I don't know what you mean."

Her gaze dropped down my body, but she caught herself and quickly looked away. She tightened her grip on the sheet like it could protect her from this conversation.

"It was good. Really good. But it was just sex."

Just sex. My chest tightened. Not with anger, though there was plenty of that brewing, but with something that felt dangerously close to hurt. "That wasn't 'just' anything and you know it."

"Oh, don't make this complicated, Flynn." She sighed, turning away to gather her scattered clothes from the floor. "It was the circumstances. The danger. The near-death experience. It's textbook. A biological imperative to affirm life after facing mortality. Let's just chalk it up to a heat-of-the-moment mistake and move on.

"A mistake?" I echoed, disbelief crawling up my throat. "Which part exactly? When you begged me to fuck you harder? Or when you came screaming my name the second time? Or maybe the third?"

Her cheeks flushed, but her eyes went cold. "Don't be crude."

"Don't be a coward."

That hit. I saw it in the way her jaw tightened, the slight flinch she couldn't quite suppress. "I'm not afraid of you." She turned away. "And we don't have time for this. I'm going to shower.

"No?" I moved around the bed, positioning myself in her path. "Then look at me."

"Flynn—"

"Look at me, Lyric."

Reluctantly, she raised her eyes to mine, and for a split second, I saw it—that flash of vulnerability, of want, before she buried it beneath layers of ice.

"Tell me last night meant nothing to you," I challenged, stepping closer. "Tell me you don't feel this—whatever the hell this is between us—and I'll walk away. I'll back off. We'll be nothing but colleagues."

She didn't respond, her throat working as she swallowed.

"You can't, can you?" I pressed. "Because you're lying to yourself."

"What do you want from me?" she asked on barely a breath of sound.

What did I want? The question hammered against my ribs. I wanted her—not just her body, but all of her. The vulnerability beneath the armor. The woman who fought like a demon and kissed like she was drowning.

The one who placed charges with surgical precision and laughed in the face of danger.

"I want you to be honest," I said finally. "With yourself, if not with me."

She shook her head, a bitter smile twisting her lips. "Honesty is a luxury in our line of work. You know that better than anyone."

"Not with each other. Never with each other." I reached for her, my fingers grazing her cheek. "I don't do this, Lyric. I don't stay. I don't... feel. But with you—"

"Don't." She jerked away from my touch and held up a hand as she backed up. "We have a mission to complete. Let's focus on that."

She disappeared into the bathroom, the door closing with a decisive click that might as well have been a gunshot. I heard the shower start, water drowning out whatever sounds she might be making in there.

I scrubbed a hand down my face, trying to process what had just happened. Last night, she'd been all fire and need, wrapping herself around me like she couldn't get close enough. This morning, she was treating me like a regrettable one-night stand.

I knew this dance. I'd choreographed it myself more times than I could count. The morning-after retreat, the casual dismissal, the strategic withdrawal. I was the king of emotional distance.

So why did it feel like my chest was caving in?

CHAPTER 16
LYRIC

The morning after always sucks.

That was one of my mother's favorite lessons—usually muttered while popping aspirin and chasing it with a little hair of the dog.

She was wrong about a lot, but she was right about this.

I turned the shower as hot as I could stand it, hoping the scalding water would wash away the feeling of Flynn's hands on my skin, his mouth on my neck. Every inch of my body ached—a delicious, bone deep soreness that came from being thoroughly, gloriously fucked.

I closed my eyes, letting the water cascade over me, and tried to forget the look on Flynn's face when I'd called last night a mistake. The hurt that had flashed through those amber eyes before he'd masked it with anger.

It wasn't a lie, exactly. It had been a mistake. Just not for the reasons he thought.

The mistake wasn't the sex. The sex had been mind-blowing—raw and primal and exactly what I'd needed. The mistake was letting myself feel something beyond the physical release. The mistake was the way my chest had tightened when I'd woken up to find him watching me with something dangerously close to tenderness.

The mistake was wanting more.

Men like Flynn Shepherd were temporary by design. They were human wrecking balls, destroying everything in their path, and leaving behind nothing but rubble. My entire career was built on maintaining control, on never giving anyone power over me.

One night with Flynn had already cracked my carefully constructed walls. A second night would shatter them completely.

I couldn't let that happen. Not when we were knee-deep in a mission that could cost lives if I lost focus. Not when I still had to face Moreau and secure Sentinel. Not when my place on this team was hanging by a thread.

I stepped out of the shower and wrapped myself in a towel, the steam following me in a cloud as I walked back into the bedroom, steeling myself for a fight.

Flynn was gone.

I should have felt relieved. Instead, something hollow opened up in my chest.

No. I'd done the right thing. The only thing. Anything else would've been reckless and dangerous. Sloppy.

I toweled myself off roughly, trying to scrub away the memories of his hands on me, his mouth, the way he'd looked at me like I was something precious instead of just another body. Another conquest.

But the ghost of him lingered everywhere—in the faint scent of his cologne that clung to the rumpled sheets, in the throb between my thighs that reminded me with every step that I'd let him in. That I'd begged for him.

"Stupid," I muttered, yanking a brush through my wet hair harder than necessary, ripping through the tangles. "So fucking stupid."

My reflection stared back at me from the vanity's mirror, lips still slightly swollen, a faint bruise blooming on the side of my breast where his mouth had nipped and sucked.

Heat flushed my skin at the memory and pooled between my legs.

Ugh. I threw down the brush in exasperation with myself and told my traitorous reflection, "No."

I couldn't afford to care about Flynn Shepherd. I couldn't afford to care about anyone.

Focus on the mission. Nothing else matters.

I dressed in a black Tom Ford jumpsuit with a deep-V that plunged nearly to my navel and a wide belt cinched at my waist with a gold buckle. I slid matching chunky gold bracelets onto my wrists and strapped on heels sharp enough to kill. Finally, I dealt with my hair, twisting it into a severe chignon with not a hair out of place.

No one looking at me would see the woman who shattered in Flynn Shepherd's arms last night.

They'd see cold, untouchable Elisa Deveraux.

And that was exactly who I needed to be right now because beneath my carefully constructed exterior, I was unraveling fast.

Even though I stopped for coffee on my way across town, nobody else had arrived yet when I stepped into the temporary command center.

Nobody except Flynn, draped in a chair like he owned the damn place. His eyes heated as he took in my outfit, lingering too long on the deep-V neckline that left little to the imagination. That persistent, nagging memory of his mouth on my breasts rushed back, sending a wave of heat through me.

"Morning, princess," he said like he hadn't just seen me an hour ago, his voice rough with an edge I couldn't quite place. Anger? Hurt? Desire? Maybe all three.

I took a seat as far from him as possible while still being in the same room and set my coffee on the table, pulling out my tablet to review the after-action report I'd thrown together after my shower.

Silence stretched between us.

"So that's how it's going to be?" he finally asked.

I looked up, keeping my expression neutral. "I don't know what you mean."

"Yes, you do." He leaned forward, those amber eyes molten. "You're going to pretend last night never happened."

"There's nothing to pretend. It happened. It's over." I turned my attention back to my tablet, though the words blurred together. "We have more important things to focus on. You know, like stopping Moreau from selling a weapon that could kill thousands."

"Right." He exhaled through his nose, his jaw tight. "The mission. Always the mission."

Before I could respond, the door swung open and the team filed in.

Trent nodded at me, his face unreadable as he settled into a chair.

Alistair was quiet as he sat beside Trent, his gaze shifting between Flynn and me. I didn't like the way it made me feel, like he saw everything. Every bruise I'd covered with foundation, even the ones I'd asked Flynn to put on me in the throes of sex. He might be our medic, but I didn't need his diagnosis. Not for this.

Nolan sauntered in behind them, looking like he'd rolled out of bed and into the first clothes he found. His trademark smirk was firmly in place as he dropped into a chair and propped his boots on the table. "As a connoisseur of explosions, I have to say on record that was a very impressive fireball last night." He eyed my outfit and his smirk widened to a grin. "And today she's dressed to kill. You might just be my soulmate, Siren."

Flynn growled softly, and I shot him a warning look. The last thing I needed was for him to go all possessive alpha male in front of the whole team. I'd never gain their respect if he treated me like I was his territory to defend instead of his equal.

"I'd be a terrible soulmate," I replied to Nolan with a thin smile. "Ask anyone."

Nolan winked. "And by anyone, you mean Shepherd?"

Oh, God.

I glanced around the table. Flynn looked like he wanted to punch something. Trent took a sudden interest in his coffee cup, twisting it in slow circles. Alistair studied the ceiling as if it might hold vital intelligence. Even Nolan seemed to realize he'd stepped in something, his grin faltering.

They knew. Of course they knew. A team like this didn't miss anything.

I wanted to melt into the floor.

Thankfully, Ozzy saved me from having to respond by bursting into the room just then, juggling a laptop, at least three tablets, and a travel mug of coffee the size of a small bucket. His dark eyes were bloodshot, and the scowl on his face could have curdled milk. "You motherfucker," he said to Flynn. "You stole my tech."

Flynn's mouth twitched. "Borrowed."

"Borrowing implies returning it intact," Ozzy muttered, dropping into a chair and lifting the coffee bucket—it really couldn't be called a mug—to his mouth. Printed on the bottom was a hand throwing up a middle finger. "That EMP grenade was one of a kind."

"And it worked beautifully," Flynn replied, unrepentant. "Consider it field testing."

Before Ozzy could retort, the door swung open again with enough force to rattle the hinges. Ethan strode in, every line of his body rigid with barely contained fury. The room went silent.

"Would someone like to explain why half of Monte Carlo is on fire?"

I kept my expression neutral, but my pulse kicked up a notch. The tension in the room was thick enough to choke on.

Flynn lounged deeper in his chair, appearing completely unfazed by Ethan's temper. "Technically, it's more like point-zero-five percent. One block. Not even the whole block. And you did tell us to sabotage what we could."

"Not helping," I muttered under my breath.

Ethan's gaze snapped to mine. "Did I tell you to detonate a thermite compound in the middle of the city?" His voice had gone deceptively calm, but the muscle jumping in his jaw told a different story. "Or was I hallucinating when I specifically ordered you to gather intel, sabotage what you could, and exfil without drawing attention?"

I held his stare. "The truck was moving some of the technology. We couldn't let it reach its destination."

"So you blew it up." It wasn't a question.

"We neutralized the threat," I corrected.

"It took Maya years to establish this cover." Ethan's voice broke on her name, and something twisted in my chest.

It was common knowledge that Ethan and Maya had been lovers, but it wasn't until this moment that I realized he had actually been in love with her.

I glanced over at Flynn. He was watching Ethan with sympathy in his eyes. Then his gaze met mine, and the depth of feeling, the vulnerability, I saw there made my stomach flip. I tore my eyes away, focusing back on Ethan.

"Years," Ethan repeated. "And you nearly burned it to the ground in one night." He slammed a tablet down on the table. News footage filled the screen—flames licking the night sky, emergency vehicles with flashing lights, reporters gesturing dramatically at the wreckage. "This isn't how Edge operates."

Flynn snorted, and my gaze snapped back to him. I couldn't seem to keep it off him. The vulnerability was gone, and he was back to his usual cocky self. "Now that's a load of bullshit. Every operative in this room has done something that left a smoking crater at one point or another. Hell, that's Nolan's favorite pastime."

"Ah, he's not wrong," Nolan said.

Flynn continued, his casual tone contradicting the dangerous glint in his eyes: "Just last month, Trent tanked two years of undercover work to save a woman from that doomsday cult, and then the earthquake device they had practically ripped California off the map. But you didn't ride his ass about it."

"There were extenuating circumstances," Trent said coldly.

"Ah, but what about that time Alistair and Rafe accidentally burned down an entire warehouse in

Budapest? No extenuating circumstances there," Nolan said, all innocence. "And the time Leo punched a tank-sized hole through that villa in Odessa just because the Russian who owned it was a right gobshite." He ticked off each example on his fingers, clearly enjoying himself. "And let's not forget Oz hijacked a Chinese defense satellite, crashed it, and nearly started World War Three."

"That was justified," Ozzy muttered into his coffee.

Ethan's jaw clenched. "Enough."

"No, I don't think it is," Flynn said, his gaze locked on Ethan. "What about when Maya blew up a yacht in Singapore last year? Thirty-foot fireball visible from the mainland. Made international news, and I don't recall you giving her any kind of grief about it."

The room fell silent. No one breathed. I wanted to kick Flynn under the table, and cursed myself for sitting so far away from him. What did he think he'd achieve by jabbing at a wound Ethan hadn't even begun to let heal?

Flynn leaned back in his seat again, folding his hands behind his head. "Seems like the problem isn't the tactics, it's that Lyric's the one using them."

Ethan's face went pale, then flushed with anger. For a heartbeat, I thought he might actually hit Flynn. Instead, he braced his hands on the table and leaned forward, his voice dropping to a dangerous whisper. "I didn't ask for your opinion, Shepherd, and you're way out of line. You're not even officially part of this team."

"No, and that's the way I like it."

I watched Flynn's face harden, those amber eyes

turning molten with challenge as he stood and faced Ethan across the table. The temperature in the room seemed to drop ten degrees.

"Then why are you still here?" Ethan asked, still in that deadly quiet tone. "If you prefer being a lone wolf…" He jerked his chin. "There's the door."

Flynn's jaw tightened. "Because a long time ago, I gave you my word that whenever you needed help, I'd be here for you. And *you need help* right now, E. So here I am."

I found myself holding my breath, watching the silent standoff between these two men who clearly shared a history that went far deeper than I'd realized.

"You hired me for my expertise, E," Flynn added quietly after a long, charged moment. "And my expert opinion is that Lyric did the smart thing by taking dangerous technology out of play. She might've even turned Sentinel to slag last night. Problem solved."

"No, problem multiplied," Ethan countered and straightened, running a hand over his face. His expression was still rigid but marginally less murderous. "The local authorities are involved. Interpol is sniffing around. And Moreau knows someone is targeting his operation."

Ozzy cleared his throat. "Actually, he doesn't."

All eyes turned to him. He spun his tablet around, showing surveillance footage of the crash site. "I intercepted the comms from Moreau's security team. They think it was the Chinese. Remember the buyers at the hangar? Wei Zhao? Apparently, you were watching their negotiations break down."

"That's... convenient," Trent said, leaning forward with newfound interest. He looked at Ethan. "Could mean Lyric's cover is still uncompromised."

Ethan paced the length of the table, his anger morphing into something more focused. "Is Elisa Deveraux still viable?"

A fair question. I'd been wondering the same thing since we left three bodies cooling in that parking garage.

Even though he'd asked the room and not me specifically, I answered. "So far, yes. We killed all of the guards who saw my face, and I haven't heard from Moreau. The invitation is still in my possession." I pulled it from my pocket and placed it on the table. "If he suspected me, he'd have sent someone for this already."

"Or he's watching to see what you'll do," Alistair said quietly, speaking for the first time.

Flynn's eyes met mine across the table. We both knew Alistair was right. Moreau was too careful, too calculating to leave things to chance. If he had even a whisper of suspicion about me, he'd be setting traps.

"Then I'll give him what he expects," I said firmly. "Elisa Deveraux will arrive at the auction with her security detail, ready to buy Sentinel by any means necessary."

"And if he's waiting with a bullet instead of an auction paddle?" Trent asked.

I shrugged. "Then I'll deal with it."

"We'll deal with it," Flynn corrected, his voice brooking no argument.

Ethan studied us both, his expression unreadable. Something passed between him and Flynn—some silent communication born of shared history that excluded the rest of us.

For the first time, I wondered about that history. Flynn had made it very clear he'd only taken this job initially because of Ethan.

"It gets better," Ozzy continued, swiping to another screen, drawing me out of my thoughts. "Moreau's people are in full panic mode. They're moving the auction up. Tomorrow night, not this weekend."

My heart skipped. "Tomorrow? Where? Still at the docks?"

Ozzy scowled at me. "Still working on that, but I've got algorithms scanning every communication channel Moreau's ever used."

Nolan raised a hand. "Uh, question. Why don't I just fly over the hangar and drop a few high-yield thermo-barics and…" He gestured with his hands to mimic an explosion. "… boom. Call it a day?"

"Because we need confirmation," Ethan said, shutting him down with a look. "We need to verify Sentinel was actually in that truck. And if it wasn't, we need to find it before Moreau sells it to the highest bidder." He pinned me with his stare. "If that technology gets loose, it's a global security nightmare. One rogue drone could assassinate a world leader. A swarm could take out an entire government."

"And they already evacuated the hangar," Ozzy said without looking up from his laptop screen. "You just want to blow shit up."

"Well, yeah." Nolan grinned unapologetically. "That is literally my job description. Fly things. Blow things up. Look good doing it."

"That ego of yours is so big, I'm surprised your Irish ass ever gets airborne," Alistair muttered, but there was a hint of fondness in his exasperation.

"Have you been admiring my Irish ass, Preacher?"

"Every time I have to stitch it back together, I wonder what poor life choices brought me here."

The banter rolled on. It was like hearing a language I almost understood—Nolan's swagger, Alistair's dry comebacks, Ozzy's irritated grunts as a few jabs were aimed in his direction, the half-smiles that flickered across Trent's usually stoic face. A language built over years of missions, shared trauma, and inside jokes. And I wasn't fluent yet. Maybe never would be.

"Children," Ethan snapped, his already thin patience clearly fraying. "Focus."

As the jokes subsided, he spread his hands flat on the table, leaning in. "The window just narrowed significantly. We have less than twenty-four hours to locate the auction site and prepare infiltration. Lyric's cover is our only available access point, so we're going to assume for now it's still intact. Flynn will stay as her security. Oz—" He looked over at the tech guy. "Get me into Moreau's systems. I want to know every-fucking-thing he does from here on out."

"That kind of hacking takes time," Ozzy said, never taking his eyes off his screen.

"You have twenty-four hours."

"Jesus fucking Christ. I'm a hacker, not a magician."

"Just get it done." Ethan turned to his second-in-command. "Trent, let's see if we can get Decker here before the auction. We're going to need his expertise on this."

"Wouldn't be surprised if the shady bastard already had an invitation to the auction," Nolan muttered.

"Yes, Maverick, we all know your feelings about him," Trent replied dryly, already pulling out his phone.

I hadn't met anyone on the team named Decker yet, and I resisted the urge to ask who he was. Not knowing was just another reminder that I was the outsider here, the replacement part slotted into a machine that had been running smoothly before I arrived.

Ethan continued, "Nolan—"

"Aye. Air support. I know the drill."

"Air support with *discretion*." Ethan's emphasis on the last word wasn't subtle. "No 'fireworks' unless I specifically authorize it."

Nolan looked wounded. "You take all the craic out of flying, boss."

"I'm not here for your entertainment," Ethan said, then finally turned to Alistair. "I want every medical contingency covered. Have trauma gear ready for exfil. We don't know what we're walking into."

Alistair nodded. "We're not losing anyone on this mission."

Unlike their last mission.

Although he didn't say it out loud, Maya's ghost still lingered in the room. Would she always be here?

Ethan nodded once, something painful passing

across his features before his professional mask slipped back into place. "Kate?"

"Here," Kate piped up from the speakers of Ozzy's computer, and I realized with a jolt she'd been listening in this whole time.

"Comb through Moreau's communications. I want surveillance on every dock, every helipad, every private airfield within fifty miles. I want to know where this fucking auction is happening before we send people into a potential trap."

"Already on it," Kate said. "I'm cross-referencing with satellite imagery of unusual activity patterns in the area."

"Alright." Ethan straightened, his gaze sweeping over each of us. "Let's get to work."

But as everyone else rose to leave, he caught my eye.

"A word?" he said, nodding toward the balcony.

I followed him outside, where the morning air carried the scent of salt and distant smoke—remnants of our handiwork.

Ethan closed the door behind us. "I need to know you're not compromised."

"Excuse me?"

"Flynn," he said simply.

My spine stiffened. "What about him?"

"Don't insult my intelligence, Lyric. I've known Flynn for years. I know how he operates, and I know what I'm seeing between you two."

I kept my expression carefully neutral. "Whatever you think you're seeing, it doesn't affect my ability to do my job."

"Doesn't it?" Ethan challenged. "You went rogue last night. Both of you. And while it may have worked out this time, I need to know that when the moment comes—and it will come—you'll make the right call. Even if it means leaving him behind."

The thought made my chest tighten painfully. "I'll do whatever the mission requires."

"Good," Ethan said, but his expression told me he didn't believe me. "Because Flynn has a habit of getting people killed."

The words hit like a physical blow. I kept my face carefully blank, but my pulse quickened. "What does that mean?"

Ethan turned to face the railing, his knuckles white against the metal. The morning sun cast harsh shadows across his face, highlighting the exhaustion etched there. "There's a reason he works alone."

Before I could ask what he meant, the balcony door slid open. Flynn stood there, his arms crossed. "You telling her all my dirty secrets, E?"

CHAPTER 18
FLYNN

The first rule of surviving enemy territory: never get caught with your guard down. I'd lived by that rule for fifteen years. But watching Lyric cross the hotel suite, her shoulders rigid with tension, I knew I was about to break it.

We'd left the team an hour ago. Lyric ordered a car to pick up Elisa and her bodyguard outside a private fashion atelier on Avenue de Grande Bretagne. It meant we had to walk to the place and then spend a painful forty minutes browsing the ultra-expensive designer gowns and suits, playing the part of the wealthy heiress and her security, before slipping out a side door to the waiting car.

If Moreau's people checked, it would hold.

Now we were back in the suite, and the silence between us felt like a physical thing, thick and suffocating. She hadn't spoken a word since we'd left the command center. Not while shopping, not in the car, not in the elevator, not now.

"We need to talk," I said as soon as the suite's door shut behind us, unable to stand the quiet any longer.

She dropped her clutch on a side table and kicked off her sky-high heels. "No, we don't."

I watched as she crossed to the fridge and pulled out a bottle of water. And, yeah, it probably made me a pig, but I couldn't help but watch her gorgeous ass sway as she moved.

Jesus, that jumpsuit should be illegal.

My cock went semi-hard and my hands itched to grip those curves again, to hear her gasp my name. But the ice in her voice told me she was still freezing me out. I stepped closer, closing the distance she kept trying to put between us.

"Yes, we do. What exactly did Ethan tell you?" I asked, knowing Ethan well enough to guess. He'd given her the sanitized version, the official report, the one that painted me as the reckless liability.

She unscrewed the cap and took a long drink, her throat working as she swallowed. When she finally looked at me, her eyes were guarded, wary.

"That you have a habit of getting people killed." She set the water bottle down with deliberate care. "That there's a reason you work alone."

I laughed, but it was a harsh sound even to my own ears. "That's it? A decade of history and that's all he gave you?"

"Should there be more?"

I ran a hand through my hair, suddenly restless. The walls of the suite felt too close, the air too thin. "Yeah. There's more."

Lyric crossed her arms, creating another barrier between us. "Then tell me."

I moved to the window, staring out at the glittering coastline of Monte Carlo. All that money, all that glamour, hiding rot and corruption beneath. Kind of like the mission reports that buried the truth under bureaucratic bullshit.

"Sana'a, Yemen. Seven years ago." I kept my back to her, watching her reflection in the window instead of turning to face her directly. "Ethan was running a covert extraction. High-value asset with intel on terrorist cells operating throughout the region. I was his intelligence officer."

I felt her shift behind me, but she didn't speak. Waiting. Patient. Like she knew this wasn't going to be easy for me.

"The asset had information on weapons deals, personnel movements, financial networks—the kind of intelligence that could cripple operations across three countries."

I closed my eyes briefly, the memories still razor-sharp despite the years. The heat. The dust. The coppery tang of blood in my mouth.

"My intel was solid. I'd spent three months mapping security rotations, identifying weak points, and tracking the movement patterns of everyone in that compound. But what I didn't know—what none of us knew—was that someone had sold us out."

"And people died," she said quietly.

I turned from the window to find Lyric watching me. She hadn't moved, arms still crossed, and her expression was still guarded, but I sensed a thawing in the ice.

"Three good men. Ambushed the moment they breached the compound." The memory crashed over me—gunfire, shouting, the radio crackling with desperate calls for backup. "The asset was already dead when they got there. Executed. The whole thing was a setup."

Her brow furrowed. "Ethan blames you?"

"Ha, yeah." I rubbed a hand over my face, trying to scrub away the memories. "But, also, no. Saying he blames me is too simplistic for what happened. The truth is, it's complicated. He was team leader. The call to continue the mission after the initial ambush was his, but I was the one who pushed for it."

I crossed to the bar and poured two fingers of whiskey, needing something to steady the tremor in my hands. "I told him the intel was still valuable, even without the asset. I insisted we could still complete the objective, and Ethan trusted my judgment. He always had before." I knocked back the whiskey in one burning swallow. "But it was chaos. The team was pinned down. Ethan made the call to abort, but I was so sure there were documents, hard drives, information we could salvage." I turned the glass in my hand, watching the amber liquid catch the light. "So I ignored his order to retreat, and I got shot for my trouble."

Lyric's eyes widened slightly. "How bad?"

"Bad enough." I set the glass down and lifted my shirt, revealing the puckered scar just below my ribs. She must have seen it last night—it was hard to miss—

but never asked about it. "Caught a round that shredded my liver. By all rights, I should have bled out in that compound."

She moved closer almost unconsciously, her eyes fixed on the scar. "But you didn't."

"No." I lowered my shirt, remembering the pain, the certainty that I was dying. "Because Ethan came back for me. Against protocol. Against orders. He led three men back into that death trap. And he and I were the only ones who made it out. Barely. He carried me out through a hail of gunfire. He didn't leave me behind, even though every manual, every protocol, every ounce of common sense said he should have. I dug my own grave, and he should've let me lie in it."

Lyric's expression softened just a fraction. "He chose to go back."

"Yeah. That's what makes it worse." I knocked back the second drink, welcoming the burn. "We've known each other since Ranger School. Saved each other's asses more times than I can count. When he made team leader on that Yemen op, I was his first pick. He trusted me, and I got his men killed. So when I healed up, I went freelance. Figured if I only had to worry about my own neck, I couldn't get anyone else killed."

Lyric's gaze was steady. "And now he keeps you at arm's length, but still calls when he needs you."

"Yeah." I downed the second whiskey, welcoming the burn. "He can't forgive me, but he knows I'm loyal. I owe him a debt I can never repay."

"That's kind of bullshit."

A laugh burst out of me at her blunt assessment. "You think?"

"I do." She moved closer. "You both made choices that day. He chose to trust your intel. He chose to go back for you. And yes, you chose to push forward when you should have retreated. But war is messy. Operations fail. And from what I've seen, you'd have done the same for him if your roles were reversed. You'd have gone back."

I would've been thrilled to see the ice in her eyes thawing if I hadn't had to flay myself open to get that hint of warmth again. As it was, I felt naked and raw in a way I hadn't in years. And I hated it.

"Yeah, in a heartbeat," I admitted roughly. "But how do you know that?"

"Because, now, you keep coming back. You keep jumping when he says jump and taking jobs you don't want. For him. Because you love him, even when he's an ass."

I turned away from her, staring back out at the glittering coastline. Her words hit too close to home, like a bullet finding the gap in body armor.

"Love's a strong word," I muttered, but we both knew she was right.

"If not love, then why else do you keep coming back?" She moved to stand beside me at the window, close enough that I could feel the heat of her without touching.

I shrugged, trying for nonchalance and failing miserably. "Maybe I miss his sunny personality."

She didn't smile at the weak joke. Instead, her eyes

softened with something dangerously close to understanding.

Restless, I went back to the bar and poured another drink, offering her the glass this time. She hesitated before taking it, her fingers brushing mine in the exchange. The brief contact sent electricity racing up my arm.

Lyric took a small sip, her eyes never leaving mine over the rim of the glass. The jumpsuit's neckline dipped low enough for me to catch a glimpse of the mark I'd left on the curve of her breast. I wanted to put my mouth there again, to taste her skin, to hear those soft sounds she made when I—

"Maybe because you miss having someone watch your six."

Her words stilled me. I looked away, not wanting her to see how close to the mark she'd hit.

"Nah." I waved a dismissive hand in the air. "I just like the paycheck."

She set a hand on my forearm and waited until I met her gaze. "Either he forgives you or he doesn't. This half-in, half-out thing you've got going on isn't fair to either of you."

Well, damn. She wasn't going to let me off the hook.

But two could play that game.

I set down my glass and held her gaze as I closed the distance between us. "And what about this half-in, half-out thing we've got going on?"

Lyric's eyes went wide, then narrowed, that familiar wall slamming back into place. "We don't have anything going on."

"Bullshit." I stepped closer, close enough to catch the faint scent of her perfume. "You can't even look at me without remembering last night. I see it every time it crosses your mind. Does thinking about it make you wet for me, Lyric?"

She took a step back, but I matched it, unwilling to let her retreat this time.

"Flynn, don't." She lifted her chin in that defiant angle I was coming to recognize. "We already did this. Last night was a mistake. There's nothing more to discuss."

"I disagree." I took a step toward her, watching her body language for signs she wanted me to back off. She didn't retreat, but her grip on her glass tightened. "What happened between us wasn't just blowing off steam. It wasn't a mistake. And it sure as hell wasn't something you can dismiss with some bullshit about adrenaline."

"What do you want me to say?" Her voice held a warning, but there was something else there too—a tremor she couldn't quite hide. "That it meant something? That we're suddenly in a relationship? We barely know each other."

"I know enough." Another step closer. "I know you're stubborn and brilliant and dangerous. I know you fight like you've got something to prove. I know you taste like honey when you come in my mouth. And I know last night was a hell of a lot more than just sex for both of us."

Her throat worked as she swallowed. Her facade cracked—just a bit—showing a flicker of vulnerability, of longing. But then it was gone, replaced by those cold steel walls she liked to hide behind.

"It doesn't matter what it was," she said, her voice steady again. "It can't happen again."

"Why not?"

"Because I'm still trying to establish myself on this team. Because I'm responsible for securing Sentinel. Because Ethan already doesn't trust me, and if he thinks I'm compromised because of you—"

"So this is about Ethan?"

She stepped around me and quickly put the length of the room between us. "It's about the job. It's always about the job, Flynn. You know that better than anyone."

I watched her, the careful way she moved, the tension radiating off her. If I dug my fingers into those tight knots in her shoulders, would she moan? I desperately wanted to find out, but stayed where I was. She was already spooked, and I knew better than to push a wild animal when it was cornered.

"Maybe the job doesn't have to be everything for us," I said.

Her flinch told me more than a thousand words could have. Her hesitation to admit we had something more than sex wasn't just about professionalism or Ethan's approval. This reluctance was deeper, rooted in who she believed herself to be.

"Look at me," I said softly.

She turned, her expression a careful mask.

"I'm not asking for forever, Lyric." *Yet,* I thought.

"I'm just asking you not to pretend last night didn't happen."

She made an exasperated sound and flapped her arms in exasperation. "What difference does it make?"

"Because I'm not walking away from this." The words surprised even me as they left my mouth, but I knew they were true. "From you."

Her eyes widened, something like panic flashing across her face. "Flynn—"

"I'm not saying we need to define anything. I'm not asking for promises. But I'm not going to let you shut this down before it even has a chance."

She looked away, her jaw working. "You don't understand."

"Then talk to me, princess. Tell me why this won't work."

She was silent for so long, I thought she wouldn't answer. When she finally spoke, her voice was so quiet I had to strain to hear it.

"I can't be what you want."

"You don't know what I want."

Her eyes met mine, suddenly fierce. "Yes, I do. You want the woman from last night. The one who let go, who didn't think about consequences. But that's not who I am, Flynn. I can't afford to be that person."

"Why not?"

"Because people die when I lose focus!" The words exploded out of her, raw and jagged. She took a shuddering breath. "I can't... I won't let that happen again."

There was so much pain in her voice, and I wanted to pull her into my arms, to promise her everything would be okay, but I knew better. Instead, I stayed where I was, giving her the space she needed.

"What happened wasn't your fault," I said quietly.

Her laugh was bitter. "You don't even know what I'm talking about."

"I don't need to. I recognize the look." I'd seen it in the mirror enough times. "You're carrying something heavy. And you think being alone makes it easier to bear."

"Pot, meet kettle," she said bitterly.

"Fair enough." I couldn't argue with that, and I conceded the point with a slight nod. "The difference is, I'm willing to admit that maybe the lone wolf lifestyle isn't all it's cracked up to be. I never thought so until last night. Until you."

In that moment, the wall between us dropped completely, and she looked utterly vulnerable standing there.

"Flynn." My name fell from her lips like a plea. "It's not that simple."

"It could be," I replied, stepping closer.

A battle played out behind those green eyes. "I came here to do a job. To prove myself."

"And you can still do that. This doesn't have to be either, or. This changes nothing about the mission."

"It changes everything." She shook her head, curling her arms around herself like armor. "I spent years building myself into someone who could handle this kind of work. Someone focused. Untouchable."

I reached for her hand, half-expecting her to pull

away. She didn't. "I hate to break it to you, princess, but you're very touchable."

A reluctant smile tugged at her mouth, but faded as quickly as it had appeared.

"You know what I mean." She pulled her hand away, but not before I caught the tremor in her fingers. "This isn't who I am. I don't do... whatever this is."

"And who exactly are you, Lyric Renard?" I closed the distance between us and brushed my knuckles down her cheek. "The ice queen who pretends nothing matters? Or the woman who was all fire and need in my arms last night?"

Her breath hitched. "Both. Neither. I don't know anymore." That admission seemed to cost her something. "I've spent my entire life becoming whatever person the mission needed."

"Maybe it's time to find out." I lowered my head with every intention of kissing her senseless, but Elisa Deveraux's phone buzzed across the table, shattering the moment.

Lyric jerked away, relief and regret warring in her eyes. "I have to get that."

I muttered a curse, but released her, hating every step she took toward that damn phone.

She snatched it up, and she was suddenly Elisa again. It was unsettling how quickly she could transform—her posture straightening, her expression cooling into elegant disdain. The vulnerability vanished like it had never existed.

"It's Moreau telling me about the auction being moved up. He's sending a car to collect me in an hour."

She made a disgusted face. "Ew. He just suggested I pack my smallest bikini."

"So we were right. The auction's on his yacht." My gut twisted at the thought of Moreau seeing Lyric in a bikini. "The man's predictable, I'll give him that."

Lyric's face tightened as she typed a response. "I'm telling him I'll be ready, but Colt Mercer will be accompanying me as my security."

"And will he agree to that?"

"He'll have to." Her fingers flew across the screen. "Elisa Deveraux doesn't go anywhere without protection. It's part of her brand."

I watched her slide back into character, her posture straightening, her expression shifting, becoming more aloof, more calculating. It was fascinating to witness—like watching someone put on an invisible mask.

"We need to tell Ethan."

"I'll do that," I said. "You go pack."

She set her phone down and moved toward the bedroom.

I waited until she was at the doorway before calling after her. "Lyric."

She paused, her hand on the doorframe, but didn't turn.

"You're right—I do want someone to watch my six, and I want that someone to be you." I held her gaze, making sure she understood. "I'm tired of being alone, so I'm not walking away from this. From us. Get used to it."

She glanced back at me, and a whole lot of emotion flickered across her face—fear, hope, longing. She locked it down fast, but I saw the woman from last night, the one who'd wrapped herself around me like she never wanted to let go.

The woman I was falling in love with.

Or, hell. Maybe I'd already nosedived off that cliff and was just in free fall. It was hard to tell when I couldn't think straight around her.

Lyric's lips parted like she wanted to say something, but then she shut them tight and turned away. And, like that, she was Siren again. "We'll talk later."

CHAPTER 19
LYRIC

I'VE SPENT MY ENTIRE CAREER BUILDING WALLS BETWEEN who I am and who I pretend to be, but those walls were crumbling like sand castles against the tide of Flynn Shepherd.

The first rule of undercover work: never let yourself believe the lies you're telling. You're always acting, always wearing a mask.

That's what made Flynn so dangerous. He made me want to slip off all the disguises and just be... me. Whoever that was.

I hadn't been "just Lyric" in so long I wasn't sure I remembered how.

But I couldn't be Lyric now. I had to be Elisa. And tonight, she had to be perfect.

I walked across the deck of Moreau's yacht, champagne glass in hand, the salty Mediterranean breeze flaring my gauzy swimsuit cover-up behind me like a cape. The sun was setting, splashing the horizon with flaming oranges and pinks.

I could feel both Moreau's and Flynn's gazes on me. Moreau's was lecherous. Flynn's was like a caress I felt through every nerve ending in my body. He stayed at a respectable distance, tracking my every move from where he stood at the railing, playing the part of the vigilant bodyguard.

And yet he might as well be touching me for all the heat his gaze sent radiating through my body.

I shifted my weight, feeling the slide of silk against my skin, and took a slow sip of champagne. The bubbles sparkled on my tongue as I let my gaze wander over the assembled crowd. A dozen of the world's most dangerous people mingled on the deck, all dressed in resort wear that probably cost more than most people's cars. Moreau was holding court in the middle of the crowd, but his eyes kept finding me across the deck, his smile predatory.

"You're drawing his attention," Flynn murmured as I passed him, his voice low enough that only I could hear.

"That's the point," I replied through my smile, not breaking stride.

I felt rather than saw Flynn stiffen beside me. The muscle in his jaw ticked—a clear sign he was fighting to keep his composure. To anyone watching, he was the consummate professional. Only I could see the storm brewing behind those amber eyes.

Moreau broke away from his circle of admirers and made his way toward me, his gaze drifting down my body with unhurried appreciation. The yacht was massive, but suddenly there wasn't enough air.

"Ms. Deveraux," he said, taking my hand and bringing it to his lips. "You look ravishing. The sea air agrees with you."

"As does your champagne," I replied, tipping my glass toward him. "Excellent vintage."

"Only the best for my guests." His hand settled at the small of my back, fingers splaying possessively. "I was disappointed by our last encounter. I hope tonight will be more... satisfying."

I forced myself to lean into his touch, though every nerve in my body screamed in protest. "I'm here to do business, Mr. Moreau. The rest depends on how impressed I am by your merchandise."

His laugh was low and intimate. "Always the negotiator. I admire that about you."

From the corner of my eye, I saw Flynn shift his weight, his hand drifting toward the concealed weapon beneath his jacket. I gave him the slightest head shake—a warning to stand down.

"So, where are we going?" I asked, deliberately stepping away from Moreau's touch.

"Patience, Ms. Deveraux." Moreau's smile didn't reach his eyes. "We'll reach our destination by midnight."

I gave playful pout. "No hints? Not even for me?"

"Especially not for you." His gaze flicked to Flynn, then back to me. "Your... guard dog seems tense tonight. Perhaps he should try to relax. This is a social gathering, after all."

"Colt takes his job very seriously." I sipped my

champagne, letting the bubbles dissolve on my tongue. "It's why I keep him around."

"Is that the only reason?" Moreau stepped closer, invading my space again. His cologne was expensive but cloying, like something rotting beneath the surface. "I've noticed how he watches you. Not quite professional, is it?"

My heart stuttered, but I kept my expression bland. "I already told you we're lovers. He can be possessive. But I assure you, in the end, he knows his place."

Moreau's eyes glinted with something dark. "Does he? I wonder." He leaned in, his breath hot against my ear. "Perhaps we should test those boundaries tonight."

I suppressed a shiver, keeping my expression carefully neutral. "Are you trying to make him jealous, Monsieur Moreau? That seems beneath you."

"Can you make a dog jealous?"

I felt Flynn's presence before I saw him—the shift in air pressure, the subtle change in Moreau's expression. Then Flynn was there, a solid wall of controlled aggression at my shoulder.

"You want to touch her, you go through me," Flynn growled, his hand closing around my wrist with possessive force, yanking me back against his chest.

The shift was so sudden, so unexpected, that for a moment I couldn't process what was happening. Flynn had broken character. The careful facade of professional detachment had cracked, revealing something raw and dangerous underneath.

Moreau's eyes lit with triumph, a slow smile spreading across his face. He hadn't been testing me;

he'd been baiting Flynn. And Flynn had taken it, hook, line, and sinker.

"I guess so," Moreau laughed, clearly delighted by this development.

I dug my nails into Flynn's hand, trying to get him to release me without making a scene.

He didn't.

I wanted to kick him.

Instead, I pasted on a placating smile. "Oh, there's a bit of a chill in the air now, isn't there? I think I should like to freshen up and change before we reach our destination."

Moreau's gaze dropped to my chest. I wasn't lying about the chill, and my nipples had pebbled under my bikini top. I let him look, even though I could all but feel Flynn spitting fire beside me.

After an uncomfortably long perusal, Moreau inclined his head. "Of course. The staff will show you to your cabin."

Flynn's hand was firm at my elbow as he guided me away, his grip just shy of painful.

"Oh, and Elisa?" Moreau called after us. "Dress for a party."

The moment we were out of earshot, Flynn leaned in, his breath hot against my ear. "What the hell was that?"

"That was me doing my job," I hissed, maintaining my smile for the benefit of watching eyes. "So back off."

"Your job isn't to let him paw at you like a piece of meat."

When we reached the lower deck, I rounded on him.

"This is exactly why you-know-who had concerns. You can't separate personal from professional."

Flynn's eyes blazed. "He's testing us. Testing you."

"He's just a predator who thinks he's found new prey to play with."

A crew member in white appeared at the end of the hallway, and I immediately slipped back into character, leaning into Flynn with a sultry laugh. "You're so protective, darling. It's why I keep you around."

The young woman led us to our cabin—singular, I noted with a twist in my stomach. One bed. Spacious, but still just one.

I had no idea if we would be on the boat overnight. If so, Moreau either expected Colt Mercer to sleep elsewhere or expected me to end up in his bed.

I didn't like either option.

But sharing that bed with Flynn wasn't a good idea, either. I wouldn't be able to keep my hands off him.

As soon as the door closed behind us, Flynn scanned the room for surveillance devices while I cleared the bathroom. The cabin was luxurious. All cream and gold, with floor-to-ceiling windows offering a panoramic view of the darkening sea.

"Clear," Flynn said after several minutes.

"Figured as much." I dropped onto the edge of the bed, kicking off my heels and rubbing my sore feet. I hoped to hell my next cover wasn't the kind of woman who wore stilettos with her bathing suit. What I wouldn't give for a pair of combat boots right now. "He's built his empire on discretion. If it got out he was bugging his clients' cabins, he'd lose his customer base."

"Or maybe he's just smart enough to have devices we can't detect," Flynn said, his voice still edged with irritation as he prowled the perimeter of the room. "Don't underestimate him."

I watched Flynn's restless movements, the way his shoulders remained tense beneath his tailored jacket. He was still angry at Moreau, at me, at this entire situation. I needed him to calm down before he did something stupid that got us both killed.

"I'm not underestimating him," I said, keeping my voice even. "But I need you to get your head on straight. What happened up there can't happen again."

"You expect me to stand there while he puts his hands all over you?"

"Yes, that's exactly what I expect."

Flynn stopped his pacing to look at me, his eyes burning until he saw my wince when I hit a sore spot on the arch of my foot. He crossed the cabin in two strides and sat beside me, pulling my foot into his lap.

"What are you doing?" I asked, trying to keep my voice steady.

"Taking care of my asset," he replied, his eyes never leaving mine as his fingers worked magic on my aching foot. "Isn't that what good security does?"

I should have pulled away. Should have maintained that professional distance I'd been preaching about. Instead, I let my head fall back slightly as his thumb found a particularly sensitive spot and bit back a moan that would have sounded entirely too sexual.

"God, that feels good," I admitted before I could stop myself.

A smile tugged at the corner of his mouth. "I know."

There was too much heat in those two words, too much memory of the night before. My body responded instantly, a flush creeping up my neck and pooling between my legs as his strong fingers worked their way up my calf, kneading tense muscles with just the right pressure.

"Flynn," I murmured, his name somewhere between warning and invitation.

"Tell me to stop," he challenged, his hands pausing against my skin.

I didn't. Couldn't. Instead, I watched him through half-lidded eyes as his touch slid higher, past my knee to my thigh, leaving a trail of heat in its wake.

The yacht pitched gently beneath us, the distant sound of music and laughter floating down from the deck above. We were in a bubble, suspended in time, and I was acutely aware of every inch between us—the space narrowing with each breath.

I knew exactly what he was doing. Taking what Moreau wanted. Claiming me like a dog marking his territory.

And, dammit, I didn't care.

His fingers slipped beneath the edge of my bikini bottoms, and I gasped as he found me already slick with need.

"Already so wet for me," he murmured, his voice like a rough caress down my spine. "How often did you think about my cock today, princess?"

I couldn't answer. Could barely think as his fingers circled my still-sensitive clit, sending a tremble through my legs. I fell back on the bed and gave in to the flood of sensation.

"I love seeing you like this, all spread out like a feast for me."

I studiously ignored his use of the L-word and lifted my hips, grinding against his hand. "Oh, just shut up and finger fuck me before I change my mind."

"Yes, my princess." A wolfish grin spread across his face as he pushed the fabric aside and shoved two fingers deep into my pussy. He worked them in and out, fast and hard, the heel of his palm grinding against my clit with each thrust.

"Oh… yes!" My hands fisted in the expensive bedspread, my breath coming in short, desperate pants.

God. This man knew how to use his hands. He knew exactly how to touch me, how to build the pressure until I was trembling on the edge, desperate for the release only he could give me.

"You're so fucking beautiful like this," he said, his free hand sliding beneath my bikini top to roll a nipple between his fingers. The dual sensation—his fingers inside me, his hand on my breast—sent sparks dancing behind my eyelids.

I bit my lip to keep from crying out as the pressure built, coiling tighter with each stroke of his fingers. My thighs began to tremble, my inner walls clenching around him as he drove me higher.

"Look at me," he commanded, his voice low and fierce. "I want to see you when you come."

My eyes fluttered open to meet his, and the raw hunger I saw there nearly pushed me over the edge. His gaze devoured me, possessive and primal, like nothing else in the world existed but my pleasure.

"That's it," he growled, curling his fingers to hit that perfect spot inside me. "Give it to me, Lyric."

The orgasm crashed through me without warning, violent and all-consuming. I arched off the bed, my body convulsing around his fingers as ecstasy pulsed through every nerve ending. I bit down on my fist to muffle my cries, aware even in this moment of bliss that we weren't alone on this yacht.

Flynn didn't stop, drawing out my climax until I was shaking, oversensitive, my hand shooting down to still his wrist.

"Enough," I gasped, collapsing back against the sheets.

He withdrew his fingers slowly, making me shudder with aftershocks, then brought them to his mouth, sucking them clean with a look of pure satisfaction.

"I'll never get enough of your taste."

I reached for his belt, suddenly desperate to feel him inside me, to take him as deep as he could go. "I want—"

A sharp knock at the door froze us both.

"Ms. Deveraux?" A crisp female voice called through the door. "Mr. Moreau requests your presence on deck in fifteen minutes. We'll be arriving at our destination shortly."

The bubble burst, leaving me suddenly, painfully aware of where we were and what we were suppose to be doing. Just like that, I was back on mission, the haze of pleasure evaporating.

I scrambled up from the bed, hastily adjusting my bikini, trying to ignore the way my legs trembled beneath me.

"Tell Monsieur Moreau I'll be right there," I called out, my voice impressively steady.

The footsteps retreated down the hallway. I turned to Flynn, who looked like he was ready to finish what we'd started, his eyes still dark with desire, his erection obvious against his tailored pants.

"Don't even think about it," I warned, pointing a finger at him. "We have to focus."

He sighed, running a hand through his hair. "You're right."

That easy acquiescence surprised me. I narrowed my eyes, suspicious.

"What? I can be reasonable," he said, adjusting himself with a grimace. "Sometimes."

I snorted and moved to the closet where my bag had been placed. "We need to be careful. Moreau's watching us too closely." I pulled out a sleek dress the color of blood that hugged every curve—the kind of thing Elisa would wear to an auction of illegal weapons. "He's looking for weaknesses."

"And he found one," Flynn said quietly.

Our eyes met in the mirror as I slipped the cover-up off my shoulders. "Me?"

"No." His expression was a complicated mix of frustration and hunger. "Me."

I stared at him. Flynn Shepherd, the lone wolf who

never needed anyone, had just identified himself as the weak link in our operation. Because of how he felt about me.

"Flynn—" I started, but he cut me off with a shake of his head.

"I know what you're going to say. My feelings are a liability. I'm compromising the mission." He crossed to the window, staring out at the darkening sea. "But the problem is I don't give a damn about the mission when he puts his hands on you."

"We can't afford that mindset. Not now. Not with Sentinel in play."

"I know," he said, his voice rough. "But I'm not sure I can stop it."

I stepped behind the dressing screen, stripping off my swimsuit and sliding into the dress. The silk fit like liquid, the neckline plunging dangerously low, the double slits all the way to my hips allowing me easy movement.

"You have to," I said, stepping out from behind the screen. "For both our sakes."

Flynn turned, and the naked hunger in his eyes as he took in my appearance made my breath catch. "Christ, Lyric."

"Like what you see?" I couldn't help the teasing smile that played across my lips, even as I knew I was playing with fire.

"You know I do." His voice was rough gravel. "Every man on that deck is going to want you."

"But only one of them is going to get what he wants." I stepped closer, adjusting his tie that had come loose during our moment of indiscretion. "Moreau. Because he has what we need."

Flynn's jaw tightened and he caught my wrist, his thumb brushing over my pulse point. "I don't like it."

"I don't need you to like it. I need you to keep it together tonight. No matter what happens, no matter what I have to do—"

"What you have to do?" His voice was dangerously quiet. "What exactly are you planning to do, Lyric?"

I met his gaze unflinchingly. "Whatever it takes to secure Sentinel."

"Including sleeping with him?" The words were barely more than a growl.

"If that's what it takes to maintain cover and complete the mission, then yes." I kept my voice steady, though the thought made my skin crawl. "That's the job, Flynn. Sometimes it's ugly."

"No. That is not happening."

"You don't get to decide that."

His grip tightened. "The hell I don't."

"Stop it." I yanked my wrist from him and shoved both hands against his hard chest. He didn't move. "I don't need your permission. I've been doing this long before you crashed into my operation, and I'll be doing it long after you're gone."

Hurt flashed in his eyes and he backed up a step. "I told you I'm not going anywhere. I never thought of myself as a one-woman man. I thought I liked my freedom, but I was wrong. You're it for me."

I stared at him in complete shock. Who says something like that after less than a week? It was insane. Impossible.

And yet his words resonated in me like a tuning fork struck at just the right frequency.

"Flynn, you can't—"

"I can. I am." He gave a short, disbelieving laugh. "Figures I've spent my life running from connections, and now I find the one woman who makes me want to stay, and she's doing the same damn thing. That's karma for you."

I turned away, busying myself with jewelry—sliding diamond studs into my ears, clasping an obscenely expensive necklace around my throat. Fashion for Elisa, armor for me. "We have a mission."

"And we'll complete it. But don't ask me to stand by while you offer yourself to that monster."

He grabbed my shoulders and turned me to face him. "I can't do it, Lyric. Not when I know what it's like to have you. Not when I..." He paused, his jaw working before the next words came out, like he wasn't sure he should say them. Like it cost him something. "Not when I love you."

A tremor ran through me, but I forced myself to stay steady. To keep my voice neutral, my face blank. "Then you're a fool, because I don't know how to love. And even if I did?" I looked him dead in the eye. "I would never love you."

CHAPTER 20
LYRIC

I wouldn't love you.

The moment the words left my tongue, I wanted to call them back. I watched Flynn's face shutter closed, the warmth in his amber eyes going cold in an instant. He didn't argue. Didn't try to change my mind. He simply nodded once, stepped back, and slipped into his role as my security detail, as if the man who'd just declared his love had never existed.

It was better—cleaner—to sever the connection now.

At least that's what I tried to convince myself as I turned to the mirror and tamed my hair into a French twist. But the ache in my chest suggested otherwise.

The yacht's engines slowed, signaling our arrival at our destination.

"It's time to go," Flynn said.

Those four words were so coated in ice, I was surprised I didn't get frostbite. But I deserved it. He'd given me his heart, and instead of accepting it, treasuring it, I'd weaponized his vulnerability and used it against him.

I was a grade-A bitch.

Still, the mission came first. It had to. I knew with a bone-deep certainty that Sentinel hadn't been on that truck, and it was too dangerous a weapon to let anything stand in the way of securing it.

Flynn had lost sight of that, so I couldn't.

I applied a final coat of lipstick the color of fresh blood, then squared my shoulders, lifted my chin, and stepped into the skin of Elisa Deveraux again. My posture straightened, my walk became a prowl, and my voice dropped to a cultured purr that held nothing of Lyric Renard's directness.

We stepped onto the deck just as the yacht nosed into a narrow inlet between soaring cliffs. A stone mansion perched on the cliff face, windows blazing with light. Smaller boats were already ferrying guests to shore. Beyond that, the jungle loomed—too contained to be wild, too quiet to be natural. Even from the water, I could spot cameras tucked in the foliage and sensor lights tracking our approach. This wasn't just a private island. It was a hidden compound. And as I took it all in, one thought curled cold in my gut: the team had no idea this place even existed. If this went sideways, no one was coming to save us.

One look at Flynn told me he was all too aware of that fact, too.

Moreau waited at the railing, his smile rapacious as he watched my approach. "Ah, Elisa. Magnificent as always. I trust your accommodations are satisfactory?"

Heat flushed by body at the memory of Flynn's fingers moving inside me and I hoped to hell I wasn't blushing. "More than. Thank you."

"I'm sure." That predatory smile turned knowing. His gaze flicked to Flynn, then back to me.

"Your guard dog seems... subdued. Have you muzzled him?"

"I've reminded him of his place," I said coolly. "He won't interfere with our business again."

"A pity. I rather enjoyed his jealousy." Moreau stepped closer, his cologne enveloping me like a toxic cloud. He dragged a finger over the curve of my shoulder. "I'm interested to see how he'll react when I finally take what he's so possessive over."

Ugh. Like I was nothing more than an inanimate object to be possessed by men.

"He'll do exactly as I command." And I wanted to command him to pull his weapon and end Moreau right here and now. Or, even better, tell him to give me his gun so I could do it myself.

I stepped toward the railing, away from Moreau's touch, on the pretense of studying the island. "Impressive fortress you've built here. Very isolated."

"Yes, well. Privacy is essential in our line of work, wouldn't you agree?" Moreau offered his arm. "Shall we? The auction begins at midnight."

The last thing I wanted to do was touch him, but I placed my hand on his arm. "What ever will we do until then?"

"Play," Moreau said, his eyes darkening. "I have

entertainment planned that I think you'll find... stimulating."

The way he said it made my skin crawl, but I maintained Elisa's cool facade. "I'm intrigued."

As we boarded the small launch that would ferry us to shore, Flynn positioned himself behind me, his presence solid but distant. He wasn't looking at me anymore—his eyes constantly scanning, assessing threats, exit points, potential weapons. Back to being a professional, with nothing of the man who'd touched me so intimately just minutes ago.

The boat ride was mercifully short. We disembarked onto a private dock where uniformed security stood at attention. Up close, the mansion was even more imposing—a modernist monstrosity of glass and stone that seemed to grow from the cliff face, its angular lines jutting out over the sea like a challenge to gravity itself. Stone steps carved into the rock led upward, illuminated by small lights embedded in the stone.

Thankfully, one of Moreau's guards pulled him away at the top of the stairs.

"Will you excuse me?" He gestured to the torch-lit path leading through a manicured jungle toward the house. "Please, go in and enjoy yourselves."

I watched Moreau's retreating form with a mixture of relief and dread. The moment he was out of earshot, Flynn stepped closer, his body heat radiating against my back.

"Comms?" I murmured, my voice professional, detached.

"No signal. We're on our own."

"Figured as much."

His gaze scanned the perimeter. "I count sixteen guards on rotation, armed with modified MP5s. Four snipers on the roofline. At least two more in the tree cover."

I kept my smile fixed in place as we passed other guests. "They don't know about this place?"

I didn't have to specify who 'they' were. Flynn knew I was talking about Ethan and the team.

"No." That single sound held volumes of tension. "I don't like this."

The interior of the mansion was a stark, open space with floor-to-ceiling windows facing the Mediterranean. Servers circulated with trays of champagne and delicate hors d'oeuvres, while a string quartet played softly in one corner. Despite the elegant setting, there was nothing soft about the gathering.

These people were all killers in evening wear.

I recognized most of them from intelligence briefings. Richard Halston, owner of the Halston paramilitary group, held court near the bar, his silver hair immaculate, his smile too big and too white. Across the room, Arkady Reznikov—"The Curator" as he was known in certain circles—examined a small sculpture with detached interest.

Flynn leaned close. "Emilio Benítez is here," he murmured, his breath warm against my ear. "By the windows."

I followed his gaze to the older Latino man, who stood apart from the crowd, his weathered face impassive as he surveyed the room. El General, as he was known to his followers, had traded his uniform for an expensive suit, but nothing could disguise the hardness in his eyes.

"And Drexel," I added, spotting the tech mogul holding court with a circle of admirers. Evan Drexel's boyish face and exuberant gestures made him look harmless, but I knew better. His quantum computing empire was built on buried bodies and stolen technology.

I squeezed Flynn's arm once, then released him. "Time to mingle. Keep an eye on me, but not too close."

He nodded, professional distance firmly in place. Only the slight tightness around his mouth betrayed any emotion.

I slipped into the crowd, a smile fixed on my face as I moved from group to group. I laughed at Halston's dry jokes about geopolitical collapse, raised an eyebrow at Reznikov's thinly veiled proposition, and asked Benítez pointed questions about South American political stability that made his eyes narrow with suspicion.

"You're well-versed in my country's politics, Ms. Deveraux," he said, his accent thick but his English perfect.

I sipped my champagne. "I know where my investments will be safest. Politics is just another market to navigate."

He laughed, a sound like gravel. "A pragmatist. I approve."

Throughout it all, I was acutely aware of two sets of eyes following my every move. Flynn's—steady, watchful—and Moreau's—calculating, hungry, never straying far from me.

I excused myself from a tedious conversation with an Eastern European arms dealer and made my way to the terrace for air. The night was cool but humid, the scent of salt and exotic flowers heavy on the breeze. Below, the Mediterranean stretched black and endless, dotted with the lights of distant ships.

"Playing your part beautifully, I see."

I turned to find Flynn behind me, close enough to speak privately but maintaining a professional distance.

"That's the job," I replied, keeping my voice light for any listening ears.

His eyes met mine, and for a moment, I glimpsed the raw hurt beneath his professional mask. "Is that what you've been doing with me? Playing a part?"

Before I could respond, I spotted Moreau approaching and backed away from Flynn.

"Ms. Deveraux. You're neglecting your host."

I turned, forcing a smile. "My apologies. I was just admiring your stunning view."

"There are better views inside," he replied, his hand sliding to the small of my back as he guided me toward the house. "I have something special to show my most valued guests. Alone." He shot a look at Flynn. "I assure you, Mr. Mercer, I'll take very good care of her."

None of us missed the double entendre in his words.

I allowed myself to be led, casting one last glance over my shoulder at Flynn. His face was carefully blank, but his eyes burned with a promise.

I would not be facing this snake pit alone.

As we returned to the crowded ballroom, Moreau's hand remained possessively splayed across my lower back. Every instinct screamed at me to twist his wrist until bones cracked, but Elisa Deveraux would never. She'd smile her enigmatic smile, drop her shoulders just slightly to suggest receptiveness without promise. So that's what I did, even as my skin crawled beneath his touch. I scanned the room, noting Flynn had positioned himself near the bar with clear sightlines to me. His face remained professionally blank, but his eyes never left us —a predator tracking its prey.

Or… maybe its mate.

I pushed that thought away and focused on the gathering of war criminals and arms dealers laughing over champagne like they were at a charity gala instead of a weapons auction.

"More champagne?" Moreau signaled a server without waiting for my response. The server appeared instantly, holding out his tray with a slight bow.

I accepted the crystal flute, using the movement to create distance between us. "Thank you."

A commotion at the entrance drew everyone's attention. The security detail at the door was suddenly alert. Vidal cut a path through the crowd and headed straight for Moreau. Once he reached us, he whispered something that made Moreau's eyebrows rise.

"Interesting. It seems we have an unexpected guest," he said to me, then nodded to Vidal. "He's unexpected, but not uninvited. Let him in."

A few moments later, the crowd parted like the Red Sea for a man who oozed money and arrogance.

"It's the Ace of Spades," someone whispered nearby, and I felt the room's energy shift.

Unlike the other guests who projected their power through volume or posturing, he radiated quiet, lethal competence. He moved with the unhurried grace of a predator who knew he had no natural enemies, acknowledging greetings with slight nods or the barest hint of a smile. His suit was a deep charcoal gray with a subtle sheen and cut to kill. No tie. Collar open, showing a hint of tanned skin on his chiseled chest. His face was all angles, shadowed with stubble that made him look roguish rather than sloppy, and his dark blond hair was styled in that carefully disheveled way that suggested he'd just finished fucking someone senseless. Steel gray eyes swept the room in one economical glance, missing nothing, cataloging everything.

And a half-step behind him, silent as a shadow, was Trent Dalton, his face impassive.

What. The. Actual. Fuck.

I didn't let my shock show. Elisa wouldn't recognize these men, so I maintained my expression of mild curiosity even as my mind raced. No one had told me Trent was coming. And, if I had to guess, the man with him was the mysterious Decker that Nolan didn't like.

No one had said anything about backup. The implication was clear: they didn't trust me to handle this alone.

Decker looked exactly like what he was pretending to be—a high-level arms dealer with connections in every dark corner of the world.

Or maybe he wasn't pretending?

Trent played his part perfectly, the silent enforcer whose mere presence was enough to make people step back.

"Decker," Moreau said, his voice pitched between surprise and pleasure. "I wasn't aware you'd received an invitation."

Decker's smile was sharp as a blade. "I didn't. Have to say, I'm hurt, Nico."

"I'd heard you retired."

"You know I never miss a good party. Especially when such unique items are on the menu." Decker clapped Moreau on the shoulder like they were old friends. "Now, tell me what treasures you've brought us this time."

I watched them move away, deep in conversation, Decker slipping into Moreau's orbit like he'd always belonged there. My blood simmered with irritation. Had Ethan sent them because he thought I couldn't handle the mission? Was this another test? Or worse, a sign that I'd already failed?

I caught Flynn's eye across the room. He gave a slight shrug, eyebrows raised in subtle surprise. So he hadn't known either. That was something, at least—I wasn't the only one being kept in the dark.

I circulated among the guests, maintaining Elisa's persona while cataloging every scrap of information I could. The Yemeni arms dealer mentioned shipments being diverted through Cyprus. The Russian operative complained about increased security along the Georgian border. The Chinese businessman kept checking his watch, clearly waiting for something specific.

All the while, I was acutely aware of Decker working the room, his laughter floating above the crowd as he charmed potential rivals and allies alike. Everyone here seemed to know him, and I repeatedly heard "Ace of Spades" muttered as he made his way around the room.

Ace of Spades.

The death card.

Why was I even here if Edge had a man like Decker in their pocket? If he was powerful enough to just show up at Moreau's uninvited, with everyone knowing who he was, why waste time with a deep cover like mine?

The sting of not being trusted mixed with something else—a growing sense that I was just a placeholder, a temporary solution until they could get a real operative in place.

I was moving toward the bar when Decker intercepted me, his timing too perfect to be coincidental.

"I don't believe we've met," he said smoothly, extending his hand. "Decker."

"Elisa Deveraux," I replied coolly and took his hand. I really didn't know what to make of him. He was with Trent, so he had to be one of the team, but he was playing this role with such natural ease that I found myself wondering where the act ended and the real man began.

"Ah." He bowed over my hand, placing a light kiss on my knuckles. "So you're Moreau's pet heiress from Paris. I've heard you're stirring things up around here."

Was he deliberately provoking me? Testing me, seeing if I'd maintain my cover?

I yanked my hand back and glared at him. "Mr. Decker, I am no one's pet."

A slow grin broke across his face. "Decker's my first name. Sinclair is the family name, but you can call me whatever you like, Ms. Deveraux."

Behind me, I heard Flynn's soft growl.

Decker's gaze shifted to him for an instant before his smile widened. So he wasn't only here to test me, but he was also appraising Flynn's performance.

Ethan really didn't trust either of us.

I don't know why that realization hurt so much. I'd known it, but having Decker and Trent here just drove the point home.

All this time, I'd thought I was a placeholder for Maya, but what if I was just a temporary solution until they could get Decker in place?

Did I really want to continue with a team that didn't trust me?

A server appeared with a lowball glass of whiskey and Decker took it without looking at the man.

"What brings you to Moreau's little soirée?" he asked, sipping the whiskey. "You don't seem like his usual crowd."

I smiled. "I enjoy auctions."

"What are you hoping to acquire tonight?"

"Something that will give me an edge." I met his gaze steadily, letting a hint of steel show beneath Elisa's polished exterior. "I don't like to lose."

"Neither do I, Ms. Deveraux." Was I mistaken, or was that a wince he hide behind his smile? "Perhaps we'll be bidding against each other."

"Perhaps." I took a deliberate sip of champagne. "Though I wouldn't count on there being an auction for that particular item. I've found there's more than one way to get what I want, and I will do whatever necessary to secure it."

A flicker of approval crossed his face, so brief I might have imagined it. "I look forward to seeing your methods, then." He leaned in close, his lips nearly brushing my ear. His cologne was just as expensive as Moreau's but much more pleasant, like spice and smoke and silk sheets after midnight—dangerous and deliberately understated. The kind of scent that stayed on your skin long after the man was gone.

"We're just back-up," he whispered. "This is your show, Siren."

Flynn materialized at my side, his body angled slightly between me and Decker. "Ms. Deveraux, Moreau is asking for you."

Decker's smile returned. He stepped back, and this time, there was no mistaking the wince and slight limp when he did. No, I wasn't mistaken before. He was in pain.

Shit. Had he also been wounded in the op that killed Maya? Was that why I hadn't met him yet? He was on medical leave with Rafe and Leo?

Decker raised his glass in a small salute. "Until later, Ms. Deveraux."

"A pleasure to meet you, Mr. Sinclair," I replied with perfect poise, though my mind was racing.

As Flynn guided me away, his hand rested lightly at the small of my back—a touch so different from Moreau's possessive grip. Even now, when I'd wounded him so deeply, Flynn's touch remained respectful. Protective rather than controlling.

"You okay?" he asked, his voice low.

"Fine." I kept my smile in place. "Just surprised to see our friends here."

"Me too." His hand brushed against mine, a brief, unprofessional touch that sent heat coursing through me despite everything. "Any idea why?"

"Insurance policy," I murmured, then tilted my head toward where Moreau stood near a hidden doorway, gesturing for his guests' attention.

"Ladies and gentlemen," Moreau called, his voice cutting through the chatter. "If you would be so kind as to follow me, it's time for the evening's entertainment."

The guests moved toward him with barely concealed eagerness, champagne forgotten in anticipation of what was to come. I let the current carry me forward, Flynn a steady presence behind me, Decker and Trent somewhere in the crowd.

Whatever Moreau had planned, we were about to see it together.

CHAPTER 21
LYRIC

We were herded like designer-clad cattle down a curved hallway that descended into a theater at the heart of the fortress. The seats were wide and plush, the asiles lined with subtle lighting that created a sense of drama.

Moreau clearly understood the value of presentation.

"Please, find your seats," he instructed, his voice amplified by hidden speakers. "The demonstration will begin shortly."

One of Moreau's men guided me to the front row. It was the last place I wanted to sit. The seat he led me to was in the middle of the row, trapped by the stage to my front and other guests to either side of me. No easy exits.

But I couldn't very well turn down a specially reserved seat without pissing Moreau off.

As I lowered myself to the seat, I kept my expression neutral, even bored, despite the anxiety creeping up my spine. A Saudi prince sat to my right and laughed too loudly at something Halston, seated behind us, whispered. To my left, a woman I recognized as a former Russian intelligence officer examined her manicure. Decker was seated beside her. And somewhere behind us, Flynn and Trent were watching, waiting, ready. I wasn't alone in this snake pit, but that knowledge was doing little to comfort me at the moment.

Moreau took center stage, arms spread wide like a conductor about to lead an orchestra. The lights dimmed, leaving him illuminated in a perfect spotlight.

"Ladies and gentlemen," he began, "what I offer you tonight is not just weaponry—it is the future." He paced the platform with the precision of someone who had rehearsed this performance. "We live in an age of regulation, of treaties, of constraints imposed by those who fear progress. But here, in this room, we recognize a simple truth: the future belongs to those bold enough to seize it."

A murmur of appreciation rippled through the audience. These people didn't just want weapons. They wanted permission to desire power without guilt. Moreau was selling them absolution as much as technology.

"Our first offering..." Moreau's voice carried through the chamber even though he had no microphone in hand. "...is already here."

The audience glanced around in confusion. There was nothing on the stage. Nothing in the air.

The hairs on the back of my neck prickled.

Moreau paced the stage, hands clasped behind his

back. "Visibility is a weakness. The moment you can be seen, you can be tracked. Targeted. Eliminated. The true advantage in warfare isn't superior firepower—it's surprise." He stopped at the edge of the stage. "The Ghoststep Cloak neutralizes that weakness."

A blur coalesced out of thin air beside Moreau, the human silhouette slowly resolving from shimmer to solid as the cloak deactivated. The figure wore a sleek, skin-tight suit the color of gunmetal. The helmet was blank and reflective, but not bulky. Almost elegant. In one gloved hand, the figure held a combat knife. The blade hovered a breath from Moreau's throat.

He didn't even blink.

"This operative has been on stage the entire time, three feet from me. Would anyone like to guess how many of your personal security details noticed him?"

Silence.

Then a low, nervous chuckle from the crowd.

The operative stepped back, sheathing the knife with a crisp motion, and saluted.

Moreau gestured to him. "Equipped with adaptive metamaterial that bends light, disperses infrared signatures, and dampens sound, the Ghoststep Cloak renders its wearer functionally invisible to sight, heat, motion sensors, and even acoustic detection. Ideal for infiltration, exfiltration, or… eliminating liabilities without alerting the rest of the room."

A bead of sweat slid down the temple of the Saudi prince.

I coached my expression into mild interest even as my pulse kicked wildly against my throat. This wasn't a weapon of mass destruction. It was quieter. More insidious. And arguably more terrifying.

Because unlike missiles or drones, this one could be *standing behind you already.*

"Next," Moreau said, after the Ghoststep operator had walked off stage. "Here's something for those who prefer a more... personal touch."

He held up what looked like an EPIPen. "The Neural Disruptor. Elegant, discreet, and utterly effective." He smiled at the audience. "I'll need a volunteer."

His gaze zeroed in on me.

My pulse stuttered. Every instinct screamed at me to refuse, but refusal wasn't an option. Not when I was playing the role of an arms dealer eager to purchase Moreau's deadly innovations. Not when Halston's gaze was burning into the back of my skull.

"The lovely Ms. Deveraux," Moreau purred, extending his hand toward me. "Would you do us the honor?"

I took my time rising from my seat, arranging my features into a mask of bored curiosity. The walk to the stage felt endless, my Louboutins clicking against the polished floor. I had no doubt Flynn was cursing me with every step I took toward Moreau.

"Stand here, if you would," Moreau directed. "This won't hurt. Much."

The audience chuckled.

I gave him a cool smile. "I've heard that before."

My comment earned a few more chuckles. Good. Let them believe I was fearless.

Moreau circled me slowly, the disruptor still in

hand. "What's remarkable about this little device," he said to the crowd, "isn't just its efficiency. It's the silence."

I never saw it coming.

A faint tap at the base of my neck. That was all.

Then everything seized.

I couldn't move. Couldn't speak. Couldn't even blink. I was locked inside my own body, aware of the stage lights, the weight of their stares, the chill of the air on my skin. A scream built in my chest, but couldn't escape.

Only my eyes worked. And they were wide.

Moreau circled me like a docent in a gallery, his voice silk-smooth. "Complete neuromuscular disruption. The subject is fully conscious, still breathing, but otherwise physically paralyzed. The duration is adjustable from thirty seconds to fifteen minutes, and it leaves no external signs, no permanent damage, and no residual trace in the bloodstream. No evidence it was ever used."

He stepped in front of me, speaking to the crowd, but looking at me now. "You'll notice the eyes. Alert. Processing. Trapped."

A bead of sweat slid down my spine.

I wanted to move. I wanted to *run.*

And I couldn't.

"Now," Moreau said pleasantly, and tapped the pen against my neck again.

Like a marionette with its strings cut, my body sagged, breath crashing into my lungs in a desperate gulp. I caught myself before I fell, staggering one step, then two, as control returned in a sudden, nauseating rush.

The crowd applauded. Some even laughed.

I forced myself upright. Forced my features into an intrigued smile even as my stomach churned. The applications for such a device went far beyond conventional warfare. Interrogation. Torture. Rape. The tool was made for violations of the worst kind.

"Effective," I said hoarsely. "I'll take six."

That got another wave of appreciative laughter.

But I didn't miss the look Flynn shot Moreau from the shadows beyond the stage lights.

If Moreau ever touched me again, he was going to die for it.

CHAPTER 22
LYRIC

THERE WERE MORE DEMONSTRATIONS. MORE HORRORS. BUT by the end, there was still no sign of Sentinel.

Maybe it had been on that truck after all?

No, it couldn't be that easy. And it was still listed for the auction as Lot Number Forty-Two.

Moreau was just saving Sentinel for his grand finale. I was sure of it. He was enjoying the theatrics of the night too much.

After the final demonstration, the room emptied slowly, the guests drifting back upstairs to the main ballroom, their conversations animated with fresh desire for the weapons they'd just seen. I made my way through the crowd, smiling at the right people, nodding at others, all while looking for a moment of space to process what we'd witnessed.

The terrace beckoned. Dark, quiet, away from the press of bodies and the constant performance. I slipped outside, the night air cool against my skin. The Mediterranean stretched before me, black and endless under a scatter of stars, while behind me, the party continued in a bubble of light and privilege. I knew I shouldn't isolate myself, but I needed just a moment to breathe and collect myself so I could be Elisa again.

The terrace was modern, like the rest of the compound, all clean lines and polished stone. Subtle lighting illuminated the space just enough to navigate without spoiling the view. I leaned against the railing, letting the sea breeze cool my skin, which still felt flushed from the awful feeling of being trapped inside my own body.

I sensed his presence before I heard him, and all of my senses prickled to high alert. I'd always been more fight than flight, but Nico Moreau triggered every primal prey instinct I possessed.

Run.

I stayed put.

"Admiring my view, Ms. Deveraux?" His voice was as smooth as the aged whiskey in his glass as he joined me at the railing.

I turned, offering him Elisa's smile. "It's breathtaking."

He stood closer than necessary, his shoulder brushing mine. Behind him, I noticed his security personnel positioning themselves at the terrace entrance, effectively cutting off any interruption. Or escape. Flynn was nowhere in sight. Neither were Decker nor Trent. I was alone with Moreau and his men.

He sipped his drink. "What did you think of my little showcase?"

"Theatrical."

"Yes, well, buyers are more willing to spend money when they know how valuable their shopping list actually is. Do you have a list, Elisa?"

I maintained my languid pose, though every nerve in my body was firing warning signals. "I never enter a marketplace without a shopping list, Monsieur Moreau."

"And what's at the top of yours, I wonder?" He leaned in, close enough that I could smell the whiskey on his breath. "The Ghoststep Cloak? The Neural Disruptor? Or are you still dead-set on Sentinel?"

"What if I want it all?"

His laugh sounded genuine.

"Ambition suits you." His gaze lingered on my face, then dragged deliberately down my body. "But you'll forgive me if I find myself... questioning your intentions."

I arched an eyebrow. "Questioning?"

"A truck carrying my merchandise was sabotaged last night."

My heart stuttered, but Elisa's face showed only mild interest. "How unfortunate for you."

He swirled the amber liquid in his glass. "Coincidentally, it happened right after I offered you the invitation to come here."

"Are you accusing me of something, Monsieur Moreau?" I let just enough ice creep into my tone to remind him who Elisa Deveraux was supposed to be—wealthy, powerful, and not someone to be trifled with.

"Mm." He took another sip. "You must understand my concern. Your documentation is impeccable, your references check out perfectly, and your financial trail is pristine. Too pristine."

I turned to face the sea again, buying myself a moment to control my expression. "I pay good money for discretion."

"As do I." His hand settled on the small of my back, fingers splayed possessively. "Which is why I know there was a breach in the security system at my warehouse exactly twenty-three minutes before the truck incident. Right as Vidal was escorting you from my suite. We found a tracker on his phone."

His hand was a brand through the thin fabric of my dress.

I forced myself not to flinch away. "Perhaps you should upgrade your security rather than harassing your guests with baseless accusations."

His fingers tightened incrementally. "There are ways to regain my trust, Elisa." The way he said my cover name made it sound like he knew it was false. "Starting with joining me in my private quarters before the auction begins. I find trust is best built in intimate settings, don't you?"

He made it sound like an invitation. But there was nothing optional about it.

I calculated my response carefully. An outright rejection would insult him, potentially closing off my access to Sentinel. Enthusiastic acceptance would seem suspicious given Elisa's previously established boundaries. I needed to navigate the narrow space between.

"That's a very... direct proposition," I said, letting a

hint of appreciative surprise color my voice. "I hadn't expected you to be so forthright."

"I'm a man who knows what he wants." His fingers traced up my arm to my collarbone. "And I think we could come to a mutually beneficial arrangement, you and I."

I tilted my head, as if considering. "What would this arrangement entail, exactly?"

"You in my bed tonight, before the auction..." His thumb brushed the base of my throat. "...will assure me you had nothing to do with my security breach, and win you certain advantages during bidding."

"Insider trading, Monsieur Moreau?" I raised an eyebrow, injecting just the right amount of playful reproach. "How scandalous."

"Business and pleasure often mix well in my experience." His eyes dropped to my lips. "What do you say, Elisa? Shall we explore what else we might... exchange?"

I placed my hand lightly on his chest, neither pushing him away nor pulling him closer. "You make a compelling case." I let a smile play at the corners of my mouth. "But I never make important decisions in haste."

His expression hardened slightly. "The auction begins at midnight."

"And I still have hours to consider your generous offer." I slid from between him and the railing, grateful to be out of the cloud of his cologne. "If you'll excuse me, I should freshen up before making any... significant commitments."

I could feel his frustration radiating like heat as I stepped away. This wasn't a man accustomed to waiting for what he wanted.

"Don't take too long, Ms. Deveraux," he called after me. "Some opportunities are time-sensitive."

I glanced back over my shoulder, offering a smile that promised nothing but suggested everything. "The best things are worth waiting for, wouldn't you agree?"

His answering smile was tight. "My patience has limits."

"As does my interest." I turned and walked away, forcing myself to move unhurriedly, my hips swaying just enough to keep his eyes on me rather than on my hasty retreat.

I felt exposed with every step, my back crawling with the certainty of his gaze tracking me. I nodded to a few guests as I passed through the main ballroom, maintaining Elisa's poise while scanning for Flynn. I spotted him near the bar, his eyes finding mine immediately. He was fuming mad. I gave him the barest head shake—not now—and continued toward the guest wing.

A security guard directed me to my assigned room, unlocking it with a keycard before handing it to me with a curt nod. "Mr. Moreau has arranged for your comfort. If you require anything, dial zero on the phone."

The door closed behind me with a soft click. I engaged the lock and wished there was also a deadbolt, maybe a security chain. Only then did I allow my shoulders to drop, my breath escaping in a shaky exhale.

The room was luxurious. King-sized bed with silk sheets, floor-to-ceiling windows overlooking the ocean, and a bathroom that probably cost more than most people's houses. It was also, I was certain, thoroughly bugged.

I moved to the bathroom, turning on the shower to create white noise, before pulling out my phone. I needed to contact the team, to warn them about Moreau's suspicions, to figure out our next move.

I typed a quick, encrypted message to Ethan: "Moreau suspects me. Sentinel confirmed. Auction at midnight. Need backup."

It didn't go through.

"Fuck." I erased the message and set my phone down hard enough to crack the screen, if it weren't for its military-grade durability. There had to be signal jammers in place.

I stared at my reflection and, for the first time in my professional career, I hated that I didn't see myself staring back. I scrubbed at the makeup, yanked at my hair until all the pins clattered into the sink.

I'd lied to Flynn earlier. I did know how to love, and that was the problem. I knew exactly how it felt to love someone so much that losing them tore you apart. I knew the cost of letting someone matter that much.

My sister's face flashed in my mind. Elodie laughing, alive.

But she wasn't alive. She was gone forever because I'd let my focus slip for one crucial moment.

I couldn't make that mistake again. Not with Flynn. Not with anyone.

I steeled myself, tucking away anything soft, anything vulnerable. There would be time for feelings later, if we survived. Right now, I needed to be Siren.

Cold. Professional. Deadly.

Then I stepped into the shower, letting the hot water wash away Moreau's lingering touch, along with any doubts about what needed to be done.

CHAPTER 23
FLYNN

I'D COUNTED EVERY EXIT TWICE, MAPPED EVERY SECURITY camera, and memorized the guard rotation schedule by the time I heard the shower turn off. Seventeen minutes. That's how long she'd been in there, washing away Moreau's touch while I paced the polished marble floor like a caged animal. My reflection in the floor-to-ceiling windows showed a man barely holding it together—hair disheveled from running my hands through it, jaw tight enough to crack teeth. Behind me, the king-sized bed with its silk sheets and too many pillows sat pristine and untouched, mocking the chaos in my head.

The way Moreau had been looking at her since we set foot on his yacht made my skin crawl. I'd seen that look before—on warlords, arms dealers, men who collected beautiful things like trophies. And the way she'd played along, smiling, leaning in when he whispered in her ear—it was textbook undercover work, but it scraped something raw inside me.

The bathroom door opened in a billow of steam, and

there she was, wrapped in a plush white towel, water droplets still clinging to her shoulders. Her platinum hair was darker when wet, slicked back from her face. She looked younger, more vulnerable somehow, without her carefully constructed Elisa armor.

"What the hell are you doing here?" she demanded, glancing at the door. "How did you get in?"

I didn't move from my position by the window. "Security in this place is good, but not good enough. Not when they've got four cameras down in the east wing that they're scrambling to fix."

Her gaze swept the room before she lowered her voice to a hiss. "You shouldn't be here. If Moreau has the rooms bugged—"

"He doesn't. His business is built on his discretion, remember?"

"I don't trust his discretion—"

"I also did a sweep when I came in. We're clear." I took a step toward her, unable to stay still. "What the hell did he say to you?"

Her eyebrows shot up. "Who, Decker?"

"Don't play dumb." My words came out harsher than I intended. "Moreau. That little dance on the terrace."

"That 'little dance' is me doing my job. You know, the one where I get close enough to Moreau to access Sentinel?"

"There's close and then there's what he was suggesting. He wants you in his bed, Lyric."

"Yeah, it's called a honeytrap," she said in a tone

that suggested she thought I was a sandwich short of a picnic.

"That isn't part of the plan."

"Yes, it is. Always has been. Ask Trent. Or Decker. He probably knows since he's also apparently part of this team that doesn't fucking trust me."

The bitterness in her voice surprised me. "I didn't know they were coming, either—" I stopped, shook my head. She was trying to distract me. "But that's not the issue right now."

"Oh?" Her tone went syrupy sweet. "So, tell me, what is the issue?"

"The job is to bid on Sentinel, not to fuck the arms dealer!"

"Lower your voice," she whisper-yelled, closing the distance between us. "Sometimes maintaining cover means doing things we'd rather not do. You know this. You've done this."

"Not this." I jabbed a finger at her. "This isn't just about the mission for you. This is about proving something. To Ethan. To the team. To yourself."

She didn't flinch outwardly, but I saw it in her eyes. "And what if it is? What business is that of yours?"

"Because I care about what happens to you!" My voice cracked. It wasn't just caring, but I knew if I threw the L-word at her again, it would send her running— and she'd land in Moreau's bed just to spite me. "I want you safe. I want you to come back from this mission whole, not splintered into pieces because you pushed yourself too far."

She laughed, a sharp, bitter sound that held no

humor. "Whole? I haven't been whole in years, Flynn. That ship sailed a long time ago."

"Lyric—"

"Get it through your thick skull." She tapped my forehead with each word. "I make the calls on how I handle my cover. Not you."

I caught her arm as she tried to move past me. "How far are you willing to go, huh? Where's the line?"

She whirled and shoved against my chest hard enough to make me step back. "There is no line! There's just the mission. There's just the job. There's just what needs to be done!"

Jesus. She really didn't believe there was a limit, did she? My gut clenched at the thought of her crossing lines she couldn't uncross, all for a mission, for approval, for whatever drove her to push herself over every edge.

I stepped closer, eliminating the space between us.

"And what about after?" I asked softly. "When the mission's over and you've crossed every line, compromised every part of yourself, what then? Who are you then, Lyric?"

Her eyes flashed dangerously. "It's my op. My body. My choice."

"Your op, yeah." I pulled her in so tight against me until I could feel her shuddering breath on my face and her pounding heart against my chest. I could smell her shampoo, something clean and citrusy, and underneath it, her skin. Steam from the shower still clung to her, making her almost glow in the dim light. "But last night, that pussy was mine. Every whimper. Every goddamn moan. You gave it all to me, and that gives me a say now. No other man is going to touch you while I'm still breathing."

"You don't get to decide that. You're not my handler," she breathed. "You're not my keeper. And you're sure as hell not—"

"Say it," I challenged, my face inches from hers. "I'm not your what?"

The silence between us crackled with electricity. Her chest heaved with each breath, and the edge of her towel slipped to show the curve of her breast. I was suddenly, painfully aware of how close we were standing, how little she was wearing, how easy it would be to—

"You're not mine," she whispered, her voice catching on the last word.

Something inside me broke at that—at the wounded defiance in her eyes, at the way she was staring at me like I was both the problem and the solution. I wanted to shake her. I wanted to walk away. I wanted to drag her into my arms and not let go until she understood.

"Yes, I am. Wholly, violently, maddeningly yours. You had me the second you moaned my name, the second your nails clawed down my back and marked me as yours." I caught her face between my hands, unable to keep myself from touching her any longer. "Even if you don't want me. Even if you walk out that door and straight into his bed, I'll still be yours. And God have mercy on the bastard if he touches you, because I won't."

Her eyes darkened, pupils dilating as she stared up

at me. For a heartbeat, I thought she might push me away. Instead, she grabbed the front of my shirt and yanked me toward her. Our mouths crashed together with bruising force, teeth clashing before we found our rhythm. The kiss wasn't gentle. It was all fire and fury, a continuation of our argument by other means.

I backed her against the wall, lifting her by the backs of her thighs. The towel came loose in the process, falling forgotten to the floor. Her legs wrapped around my waist as I pressed her harder against the wall, my mouth leaving hers to trail hot kisses down her neck.

"I hate you," she gasped even as she clawed at my shirt, popping buttons in her haste to get to skin.

"I know," I growled against her throat, my hands sliding up her bare sides, feeling her shiver against me. "Tell me to stop and I will."

She answered by ripping my shirt open the rest of the way, buttons scattering across the marble floor like tiny gunshots. Her fingernails raked down my chest, leaving trails of fire that went straight to my cock. I groaned into her mouth as she bit my lower lip hard enough to sting.

"Bed," she gasped against my mouth, and I didn't need to be told twice.

I carried her to the bed, our mouths never breaking contact, my hands gripping her ass, fingers digging into her soft flesh. We fell onto the silk sheets in a tangle of limbs, her naked body writhing beneath me as I struggled out of my remaining clothes.

"You drive me fucking crazy," I muttered, pinning her wrists above her head with one hand while the other trailed down her body. She was already wet, her thighs parting eagerly despite the anger still flashing in her eyes. I slid my fingers through her slick folds, watching her arch into my touch despite herself.

"Feeling's mutual," she gasped, her head thrown back as I circled her clit with my thumb.

"You want to be reckless? Want to push every boundary?" I growled, working my finger in and out of her soft, slick heat. "Let me show you what reckless feels like."

She arched against my hand, a soft moan escaping her lips. "Flynn—"

I silenced her with my mouth, swallowing whatever she was about to say. I didn't want words right now. Words were where we got lost, where we hurt each other. This—her body trembling beneath mine, her pulse hammering against my lips as I kissed down her throat—this was honesty.

I knew her body now, knew exactly how to touch her to make her come apart. Her hips bucked against my hand, seeking more friction, more pressure.

"Tell me you're mine," I demanded against her ear, nipping at the sensitive skin beneath it. "Say it."

"I'm not—" she gasped as I curled my fingers, hitting that spot that made her eyes roll back. "I can't—"

"You can." I withdrew my fingers, and she cried out, bucking up to keep them until I wedged my hips between her thighs and positioned myself at her entrance. I dragged the head of my cock through her folds. "Say it, Lyric."

Her eyes flew open, blazing with defiance even as her body trembled with need. "Make me."

The challenge in those two words snapped the last thread of my control. I thrust into her hard, burying myself to the hilt in one swift movement that had us both gasping. I wasn't wearing a condom and the sensation was indescribable—her hot, silky walls gripping me without any barrier between us. I nearly lost myself right then, overcome by the raw intimacy of it.

"Fuck," I breathed, my forehead dropping to hers as I fought for control. "You feel—"

"Move," she commanded, her nails digging into my shoulders.

I withdrew slowly, savoring every inch of friction, before slamming back into her. She cried out, her back arching off the bed. I set a punishing pace, driving into her with all the frustration and fear and need that had been building since the moment she walked into the mission briefing.

"Say you're mine," I demanded again, my voice rough with exertion.

She shook her head, her eyes squeezed shut, lips parted around breathless moans. Even now, she was fighting me, fighting this connection between us.

I shifted my angle, hitting deeper, and her eyes flew open. "Flynn!"

"Say it." I slowed my thrusts, making each one deliberate, deep, torturous. "Say you're mine, Lyric."

"I—I can't—" Her voice broke on a sob as I ground against her, circling my hips to hit that spot inside her that made her walls clench around me.

"Why not?" I whispered, pressing my lips to her temple, tasting the salt of her sweat. "Why won't you let yourself have this?"

Emotion flickered across her face. Vulnerability, fear, something else I couldn't name. For a moment, I thought she might actually answer, might let me see past her walls.

Instead, she hooked her legs around my waist and flipped us over with surprising strength. Now straddling me, she took control, rising up on her knees before sinking back down, taking me impossibly deeper.

"Fuck," I groaned, my hands flying to her hips, guiding her movements. The sight of her above me, wild and beautiful in the dim light, her body gleaming with sweat as she rode me—it was almost enough to make me forget my question.

Almost.

"You're running away again," I panted, sitting up so we were chest to chest, my arms wrapped around her back as she continued to move against me. "Even now."

"Shut up," she whispered, burying her face in my neck. "Please, just—shut up."

I felt wetness against my skin—tears, not sweat— and something in my chest cracked open. I cradled the back of her head, gentling my touch even as our bodies continued their frantic rhythm.

"I've got you," I murmured into her hair. "I've got you, Lyric."

She came with a broken cry, her body shuddering around mine, walls pulsing and clenching.

My protective instincts, the ones that had sparked our fight, transformed into something more primal. I turned us again, pressing her into the mattress, my body covering hers. My mouth found the curve where her neck met her shoulder, and I bit down gently, marking her, claiming her in some ancient, instinctual way.

Mine, my brain chanted with each thrust. *Mine, not Moreau's, not anyone's.*

"Flynn," she breathed, her head falling back as her nails dug into my shoulders and her legs trembled around my hips. "Oh, God. It's too much."

I kissed a path from her collarbone to her breast, relishing the way she arched into my touch. Her fierce independence was melting beneath me, her usual iron control surrendering to sensation. It was the greatest victory I'd ever won—Lyric Renard, coming undone in my arms.

CHAPTER 24
FLYNN

"Look at me," I commanded, my voice hoarse.

Her eyes fluttered open, locking onto mine, and the intimacy of that connection hit me harder than any physical sensation. In that moment, all her walls were down, all her defenses stripped away. I saw her—not Siren, not Elisa Deveraux, but Lyric—and she saw me.

I came with a force that stunned me, my release tearing through my body like a storm. Her name was a prayer on my lips as I poured myself into her, unable and unwilling to pull away. The intensity of it—of being inside her with nothing between us—left me shaken to my core.

We collapsed together, a tangle of sweat-slicked limbs and ragged breaths. Slowly, reality reassembled itself. The distant sounds of the party filtered back in. The breeze from the partially open terrace doors cooled the sweat on our skin. I kept her close, my arms wrapped around her like I could protect her from everything—Moreau, the mission, her own demons—if I just held on tight enough.

Her head rested on my chest, her breathing gradually slowing to normal. I traced gentle patterns on her back, feeling the knobs of her spine, the delicate wings of her shoulder blades.

"I love you," I whispered into her hair. "I know you don't want to hear it, but it's true."

Her body stiffened in my arms, muscles tensing as if preparing for flight. I tightened my hold slightly, not enough to trap her, just enough to let her know I wasn't letting go easily this time.

"Why?" she finally asked, her voice so quiet I almost missed it. "Why would you love me?"

She sounded genuinely confused, as if the concept of being loved was fundamentally incomprehensible to her.

"What do you mean, why?" I pulled back enough to see her face, though she kept her eyes downcast. "Because you're brave and fierce and brilliant and you fuck like a goddess."

That got a small laugh out of her, as I'd intended.

I caught her chin in my hand and lifted until her eyes met mine. "And because you make me laugh even when everything's going to hell. And because you watch jellyfish with such childish wonder and eat pistachio gelato when literally any other flavor would be better."

A scowl drew her brows together. "Pistachio is the best."

I smoothed the furrow in her forehead with my

thumb. "And mainly because when you smile at me—really smile, not that cover identity bullshit—it feels like I've won the goddamn lottery."

She looked away, her fingers fidgeting with the edge of the sheet. "I can't... I'm not built for this, Flynn."

"For what? Being loved?" I asked, keeping my voice gentle. "Why? What happened to make you believe that?"

For a long time, I thought she wouldn't answer. Then she sighed, and her expression cracked—a hairline fracture in her perfect armor.

"I had a sister," she said, her voice so quiet I had to strain to hear it. "Elodie. She was three years younger."

Had. Past tense.

I stroked a hand over her hair and down her back. "What happened to her?"

"We traveled a lot as kids. Our mom was a commercial airline pilot. We never stayed in one place long enough to put down roots. But we had each other." Her voice changed when she spoke about her sister, softening around the edges, warming with memories. "She was everything I wasn't—outgoing, fearless, immediately likable. She collected friends the way other kids collected shells or rocks."

I remained silent, instinctively knowing that what she needed most was someone to listen.

"When I was fifteen, we were staying in Istanbul. I thought I was so mature, so worldly." Bitterness crept into her tone. "Mom was flying, so it was just the two of us in this little apartment near the Spice Bazaar. One afternoon, we went exploring. The market was crowded, noisy. I noticed this man acting strangely, following other tourists, watching them. I thought I was being so clever, playing detective."

Her fingers tightened on the sheet, knuckles going white. "I followed him, convinced I was uncovering some criminal plot. I was so focused on the wrong threat that I didn't notice Elodie had wandered off. When I turned around, she was gone."

A cold weight settled in my stomach, anticipating where this story was heading.

"We reported it immediately. The local police, Interpol, the American embassy... everyone was involved. But she just... vanished." Her voice cracked slightly. "Three years later, they found her body in a shallow grave outside the city. Three years of hoping, of imagining she was alive somewhere, and then—nothing."

I tightened my arms around her, wishing I could absorb some of her pain. "It wasn't your fault, Lyric."

"That's what everyone said," she replied, her voice hollow. "My mother never blamed me, not once. But she started drinking heavily and—I knew what she really thought. One moment of distraction. One split second where I took my eyes off her, and she was gone forever."

"You were a child."

"I was responsible for her," she countered, those fierce green eyes meeting mine. There was so much pain there, so much guilt. "I can't afford distractions, Flynn. I can't let myself feel too much, care too much, because that's when people die."

Everything clicked into place—her resistance to

connection, her absolute focus on the mission, her reluctance to let anyone close. She wasn't cold; she was terrified. Terrified of making the same mistake again, of losing someone else she cared about.

I cupped her face in my hands. "Listen to me, princess. What happened to your sister was a tragedy, but it wasn't your fault. You've been punishing yourself for years for something you couldn't control."

"You don't understand," she whispered, but there was less conviction in her voice.

"Remember who you're talking to here." I stroked my thumb across her cheekbone, wiping away moisture she probably didn't even realize was there. "After Yemen, I blamed myself for every man we lost. I thought if I'd just been smarter, faster, better, they might have lived. It took me years to realize that blame doesn't bring anyone back. It just stops you from living."

She leaned into my touch, her eyes drifting closed. When she opened them again, I saw the ice melt away.

"Flynn, there's something I need to tell you," she said, her voice taking on a new urgency. "Earlier, on the yacht, I lied when I said—"

She broke off and hissed in pain.

"What?" I sat up, and something stung my neck. I slapped at it reflexively, my hand coming away with a tiny metallic speck no bigger than a grain of rice.

Lyric's eyes widened. "Nanodrones. One of the prototypes for sale tonight."

A strange numbness was spreading from the injection site. I tried to climb off the bed, go for my weapon where it had landed with my pants, but my limbs felt leaden, unresponsive. My body was betraying me, muscles going slack even as I fought against it.

The door burst open, and Moreau walked in, flanked by four armed guards. His smile was pure satisfaction as he surveyed the scene—both of us naked, paralyzed, vulnerable.

"Uh-oh, the bodyguard caught in a compromising position with his client." Moreau's voice was silky with amusement. He tsked. "How unprofessional."

I tried to tell him to fuck off, but my tongue was swollen, useless.

Beside me, Lyric's eyes blazed with fury, the only part of her still fully under her control.

"The nanodrones are quite remarkable, aren't they?" Moreau continued conversationally, circling the bed like a shark. "Programmable to deliver precise doses of various compounds. This particular batch carried the neural disruptor from my earlier demonstration." He crouched beside me, his face inches from mine. "How does it feel, Mr. Shepherd, for your mind to be completely clear while your body is entirely helpless?"

The helplessness was worse than anything I'd ever experienced. Not even the agony of Yemen compared to watching, fully conscious but immobile, as Moreau moved from me to Lyric, his predatory gaze sliding over her naked body.

"Such a waste," he murmured.

He reached out, his manicured fingers brushing across Lyric's breast with deliberate slowness. My vision tunneled, rage building with nowhere to go as he circled her nipple, watching it harden against her will.

"Magnificent," he murmured, pinching lightly, his eyes flicking to mine to ensure I was watching. "She has exquisite skin, doesn't she? So responsive."

Lyric's eyes met mine, filled with rage. I clung to that connection, the only one left to us as Moreau continued his violation.

A cruel smile twisted his lips as he dragged his hand down her stomach, tracing the dip of her navel, following the slight curve of her abdomen. "Such a shame we couldn't come to a more civilized arrangement, Ms. Deveraux." His palm continued its journey downward, fingers dipping between her legs. "Or should I say, Agent Renard?"

Lyric's eyes screamed.

A cold, sick feeling spread through me. Moreau was getting off on this, and I realized with cold certainty this wasn't the first time he'd used this paralytic on a woman.

He withdrew his hand and wiped his fingers on the sheet with a theatrical grimace. "Tainted goods now, I'm afraid. Such a pity."

If I could have moved, I would have torn his throat out with my bare hands. Instead, I lay there, helpless, as he straightened and adjusted his cuffs.

"Bring them," he ordered his men. "And find the others. I want every member of their team in custody before the auction starts."

CHAPTER 25
TRENT

The auction opened with a pedophile's wet dream.

Lot Number One was a prototype surveillance drone disguised as a cartoon bumblebee.

Marketed as an "educational engagement tool with embedded safety protocols," it was cute enough to pass inspection in a kindergarten and small enough to nestle beside a crib mobile. The specs boasted facial recognition, real-time location tracking, and proximity-activated explosives—because why stop at watching when you can also erase the evidence?

The room buzzed with interest. One buyer inquired about the possibility of deploying it in refugee camps. Another asked about its audio feed specifically for "remote behavioral assessment."

These people toasted pedophilia over champagne.

I wanted to put a bullet in every one of them.

But I blocked it out. Let it all blur into meaningless noise. Crystal glasses clinking, the low hum of whispered deals struck by people with too much money and not enough soul. I stood with my back to the wall, scanning the crowd. My stance was relaxed, hands clasped in front of me like any good bodyguard. But my eyes never stopped moving. Three exits. Twenty-eight guests. Fourteen guards. Two snipers overhead, trying to blend in. I clocked them the second we walked in.

Decker was working the crowd a few feet away, playing the part of the arms dealer he used to be. He laughed at something the Chinese dealer said after winning the first item, raising his champagne in mock toast.

In that moment, I understood Nolan's distrust of him. He fit in too well with these people. He was too comfortable in their skin, like he'd never fully shed it himself, like slipping back into this world didn't cost him a thing.

The next item was a neurostim collar marketed for "enhanced obedience." Translation: a slave who didn't know they were enslaved. The interest was explosive, bidding fierce. Even Decker joined in, and he seemed to be enjoying himself a little too much.

I exhaled hard and blocked it out, and my thoughts slipped—like they had so often recently—to Evelyn Phillips and the little girl I'd lived with for two years while embedded in a cult that nearly triggered the apocalypse they were praying for.

Fuck.

Why did that woman continue to haunt me?

It had been a month since the extraction. She should be out of my system by now. She wasn't even my type. Too quiet. Too broken. Too many complications.

I shouldn't care. They were part of the job. Just another mission.

But, damn it all to hell, I did care. Too much. I wondered if Evelyn was sleeping through the night, or if she still startled at shadows. If the girl, Emma, still refused to let go of her hand.

I'd put them in that safe house myself. New names, new identities, new lives. No contact. No trace. And still, I couldn't shake the weight of that promise I'd made to them: *You're safe now.*

The bidding reached a fever pitch, pulling me back to the present. Three million for a collar that could turn a human being into a puppet.

I tensed as the room erupted in applause. The buyer—some European aristocrat with old money and older sins—smiled like he'd just acquired a prized thoroughbred. Next to him, his companion, a woman half his age with dead eyes, applauded mechanically.

A sudden prickle of instinct skated along the back of my neck and had me straightening away from the wall, watching the crowd more closely. It was a sense, low and sharp, that something had shifted around me. A gut instinct I'd learned not to question.

I scanned the room again, and realization hit.

Fuck.

Flynn and Lyric weren't here.

They'd been working the crowd twenty minutes ago, but I hadn't seen them since the auction started.

I tapped my ear once, activating the encrypted comm link. "Dealer, do you have eyes on Outlaw or Siren?"

Decker didn't visibly react, but his voice came through crisp in my earpiece. "Negative, Vigil. Last visual was Siren with Moreau near the terrace doors. Outlaw was at the bar watching them, looking pissed."

I kept my expression neutral as I moved toward the eastern wall, finding a better vantage point while maintaining my cover as Decker's security. Something wasn't right. Operatives don't just disappear during a mission unless they're compromised.

"I don't like this," I murmured just loud enough for the comm to pick up.

"Makes two of us." He took a slow sip of champagne, his gaze sweeping the room. "Moreau's gone, too."

"I'll check the east wing," I said quietly. "You take west. Rendezvous back here in ten."

Decker nodded, already drifting away, that easy smile back in place as he slipped through the crowd like smoke.

I moved along the perimeter of the room. Moreau's guards tracked me with their eyes but didn't interfere. To them, I was just another security detail, watching my principal's back. They had no idea I was hunting.

I had just stepped into the hallway when a murmur went through the crowd behind me. I backtracked in time to see Moreau return to the ballroom, his security detail forming a tight perimeter around him. His face was placid, but there was a cold satisfaction in his eyes that made all of my instincts fire.

I had no doubt he'd made our operatives, but Flynn and Lyric weren't with him.

What the fuck was going on?

I spotted Decker on the other side of the ballroom. Several Russian men in suits had waylaid him, chatting animatedly, which was for the better. At least I didn't have to go searching for him now. I cut through the crowd, headed back toward him.

"Mission's blown," Decker said into his champagne when I reached his side and pulled him away from the Russians.

Yeah, no shit, I wanted to say, but kept my mouth shut.

He nodded and smiled at a passing guest, still playing his part. "What's the plan now?"

I had no fucking idea.

"Ladies and gentlemen," Moreau called and held up his hands, waiting until the chatter died down. "Before we continue the auction, I've arranged one final demonstration."

My gut tightened.

This was not going to be good.

"Follow me, if you would." He gestured toward the terrace doors. "I believe you'll find this particular performance... enlightening."

The crowd moved as one, murmuring with dark anticipation.

Whatever he was about to show his guests, it wasn't just going to be tech.

As we joined the flow of bodies, I ran through all the contingency plans, but the only one that made sense was a hot extraction. We needed Nolan here with the helo ASAP, but contacting him was going to be next to impossible. Our comms worked within the house, but no signal was getting off the island.

The terrace opened onto a courtyard I hadn't seen during recon. Wide, circular, enclosed by high walls. Four exits, each manned by armed guards. Torches ringed the perimeter, their flames casting long shadows. It felt like a Roman arena. The kind that had only one purpose: Execution.

Decker let out a low breath. "Who the fucking fuck builds a colosseum in their backyard?"

I didn't respond. Didn't need to. He'd summed it up succinctly enough.

Moreau climbed a short platform at the north end, positioning himself so every eye was on him. He raised his arms like he was Caesar or some fucking thing. All he needed was a toga.

And the knife in his back.

"For those unfamiliar," he said when silence fell, his voice ringing out over the courtyard. "Sentinel MK-IV is more than a drone system. It's an autonomous hunter. Capable of identifying, pursuing, and eliminating targets without operator input. Facial recognition. Thermal imaging. DNA sequencing. This is precision death, gentlemen."

A few guests applauded. Others leaned in, intrigued. No one looked away.

"But of course, you want proof. Reliability. Accuracy. And what better proof," he said, smiling now, "than live targets?"

A door opened in the far wall of the area. Two

guards dragged Flynn and Lyric in, while another two marched behind with rifles.

My lungs locked. For a split second, I wasn't an operator. I was just a man watching two people I was supposed to protect being dragged out like animals for slaughter.

They were drugged, barely standing. Flynn's shirt was missing buttons and a sleeve, his ribs blackened with bruises. Lyric's red dress hung from one torn strap, a handprint visible on her arm.

Whatever happened, they hadn't gone quietly.

Even now, they continued to fight against their captors.

Moreau swept a hand toward them. "Our uninvited guests—American operatives who thought to infiltrate our gathering. Ms. Elisa Deveraux, better known as Lyric Renard, and her companion, Flynn Shepherd."

The guests murmured. One or two chuckled. This was theater to them.

"Fuuuck," Decker muttered.

The guards cut Flynn's restraints. He swayed, caught himself, and scanned the crowd. His eyes locked on mine for an instant before he turned to help Lyric as her bindings were also cut off. She staggered but lifted her chin. There was blood on her temple, but her eyes burned with hatred and defiance.

"We used the neural disruptor to ensure a smooth transfer," Moreau explained. "It's already wearing off, but the effects are still counteracted immediately by the antidote."

The guards jabbed them with pressure syringes,

similar to the one used during the earlier demonstration of the neural agent.

As soon as the antidote hit, Flynn exploded into motion.

He lunged at the nearest guard, his fist connecting with a brutal crack. The man dropped, but another raised his rifle and aimed at Lyric.

"Move again, and she dies," the guard barked.

Flynn froze. His chest heaved, muscles locked, one hand clenched in the guard's shirt. He didn't look scared. He looked murderous. But he dropped his grip, slowly, jaw grinding like he was chewing glass.

Lyric didn't flinch. Didn't plead. She just held her ground beside him, spine straight, eyes locked on Moreau like she could kill him with sheer willpower.

Goddammit, Flynn.

I should've expected him to go feral like that. The man had the instincts of a wrecking ball and the impulse control to match.

Beside me, Decker murmured, "We need a plan. Now."

My fingers itched for the weapon holstered at my back, but I didn't move. Not yet. If I drew now, I'd get maybe two shots before the guards reacted, and Lyric and Flynn wouldn't make it out alive.

And neither would we.

Moreau chuckled, watching the scuffle below with obvious delight. "As you can see, our guests have full motor function again. Just in time to give us a demonstration."

The crowd leaned forward in anticipation as the

drone emerged from a hidden panel in the wall. Sleek, matte black, no visible rotors, almost no sound. It hovered six feet above the ground, sensors tracking, lights pulsing red.

"Sentinel uses biometric targeting, facial recognition, and predictive pursuit algorithms," Moreau told the crowd. "It doesn't just hunt, it learns. Adapts. But I'm sure you're wondering, how far can this system go? How fast? How intelligent is it? Tonight, you'll see for yourselves. And what better way to showcase its ability than to pit it against two highly trained operatives?"

The guards backed up as the drone circled Flynn and Lyric, scanning.

"Targets acquired," it intoned, voice flat and metallic.

"Of course, we want a demonstration, not an outright massacre," Moreau added. "So we'll provide our friends with a sporting chance."

He snapped his fingers, and the guards threw a couple of small-caliber pistols and two combat knives on the ground. Then they disappeared behind the heavy door again, locking it closed with a heavy thud, leaving Flynn and Lyric alone in the arena with Sentinel.

The drone hummed, patient and predatory.

My hand drifted toward the weapon at the small of my back. I could hit the fucking thing from here.

Decker caught my arm. "I wanted a plan, Vigil. Not a suicide pact."

He was right. No doubt Sentinel had the best shielding available. A single bullet wouldn't take it out of the sky, which meant Moreau's "sporting chance" was just another show.

He absolutely wanted a massacre.

"Find the signal jammer," I ordered. "Take it out, and call in air support."

Decker nodded. "What are you going to do?"

I watched Flynn put himself between Lyric and the drone. He wasn't thinking tactically. He was thinking like a man who'd already decided he'd die for her.

But Lyric didn't stay behind him. She squared her shoulders, picked up one of the pistols, and fired. The bullet pinged harmlessly off Sentinel's shielding.

"Initiate pursuit protocol," Moreau commanded.

The drone shot forward.

I swore and turned away from the arena. What was I going to do? Whatever it took to keep them alive until backup arrived.

Even if it meant I didn't walk out of here with them.

CHAPTER 26
FLYNN

"Lyric, move!" I shouted, already diving to my right as the first drone fired.

A neurodart embedded itself in the stone where Lyric had stood a heartbeat earlier. She'd launched herself in the opposite direction, rolling behind a massive stone planter as two more darts peppered the ground around her. For a split second, our eyes met across the courtyard—a lifetime of tactical training condensed into a single glance.

The crowd erupted in excitement, their previously hushed whispers transforming into enthusiastic cheers as the "entertainment" began. From his platform, Moreau watched with the smug satisfaction of a man who'd orchestrated the perfect spectacle. I wanted nothing more than to drive my knife between his ribs, but the immediate threat of the drones demanded my full attention.

I scrambled behind a decorative column as another dart whizzed past my ear, close enough that I felt the disturbed air against my skin.

Then Sentinel broke into two pieces.

Then three.

Then four.

Jesus. Fucking. Christ.

Swarm mode. The single unit had split into a quartet of smaller, faster drones, each independently targeting and tracking. I'd read about this in the intel briefing, but seeing it in action was another level of terrifying.

"They're using thermal tracking!" I yelled to Lyric, who was pinned behind her planter, eyes calculating her next move. "And movement prediction!"

The knife and gun Moreau had tossed me both felt pathetically inadequate against the hovering death machines. I clutched them anyway, my only weapons against technology explicitly designed to kill people like us.

Two drones peeled off toward Lyric while the other pair circled my position. I needed to draw at least one away from her.

"Hey!" I shouted, darting from behind my cover and sprinting toward a decorative fountain. "Over here, you piece of shit!"

The gambit worked. Three drones immediately pivoted, sensors locking onto my movement. Neuro-darts peppered the ground at my heels as I zigzagged across the courtyard, diving behind the fountain just as a dart grazed my shoulder.

Fuck. Even that slight contact sent numbness spreading down my arm. Partial dose. Not enough to paralyze me, but my left arm hung uselessly at my side, fingers tingling with pins and needles.

So Moreau was using the non-lethal options first.

He was toying with us, but he'd lose patience soon enough and unleash the real payload.

Explosive microblades that could peel skin off bone. A neural disruptor that scrambled your brain until you forgot your own name.

Hell, maybe even the toxic fog—silent, invisible, fatal in under a minute.

And if that didn't break us, Sentinel could always scream. That low subsonic pitch that turned your guts to water and made even seasoned ops piss themselves.

This wasn't just a drone.

It was an executioner driven by a man with a god complex.

"Flynn!" Lyric's voice cut through the crowd's excited murmurs. She'd made it to a cluster of potted trees, using the dense foliage as cover. The single drone tracking her hovered nearby, its sensors struggling to get a clean lock through the leaves.

"I'm good!" I called back, though we both knew that was a lie. "Keep moving!"

I ducked under another cluster of trees and, using the reflective surface of the knife blade, mapped the drones' positions. They hovered at different heights, creating overlapping fields of fire that would make any direct movement suicidal. But they weren't the only things I was tracking.

Across the courtyard, Lyric crouched under her sad

bit of cover, pistol held ready. I raised my hand in a quick series of gestures.

Cover fire. Moving to flank. On three.

She nodded once, then mouthed: *One. Two. Three.*

Lyric broke cover first, firing two perfectly placed shots that caught one drone mid-sensor. It didn't destroy the thing—these were built too well for that—but now that it was smaller than the first time she shot it, the bullet's impact sent it spinning, temporarily disrupting its targeting system.

The distraction was all I needed.

I sprinted from my cover, keeping low, zigzagging between patches of cover. The remaining drones adjusted with frightening speed, their algorithms predicting my path with uncanny accuracy. A dart skimmed my shoulder, the fabric of my shirt tearing as it passed. Too close.

I dove behind a large stone urn, my shoulder slamming into the ornate base hard enough to send pain shooting down my arm. It fucking hurt, but it was better than taking a dart.

I signaled to Lyric again: *Your turn. I'll cover.*

She was farther from my position than I'd like, but we needed to keep moving. The longer we stayed in one place, the more time the drones had to calculate optimal firing solutions. I broke cover, knife in hand, and hurled it at the nearest drone. A desperate move, but, holy fuck, it actually worked. The blade embedded itself in the drone's propulsion system, sending it careening into a nearby column with a satisfying crunch of metal and electronics.

Three left.

Lyric used the distraction to sprint toward a grouping of stone benches closer to my position. The audience tracked her movement, gasping as she narrowly avoided another barrage of darts. I could see them placing bets, pointing excitedly as if we were racehorses rather than human beings fighting for our lives. The sight stoked the fury in my chest to new heights.

A flash of movement caught my eye—one of the drones had repositioned itself, hovering just above a decorative frieze to my left. I ducked as it fired, but I wasn't the target. The dart was aimed at where Lyric would be in three seconds if she maintained her current trajectory.

"Nine o'clock high!" I shouted.

Lyric changed direction instantly, dropping into a roll that carried her behind a decorative statue instead of the bench she'd been aiming for. The dart missed her by inches, shattering against stone.

But the drones were learning, adapting to our communication patterns. While we'd been focused on the obvious threat, the third drone had circled wide, approaching from an angle I couldn't see from my position. I heard the soft whir of its propulsion system too late.

Pain exploded in my thigh as a neurodart struck home, the needle penetrating deep muscle before deploying its payload. The effect was immediate—waves of paralyzing numbness spreading from the impact site, my leg buckling beneath me as the neural pathways misfired. I pitched forward into the open courtyard, suddenly exposed on three sides.

The crowd's excitement surged to new heights. First blood drawn. The odds just shifted dramatically against us.

"Flynn!"

I tried to drag myself back behind cover, but my leg refused to respond, a dead weight trailing behind me. The numbness was spreading fast, already creeping up toward my hip. If it reached my torso, I'd be helpless.

The drones converged on my position, sensors glowing brighter as they prepared to finish me off. From his platform, Moreau smiled indulgently, as if watching a child struggle with a particularly challenging puzzle.

A crack split the air as Lyric's Glock fired once, twice, three times in rapid succession. Perfect shots, each one catching a drone at the precise junction of its sensor array and propulsion system. The machines faltered, their flight paths disrupted as their systems attempted to compensate for the damage.

It bought her just enough time. She broke cover and sprinted toward me. Reckless. Courageous.

My Siren coming to my rescue.

The crowd gasped as she abandoned safety and threw herself into the line of fire. I wanted to shout at her to get back, to save herself, but there wasn't time.

She reached me as the drones regained stability, grabbing the back of my shirt and dragging me behind a massive stone urn. A volley of darts peppered the ground where we'd been seconds earlier.

"Can you move?" she demanded and checked the wound on my thigh.

I gritted my teeth. "I'm going to kill that French bastard."

"That didn't answer the question."

Yeah, she would catch that. "I don't know. The numbness is spreading."

Her eyes met mine, and, for a heartbeat, the warrior's mask fell, showing the terrified woman beneath. "We need to extract the dart."

Without waiting for a response, she gripped the dart and pulled it free in one swift movement. Fresh pain lanced through my leg, but the cold burn of the neural agent was already fading. Whatever was in those darts, it required continuous delivery to be fully effective.

"Two rounds left," she said, checking her pistol. "They're adapting faster than I expected."

"Moreau wasn't exaggerating about the AI," I agreed, testing my leg. The numbness was receding, but slowly. I'd be at half-capacity at best for the next few minutes.

Above us, a sharp whistle cut through the air. We both looked up to see a familiar face on the terrace above—Trent, his expression grim as he surveyed our situation. He made a quick throwing motion, and two small objects sailed through the air, landing just behind our cover. Earpieces. Then he vanished as quickly as he'd appeared.

I snatched one up and fitted it into my ear. Lyric did the same with the other. There was only static.

"Outlaw, Siren." Oz's voice was tight with urgency.

"I'm attempting to hack Sentinel's control systems, but this thing has quantum encryption and adaptive AI. Every time I find a vulnerability, it self-patches."

"Can you at least jam its targeting?" Lyric asked, ducking as the drone fired through the foliage, missing her by inches.

"Negative. It's using a closed-circuit system. No external inputs except for initial targeting parameters." Frustration laced Oz's voice. "Wait—I've got something. The drones are networked to a central hub somewhere in the estate. If I can locate it—"

His voice cut out abruptly, replaced by static.

"Oz?" I called. Nothing.

The crowd was getting restless, some of them laughing at our desperate scramble for cover. I heard someone place a bet on how long we'd last.

One of the drones hovering near me suddenly shot upward, its sensors scanning the area. It had lost visual contact. I pressed myself flat against the fountain's base, using the shadows to my advantage.

The ground trembled beneath us as a section of the courtyard's stone floor slid open. A sleek, midnight-black shape rose from the hidden compartment, twice the size of the drones we'd been fighting. Its surface was featureless except for a ring of pulsing red sensors that rotated slowly, scanning the entire arena.

"What the fuck is that?" I hissed.

Lyric's face went pale. "The command unit."

Moreau's voice carried across the courtyard, dripping with satisfaction. "Ah, you've met the mother. Isn't she beautiful?"

The massive drone hovered silently for three heartbeats before it shuddered and began to separate. Not into four pieces like before—into dozens. Each segment peeled away from the central core, becoming its own autonomous killing machine, until the air above us swarmed with miniature drones no larger than hummingbirds.

"Jesus Christ," Lyric breathed.

The crowd erupted in applause as the swarm formed intricate patterns overhead, a deadly ballet of technology that made our previous opponents look like children's toys.

"Microdrones," Oz's voice crackled back through our comms. "They're—fuck—they're networked with a hive mind. One gets a visual, they all know where you are."

The swarm suddenly froze, then converged into a tight formation that looked disturbingly like an arrow, pointed directly at our position.

"Move!" I shouted, shoving Lyric toward a narrow gap between two planters as the swarm descended.

We scrambled in opposite directions as the microdrones hit our previous position with frightening precision. Instead of darts, they released a fine mist that sizzled when it contacted stone.

Chemical agents.

The swarm split again, half pursuing Lyric while the rest regrouped to track me. My partially paralyzed leg dragged as I lurched toward a decorative fountain, the water our only hope against chemical weapons.

"Nolan's on approach," Trent's voice came through

suddenly. "Two minutes out. We need to get you to the helipad on the east side."

"Little busy at the moment," I grunted, diving behind a column as three microdrones zipped past.

The swarm hunting Lyric had her pinned behind a stone bench, the tiny machines creating a perimeter that tightened with each passing second. She fired her last round, taking out one drone, but the others immediately adjusted their formation to close the gap.

"Flynn!" Her voice held no panic, just tactical assessment. "I'm surrounded. East corner, no clear exit."

I scanned the courtyard frantically. Twenty yards separated us, with open ground and at least thirty microdrones between. My leg was regaining sensation, but still unreliable. The pistol I'd been given was empty, and I... didn't know what to do.

We were fucked.

Then, Nolan's voice crackled through the earpiece, loud and clear over the sound of approaching rotors. "Cavalry's here. And I brought the boom."

His Irish brogue was the best thing I'd ever heard in my life, and I couldn't stop the grin. If there was one thing Nolan Riley loved more than sex and whiskey, it was making one hell of an entrance.

"About damn time!" I shouted. "What's your position?"

"Making the rich and criminal very unhappy," Nolan replied cheerfully as the helicopter swooped low over the courtyard, strafing the crowd with gunfire.

The drones swarmed toward the helo, and Nolan whooped as he led them away from the courtyard, giving us a much-needed breather. But it wouldn't be long before they remembered their mission and circled back to find us.

"Flynn!" Lyric raced to my side and pointed toward the raised platform where Moreau had been moments ago. The arms dealer was no longer grandstanding. Instead, he was slipping away through a side exit, surrounded by three guards in tactical gear, clutching what looked like a reinforced metal case to his chest.

"The control system for Sentinel," I said grimly.

"Get out of there!" Nolan shouted. "I can't hold them off much longer. These fuckers are mean!"

"We need to move," Lyric said, her eyes tracking the nearest drone as it paused mid-air and seemed to recalibrate. "Use the confusion to find Moreau and get that control module. If Oz can't hack them, then that module's our next best option."

I nodded. "On three. One. Two…" I grabbed her and gave her a hard kiss that left her blinking. "Three."

We charged across the courtyard as Nolan's helicopter banked hard, drawing most of the drone swarm in pursuit. The wealthy spectators scrambled for safety, their earlier bloodlust replaced by terror as bullets chewed up marble and shattered champagne flutes. Through the chaos, I spotted a service door where Moreau had disappeared—our ticket out of this hellish arena.

"There!" I pointed, half-dragging my still-partially-paralyzed leg as we sprinted toward the exit.

A guard appeared in the doorway, rifle raised. Lyric didn't hesitate—she launched herself into a slide, sweeping his legs out from under him before he could fire. I followed through with a savage kick to his temple that left him motionless on the polished floor.

"Grab his weapon," Lyric ordered, already relieving him of his sidearm and spare magazines.

The narrow corridor beyond was dimly lit and sloped downward—some kind of maintenance passage that would lead us deeper into Moreau's compound. The walls vibrated with the distant thump of helicopter rotors and the sound of gunfire.

"Oz," I called into my comm as we moved forward, "any sign of Moreau?"

"Thermal imaging shows a group moving toward the docks. Moreau's got a boat waiting. You've got maybe five minutes before he's in international waters."

"Copy that," I said, checking the rifle's magazine. "We're in pursuit."

The passage opened into a steep, natural canyon that cut through the island's limestone core. Carved steps descended through the ravine toward the distant glimmer of water. Moreau and his guards were already halfway down, moving with purpose toward his yacht, visible at the private dock below.

"There he is," Lyric hissed, raising her weapon.

"Wait," I caught her arm. "Too far for a clean shot. We need to get closer."

We started down the steps, using the canyon walls for cover. My leg was finally regaining sensation, pins and needles replacing the deadening numbness. We'd closed half the distance to Moreau when a familiar mechanical whir echoed off the canyon walls.

"Incoming!" I shouted, pulling Lyric behind a rocky outcropping as three drones shot into the ravine behind us.

The sleek machines paused at the canyon entrance, sensors rotating as they scanned for targets. Unlike the arena drones, these were equipped with what appeared to be actual firearms—compact, high-velocity weapons designed for maximum lethality.

"Moreau's done playing games," Lyric muttered, peering around our cover.

The drones split formation, one hovering directly above while the others flanked us from both sides. No more neurodarts or chemical agents. These were programmed to kill.

"We're pinned," I growled, frustration building as I watched Moreau continue his descent toward freedom.

"Oz," Lyric said into her comm, "we're pinned down in the canyon. Any luck tapping into the drone controls?"

Ozzy's voice came through, oddly distorted by what sounded like rapid typing in the background. "Working on it. Their encryption is not exactly something I can crack while eating a sandwich."

"Work faster," I suggested, earning a growl from the other end of the line.

"Brilliant advice, Shepherd. I'll get right on that."

I risked a quick look around our cover, tracking the drones' positions. They'd spread out in a semicircle, covering all possible exit routes from our position. Smart. Whatever AI was controlling them had adapted to the chaotic environment without missing a beat.

The first drone opened fire without warning, a burst of high-velocity rounds chewing into the rock inches from my head. Stone fragments peppered my face as I ducked lower.

"Down!" I shouted, pulling Lyric tighter against me as a second drone strafed our position from the opposite angle.

Lyric returned fire, her stolen sidearm barking three times before the slide locked back empty. One round glanced off the nearest drone's housing, barely scratching its matte surface.

"Bullets aren't penetrating their armor," she hissed, ejecting the spent magazine and slapping in her last one.

I leaned out and squeezed off a controlled burst from the guard's rifle. The rounds sparked harmlessly against the drone's exterior, confirming what we already knew—conventional ammunition wasn't going to cut it.

"We need to move," I said, scanning the ravine for any possible escape route. "On my mark, break for that outcropping ten yards down."

Lyric nodded, tensing beside me like a coiled spring. I counted down silently, my fingers ticking against the rifle stock.

Three. Two. One.

"Now!"

We bolted from cover simultaneously, zigzagging across the exposed ground as all three drones opened fire. The air filled with the whine of bullets and the sharp crack of stone as rounds impacted all around us. I felt something tug at my sleeve—a near miss that sent adrenaline surging through my system.

Lyric reached the outcropping first, diving behind it and immediately returning fire to cover me. I was three strides away when my leg, still not fully recovered from the neurodart, betrayed me. My knee buckled, sending me sprawling across the rocky ground.

Exposed. Vulnerable.

One of the drones locked onto me instantly, its weapon swiveling with mechanical precision. I rolled desperately, seeking any cover, but there was nothing between me and certain death.

"Flynn!" Lyric's scream tore through the canyon as she broke cover, firing her last rounds at the drone targeting me.

The bullets still didn't penetrate, but her desperate attack distracted it just long enough for me to scramble the final distance to safety, my heart hammering against my ribs.

"Jesus," I gasped, back pressed against the rock. "Thanks for that."

She nodded, her face pale but determined as she checked her empty weapon. "We're out of ammo. And Moreau's almost at the dock."

I glanced at my rifle. Maybe five rounds left. Not enough to fight our way through three armored drones. And we'd be completely fucked if the rest of the swam stopped chasing Nolan and came for us.

"Oz," I barked into my comm. "We need some fucking options here!"

"I'm working on it!" His voice was strained, the

sound of furious typing audible in the background. "Their shielding uses a quantum matrix that—you know what, never mind the tech talk. I'm close to cracking it. Just stay alive a few minutes longer."

"Easy for him to say," Lyric muttered and swore as bullets peppered the ridge above us, raining rock fragments down on our heads.

"I've got it!" Oz shouted. "Frequency match on their quantum shielding—firing solution uploaded to your weapons systems!"

A sharp electronic ping sounded from both our weapons, and the targeting displays flickered with new data.

"What the hell?" I stared at the rifle's suddenly illuminated scope.

"Edge Ops special," Oz explained, breathless with excitement. "Your ammo is now calibrated to the exact frequency needed to penetrate their shields. You're welcome, by the way."

I didn't waste time asking questions. I leaned out from cover, sighted the nearest drone, and squeezed the trigger. The round punched through its armor like it was tissue paper, tearing into the delicate electronics beneath. The machine jerked, sparked, and spiraled into the canyon wall in a fiery burst.

"Holy shit," Lyric breathed, her eyes wide. "It worked."

"Of course it worked." Oz sniffed. "Who do you think you're talking to?"

I tossed Lyric the rifle. "Two rounds left. Make them count."

She caught it smoothly, already lining up her shot as the remaining drones adjusted their attack pattern. Her first round caught the second drone dead center, the bullet tearing through its core processor. It dropped like a stone.

"One left," I said, eyeing the final drone as it hovered just out of our line of sight.

"And a lot more drones," Lyric replied grimly as the swarm filled the sky over our heads.

"Nolan," I called into my comm. "We need an air strike on my position, now!"

"About bloody time!" Nolan's voice came back just as cheerful as before. "Been waitin' for the invitation. Inbound hot, thirty seconds. Papa's bringing the rain!"

CHAPTER 27
LYRIC

Explosions lit up the night sky in a deadly fireworks display as Nolan's missiles found their targets. The drones disintegrated in brilliant flashes, raining fragments of scorched metal and circuitry onto our position. My knees gave out, and I sank to the dirt to watch the show.

We were alive.

We had survived the unsurvivable.

I turned to Flynn, intending to throw my arms around him and kiss him—

But he wasn't beside me.

Where the hell had he gone?

I glanced around the canyon in shock and spotted him already charging down the stairs, dodging flaming debris, his attention missile-locked on Moreau.

Oh, fuck.

"Flynn, wait!" I called, but my voice was lost in the rotor noise as Nolan swooped by overhead. I scrambled to my feet and sprinted after him, weaving through the smoldering wreckage of Sentinel. The acrid stench of burnt electronics and melted composites filled my lungs as I ran.

Flynn was a man possessed, tearing down the steps with single-minded fury. I'd seen him angry before, seen him in combat, but this was different. This was raw, primal rage—the kind that burns rational thought to ash.

Moreau had reached the dock, his security detail forming a protective ring around him. The yacht's engines were already running, the low rumble echoing up the canyon walls.

Oh, no.

Flynn was going to get himself killed.

I pushed harder to catch up to him, my legs burning, my body screaming in protest—cuts, bruises, and the lingering effects of the neural disruptor making every step agony. But I kept moving. Flynn wasn't going in there alone.

"Mav," I gasped into my comm. "Target the yacht!"

"No can do, Siren," came the immediate reply. "Too close to your position. Risk of collateral is too high." Nolan's voice was tense, all playfulness gone. "I can't make that shot without taking you both out."

I swore and kept running. Flynn had reached the bottom of the canyon now, a hundred yards from where Moreau's men were loading equipment onto the boat. One of the guards spotted him and raised his weapon.

"Contact!" I shouted, but Flynn was already diving behind a stack of supply crates as bullets splintered the wood around him.

I slid into cover beside him seconds later, breathing hard. "What's the plan?"

"Kill Moreau," Flynn replied, his voice unnervingly flat. His eyes were cold, focused, pupils blown wide with adrenaline.

"Flynn, we need to think this through. There are six of them, heavily armed, and we've got—"

"I don't care." He checked the rifle he'd picked up from one of Moreau's fallen guards. "He doesn't leave this island."

The yacht's engines roared louder. We were running out of time.

"Cover me," Flynn said, and before I could stop him, he was moving.

What he did next was nothing short of spectacular. He tore through those guards like they were paper dolls with toy guns. I barely needed to provide cover fire.

Then, with a yell that was all rage, he plowed into Moreau.

The collision sent them both crashing against the yacht's railing. I scrambled down to the dock, my heart in my throat as Flynn's fists connected with Moreau's face—once, twice, three times in rapid succession. Blood sprayed across the polished deck.

"Flynn!" I called, but he couldn't hear me. Or wouldn't.

Moreau wasn't going down easily. Despite his refined appearance, the man clearly knew how to fight. He twisted away from Flynn's next blow, producing a blade from somewhere that glinted in the moonlight.

Before I could shout a warning, he buried it in Flynn's side.

"No!"

Flynn barely flinched. He grabbed Moreau's wrist, twisted until something snapped, and headbutted him with enough force that I heard the crunch of cartilage from where I stood.

I vaulted onto the yacht, weapon ready, scanning for any remaining guards. The deck was clear, but that didn't mean we were alone. I moved toward Flynn, who had Moreau pinned against the railing now, one hand around his throat.

"You're dead," Flynn growled, pressing the muzzle of his gun under Moreau's chin. His finger tightened on the trigger.

But he didn't fire.

Moreau smiled through the blood dripping down his face from his broken nose. "Do it," he wheezed. "Show your lady what kind of animal you are."

Flynn's hand trembled. The rage in his eyes was primal, unfiltered—a darkness I'd glimpsed before but never seen unleashed.

"Flynn," I murmured, approaching them slowly.

He didn't look at me, but I knew he heard me. His breathing had gone ragged, uneven.

Moreau's eyes flicked to me, then back to Flynn. Despite the blood and the gun at his head, he still managed to look smug, almost amused. "Your woman was so compliant when paralyzed. So helpless while I explored what was mine."

Flynn went rigid, his whole body tensing like a bowstring pulled to breaking. His finger tightened on the trigger, his jaw clenched tight enough to crack teeth. I could see him fighting himself—the professional operative against the man who wanted nothing more than to splatter Moreau's brains across the dock for what he'd done to me.

Then he saw me standing there, and something shifted in his expression. Without a word, he stepped back and extended the gun toward me, grip first.

"Your body, your choice," Flynn said hoarsely, extending the gun toward me.

Our eyes met, and I took the weapon from him, my fingers brushing his. The metal was warm from his grip.

Moreau's eyes widened slightly as I leveled the weapon at his head, my arm steady despite everything my body had endured in the past eight hours. He tried to maintain his arrogant composure, but I saw the first flicker of genuine fear in his eyes.

"How does it feel to be completely helpless?" I asked. "To know your life depends entirely on someone else's mercy?"

"You won't shoot me," Moreau said, though his confidence was cracking around the edges. "Your people need me alive. For information. For—"

"No," I interrupted, taking another step closer until the barrel of the gun rested against his forehead.

His throat worked as he swallowed. "Ms. Renard, be reasonable—"

"You put your hands on me while I couldn't move."

The memory of his touch crawled across my skin like insects. "You thought that made me yours."

Behind me, I heard the rest of the team approaching —Ethan's voice calling out orders, Trent's heavy footsteps hitting the dock. But they seemed distant, unimportant. There was only Moreau's fear-filled eyes, the warm metal of the gun in my hand, and the absolute certainty of what needed to be done.

I fired.

The gunshot echoed across the water, a sharp crack that hung in the air before fading into the distant sounds of chaos still emanating from the compound. Moreau crumpled, his body making a dull thud against the deck. The neat hole between his eyes leaked a thin trickle of blood, surprisingly little for the damage the bullet had done going out the back of his skull. I lowered the gun slowly, my arm feeling strangely heavy now that the deed was done.

"Lyric." Flynn's voice pulled me from my thoughts. He stood beside me, swaying, his complexion pale beneath the mixture of blood and grime. What was left of his shirt was soaked through with blood where Moreau's blade had caught him.

His legs gave out.

"Flynn!" I let go of the gun and dropped down beside him, cradling his head in my lap.

The knife wound was deep, still seeping blood at an alarming rate. The neurodart puncture in his shoulder was swollen and angry, the flesh around it discolored from the agent's effects. His injured leg was trembling with fine muscle spasms—neural pathways still misfiring from the drug.

"'M fine," he mumbled, clearly not fine at all. "Check the case. Make sure… intact."

"The case doesn't matter. Sentinel's gone," I told him, tearing a strip of fabric from my already ruined dress to press against his bleeding side.

He hissed in a breath. "Doubt it. More… of those… fuckers… out there… somewhere."

He was probably right, but I didn't care. "Shh. Stop talking and stay still. You're losing too much blood."

He caught my hand, his grip still strong despite his condition. His eyes, although clouded with pain, focused on my face with fierce intensity. "Are you hurt?"

The question nearly undid me. After everything he'd endured, his first thought was still for my safety. I shook my head, not trusting myself to speak as a wave of emotion threatened to overwhelm the clinical detachment I'd been holding onto.

"I'm sorry," he whispered, voice breaking. "I couldn't stop him. I couldn't protect you."

I knew he meant what had happened when we were both paralyzed, helpless. The violation I'd experienced while unable to move or resist. The memory was there, a dark shadow at the edges of my mind that I'd have to face eventually. But not now. Not here.

"You have nothing to be sorry for." I brushed my fingers through his sweat-dampened hair, pushing it back from his forehead. "We're alive. We completed the mission. That's all that matters."

But it wasn't all that mattered, and we both knew it. I'd been so close to telling him I loved him before the drones attacked. The words were still there, waiting to be spoken, but I couldn't get them past the growing lump in my throat.

Alistair dropped to his knees beside me and ripped open his medical kit, his expression shifting from one of professional assessment to alarm as he took in Flynn's condition. "Jesus Christ."

"You should… see the… other guy," Flynn replied weakly, attempting a bloody smile that turned into a grimace.

"You're a comedian." Alistair moved fast as he cut away Flynn's blood-soaked shirt to access the wound beneath. "Trent! I need the trauma kit from the chopper! And tell Nolan to prep for immediate evac!"

Years of ops together showed in the way the team spread out, securing the scene, gathering intel, locking down our exfil route.

I started to move back, to give Alistair room to work, but Flynn's hand caught mine in a grip that belied his weakened state.

"Don't go," he whispered.

"I'm not going anywhere," I promised, squeezing his hand. And I meant it in ways that surprised even me.

"Hang in there, Shep," Alistair said, prepping an IV. "We'll have you patched up in no time. Lyric, keep pressure on his wound. He's bleeding too much."

God, that really was a lot of blood. I pressed harder as, above us, Nolan's helicopter circled, preparing for landing on the yacht's helipad. The wind from the rotor whipped my hair around my face and sent ripples across the dark water.

"Princess." Flynn's fingers tightened around mine, drawing my attention back to him. "Does this… count as a successful date? Explosions, gunfire, saving… the world from autonomous… killer drones?"

The joke was weak, but I rewarded it with a small smile anyway. "If this is your idea of a date, Shepherd, your standards are concerningly low."

"High standards," he corrected, wincing as Alistair inserted the needle for the IV. "Just… unconventional taste."

"Next time, maybe just Thai food and a movie."

Next time. Two simple words that should have made my heart rate pick up, my flight instincts kick in, but they didn't.

"Deal," he said on a breath of sound. "Though fair warning… I have terrible taste in movies."

"Somehow, that doesn't surprise me at all."

Nolan brought the helo down with more haste than precision, the landing skids scraping against the helipad with a screech that set my teeth on edge. Flynn's blood was sticky between my fingers as I pressed harder against his wound, willing the flow to stop.

The side door slid open and Nolan stood there, his hair whipping in the rotor wash, face grim as he surveyed the situation.

"Christ," he muttered, jumping down to help. "Always with the dramatics, Shepherd."

"You… know… me…" Flynn said, gasping between each word.

"Move, move, move!" Ethan's voice cut through the rotor noise, his usual composure fractured around the edges as he gestured for the team to load Flynn into the cabin.

Trent and Decker lifted him with a brutal efficiency that spoke of too many similar evacuations. His head lolled against Trent's shoulder, face ashen beneath the grime and blood. I scrambled in behind them, my torn evening gown catching on the helicopter's door frame. I yanked it free with enough force to tear the fabric further, not caring about anything except staying at Flynn's side.

Alistair was already in the cabin, his medical kit open and ready. The calm in his movements was at odds with the tension radiating from his body as he began assessing Flynn's injuries.

"Pressure here," he ordered, guiding my hands back to the wound at Flynn.

"Don't let up," Alistair added, his voice steady despite the urgency in his eyes. He cut away the rest of Flynn's shirt to fully expose the wound. "Mav, what's our ETA to the nearest trauma center?"

"Twenty-three minutes if I push it," Nolan called back, the rotors already spinning faster as we lifted off. "Eighteen if I really piss off air traffic control."

"Make it eighteen," Ethan ordered, strapping himself in across from us.

"I'm… okay," Flynn muttered.

No, he wasn't. His face had gone from pale to gray, and his eyes weren't focusing properly anymore.

Oh, God.

Panic clawed at my throat, but I forced it down. Panic wouldn't help Flynn.

Someone put headphones on me as the helicopter lurched sideways, banking hard over the water. I braced myself against the cabin wall, my hands never leaving Flynn's wound. His blood was warm against my palms, a stark contrast to the unnatural coolness of his skin.

"BP's dropping," Alistair muttered, more to himself than anyone else as he attached monitors to Flynn's chest. The portable unit beeped to life, displaying vitals that made Alistair's brow furrow deeper. "Tachycardic. Possible pneumothorax from the impact trauma."

No one spoke. I could hear my own heartbeat, harsh in the quiet. The kind of silence that crept in when everyone was too afraid to say the wrong thing or admit how bad it really was.

But then Nolan glanced back form the pilot's seat. "Alright, you lot." His voice was light, but there was worry in his eyes as he scanned Flynn. "Time for Preacher's 'Don't Die' Checklist. Number one: Limbs attached?"

"They won't be if you don't watch where we're going," Decker muttered, tightening his harness as the helicopter dipped in strong gust of wind.

"Excuse me, do I tell you how to be all broody and morally gray? No? Then leave the piloting to me, Dealer." But he returned his attention back to the stick as he called, "Number two: Blood on the inside?"

"Not as much as I'd like," Alistair said, working focused and fast, his hands steady even as Flynn's vitals trended in the wrong direction.

"Breathing?"

Flynn stirred, waving a hand to get our attention, then pointing to my headset. Ethan unbuckled from his seat and grabbed an extra one, carefully sliding it on over Flynn's ears and adjusting the mic to rest near his mouth.

"Doing… the… checklist?" Flynn's voice was almost lost in the crackle of static.

"You know it," Nolan said. "You still breathing, Outlaw?"

"Next one… to ask… gets punched."

"So, check." Nolan glanced back again, this time his gaze meeting mine. "Did you two think before doing the dumb thing?"

"Definitely not," Ethan grumbled.

A sound that wasn't quite a laugh, but wasn't a full sob escaped me before I could stop it.

"Aye, that tracks," Nolan said. "Number five: Made your peace with God?"

"Fuck, no," Alistair muttered.

"Alright, good. That's five for five. Hear that, Flynn? We're golden."

Alistair didn't look up. "You forgot the most important one, Mav."

"Oh?" Nolan asked. "I got all five."

"It's a new one I'm adding now. No bleeding out before we land."

Flynn let out a breath that was more groan than laugh. "No promises."

Nolan made a face and turned back to the stick. "That's not how the almighty checklist works, mate."

"What exactly is the checklist?" I asked and glanced over at Ethan. He looked exhausted, tired, and worried. He just shook his head.

"It started as a joke. They were making fun of my actual checklist," Alistair explained, and knocked his knuckles against the clipboard attached to his medical bag, where he'd been recording Flynn's vitals.

"It became a tradition," Trent added. "Our little pre-mission ritual."

"Aye, we do the checklist, and no one dies," Nolan said. "That's why it's Preacher's 'Don't Die' Checklist."

"Post-mission... in this case," Flynn mumbled, his eyes fluttering. "Got it... backwards... like everything else."

I reached for his hand. His skin felt cold, clammy. I squeezed gently, and to my surprise, he squeezed back.

"You're going to be fine," I said, the words coming out more like a command than a reassurance. Like I could make it true through sheer willpower.

Flynn's amber-brown eyes found mine, a hint of that infuriating spark still there despite everything. "Worried... about me... princess?"

Yes, I was. But I rolled my eyes because, even bleeding out on a stretcher, the man couldn't stop being insufferable.

His gaze softened as he looked at me, something vulnerable breaking through the pain. "Don't... look so scared. Not... dying on you."

But the monitors told a different story. The line jumped erratically, each unsteady peak making my heart stutter in response. Alistair's movements became more urgent, his usual methodical calm giving way to the controlled urgency of a man fighting a losing battle. He reached for another syringe, injecting something into Flynn's IV line.

"Pressure's dropping," he announced, his voice tight. "He's going into shock."

"Do something," I demanded, my voice cracking despite my effort to keep it steady.

"What do you think I'm doing?" Alistair snapped, then immediately softened. "I'm sorry. I'm doing everything I can."

Flynn's grip on my hand weakened, his eyes losing focus as they drifted past me to some middle distance. The color had drained from his face completely, leaving his skin with a waxy, translucent quality that terrified me more than the blood.

"Flynn," I said sharply, squeezing his hand. "Stay with me."

His lips moved, forming words, but no sound came out. Still, I knew what he was saying.

I love you.

Oh, God. He was saying goodbye.

I tightened my hold, as if I could physically anchor him to consciousness through sheer force of will.

"Stay with me," I whispered, leaning closer. "You promised, remember? No dying."

A ghost of a smile touched his lips, but it faded almost immediately as his eyes rolled back. The monitor emitted a high-pitched, continuous beep that I could hear despite my headphones and the roar of the rotor.

"Fuck! He's crashing!" Alistair shouted, already reaching for the defibrillator. "Nolan, how much longer?"

"Ten minutes!" Nolan called back, the helicopter lurching as he pushed it harder.

"He doesn't have ten minutes!" Alistair positioned the paddles. "Clear!"

I let go of his limp hand even though it was the last thing I wanted to do.

Flynn's body arched off the stretcher, then fell back limply. The monitor continued its unbroken wail. Alistair hit him again, and again, each jolt lifting Flynn's body in a macabre dance that seemed to mock life rather than restore it.

"Come on, you stubborn bastard," Alistair muttered, his face shining with sweat as he adjusted the settings and positioned the paddles again. "Not like this. Not today."

I watched, frozen, as Alistair shocked Flynn a third time. The cabin seemed to contract around me, the walls pressing in, the air suddenly too thin to breathe. This couldn't be happening.

Not to Flynn.

Not after everything we'd survived.

Not when he was the first person I've loved since losing my sister.

Ethan moved beside me, his hand gripping my shoulder in silent support. I hadn't even realized I was shaking until I felt the steadying pressure of his fingers.

"Flynn," I whispered. "Please, stay. I want you to stay."

The monitor hiccupped, a single, faint blip interrupting the continuous tone. Then another.

"We've got rhythm," Alistair said on an exhale.

"He's holding, but just barely. The knife nicked an artery. Between that and the neural agent interfering with clotting..." He didn't finish the sentence. He didn't need to.

He met my gaze. "Keep talking to him, Lyric. He hears you."

My lungs remembered how to work again, air rushing in so quickly it made me dizzy. I reached for Flynn's hand once more, careful to stay out of Alistair's way.

"That's it." I pressed a kiss to his cold fingers. "Keep fighting. We have unfinished business, Shepherd, but I'm not telling you what you want to hear on your deathbed. I won't say it until you're healthy. So you keep fucking fighting."

CHAPTER 29
FLYNN

I gritted my teeth as I yanked the IV from my arm, the sharp sting nothing compared to the deeper ache in my side where Moreau's knife had sliced through muscle and nicked an artery. Two weeks in this sterile prison were enough. The doctors had their opinions about my recovery timeline, but I'd never been good at following other people's rules. My duffel bag sat packed and ready on the visitor's chair—the one where Lyric had spent those first critical nights, though I'd been too drugged to remember much beyond the warmth of her hand in mine.

Morning light slanted through the partially closed blinds, painting stripes across the institutional tile floor. The hospital in Nice was fancy as far as medical facilities went. Private rooms with a view of the Mediterranean for those who could afford it. Or in my case, for those whose shadowy government teams had excellent health insurance. I'd woken early, determined to make my escape before the morning rounds brought more lectures about "recovery protocols" and "physical therapy schedules."

I fumbled with the buttons of my shirt, each movement sending fresh bolts of pain through my ribcage. The neural agent had finally cleared my system, but it had left my muscles twitchy and unreliable. My leg—the one that had taken the dart during the drone attack—still throbbed when I put weight on it. The doctors had used words like "remarkable recovery" and "lucky to be alive," but all I could think about was getting out of here and finding Lyric.

She'd visited daily at first, sitting a silent vigil, her fingers laced through mine as if she could physically anchor me to this world. But then she and the rest of the team had been forced out of France by political tensions. She's called when she could, but it wasn't enough. I needed to see her. To hold her. To assure myself she was okay.

A sharp knock at the door interrupted my struggle with the buttons on my shirt. Before I could respond, Ethan Voss pushed the door open, his entrance as precise and deliberate as everything else about him. His face gave nothing away, but the rigid set of his shoulders told me this wasn't a social call.

"Going somewhere?"

"Anywhere that doesn't smell like antiseptic and death," I replied, wincing as I leaned over to grab my shoes. "I have shit to do. Got a problem with that?"

Ethan closed the door behind him, then took up position by the window, arms crossed over his chest.

Classic defensive posture. This was going to be interesting.

"The doctors say you've got another week, minimum," he said.

"The doctors can bill Uncle Sam for an empty bed." I finally managed the last button, the small victory almost worth the fire burning along my ribs. "I appreciate the dramatic rescue and top-notch medical care, but I'm done being poked and prodded."

Ethan's jaw worked, a tell I'd learned to read years ago. He was chewing on something he didn't want to say.

Fine. I'd go first.

"Spit it out, E," I said, shoving my feet into my boots. "Whatever's eating you, get it off your chest before I walk out that door."

Ethan's expression shifted, the mask of professional detachment cracking just enough to reveal a flicker of concern. "You almost died, Flynn. Twice. On the chopper and again in surgery."

"Not the first time." I straightened, ignoring the protest from my ribs. "Won't be the last."

"You're going after her, aren't you?" Ethan asked, voice carefully neutral.

"Since when do you care about my personal life?"

"Since your 'personal life' involves one of my operatives." Ethan pushed away from the window, his reflection fracturing across the glass as he moved. "She's been... different after what happened with you on the chopper. When we thought we'd lost you."

My fingers found the scar on my side, the raised

ridge of new tissue still tender beneath my shirt. I remembered fragments of that helicopter ride—pain, voices, the steady pressure of Lyric's hand in mine. And then nothing but darkness until I'd woken in the recovery room three days later.

"Fuck you, E. You sidelined her, didn't you?"

A muscle jumped in Ethan's jaw. "She requested some personal time after the initial debrief. It's protocol after a mission goes sideways."

"Bullshit." The word came out sharper than I intended. "You sidelined her. What, she didn't play by your precious rulebook? She killed Moreau instead of bringing him in for questioning?"

"That's not what happened."

"Yeah, right. I know you." I paced away from him, trying to cool the anger boiling inside me before it exploded. But then—nah, fuck that. I swung around and jabbed a finger at his face. "She's not Maya. She will never be Maya. She's her own operative. And a damn good one, considering she completed the mission with zero support from her team leader."

Ethan's posture went from rigid to granite. "Sit down and shut the fuck up for a minute."

He grabbed me by the shoulders and shoved me down onto the bed. I was strong—at least I had been before spending two weeks flat on my back healing—but Ethan was a mountain. I had no choice but to do what he said.

He paced, and I could all but see the steam rising from his head.

"You want to know why she killed Moreau instead

of bringing him in?" I asked after several charged moments of silence. "Because while we were paralyzed by those drones, he put his hands on her. Touched her when she couldn't move, couldn't defend herself."

Ethan stopped moving like he'd hit a wall, and his face drained of color. "She didn't include that in her report."

"Of course she didn't. She knows what the team thinks of her—that she's just filling Maya's shoes. That she's expendable. That her trauma doesn't matter as long as the mission gets completed. She deserves better from her team and her leader."

"You're right." Ethan's broad shoulders dropped, and he scrubbed his face with both hands. He suddenly looked exhausted. "She needs you, Flynn."

I looked up sharply, searching his face for any sign he was manipulating me. Ethan and I had history—complicated, messy history that had left us both with scars that went deeper than skin. Trust didn't come easy between us anymore.

"That's quite an admission coming from you," I said carefully. "Considering you spent the first half of the mission trying to keep us apart."

A shadow passed over his face. "I was wrong."

Now that was unexpected. Ethan Voss admitting he was wrong was about as common as snow in the Sahara.

"Say that again? I think I might still have neural damage affecting my hearing."

His lips twitched. "Don't push it, Shepherd." Then the almost-smile faded. "Maya's death... it messed me up. I couldn't see past it. Couldn't accept anyone taking her place on the team."

"Lyric never tried to take her place. She just wanted to do the job and be accepted."

"I know that. Now." Ethan looked down at his hands, flexing them as if testing their strength. "Watching you nearly die in that helicopter... it brought back Yemen. All of it."

The name of that godforsaken country hung between us, heavy with unspoken history. Seven years of silence, of blame and guilt and things we'd both said that couldn't be unsaid.

"Yemen was a clusterfuck," I said finally. "Bad intel, worse timing, and decisions made under impossible pressure."

"I made the wrong call," Ethan said flatly.

I couldn't hide my wince. I'd always wondered if he regretted coming back for me that day. Now I knew for sure. "Yeah, you should've left my dumb ass. Command would have considered me an acceptable loss."

"I don't leave my people behind," Ethan replied with unexpected vehemence. "Not then, not now."

I blinked. Despite everything, despite the years of resentment between us, Ethan had never stopped considering me one of his people.

"Don't look at me like I've grown another head." He scowled. "Going back for you was the right call, and every single man there that day agreed. I never regretted it. The wrong call—the one I regret—was moving up the timeline based on intel my gut told me not to trust. I knew it was thin, but you were so certain, and I was under pressure from command to deliver results, so I sent my guys into that kill zone. I've carried that," he added, his voice dropping to nearly a whisper. "Every mission since. Every team I've led."

I stared at him, caught off guard by this voluntary breach in his carefully constructed defenses. In seven years, he'd never once acknowledged any part of that clusterfuck had been his decision, his mistake. It had always been mine—I was the one with the dirty informant, the faulty intel. I was the one who disobeyed orders in my desperation to salvage the mission. "If I hadn't gone back in after you ordered us out, they'd all still be alive. We both fucked up."

Ethan nodded. "And Perez, Jackson, and Chen paid for our mistakes. They deserved better from both of us."

I nodded, unable to speak past the sudden tightness in my throat. Tommy Perez, with his collection of bad jokes and worse tattoos. Nick Jackson, who'd been three weeks away from becoming a father. Henry Chen, the newest member of our unit, barely twenty-two and still believing he was invincible.

"I made sure their families were taken care of," Ethan said, his eyes now fixed on some point beyond my shoulder.

I hadn't known that. It was so characteristically Ethan, handling the responsibility without fanfare, without seeking absolution or recognition.

"They were good operators," I said. "Good men."

"Yes." Ethan's agreement was simple but heartfelt. "The best."

It wasn't warm and fuzzy, but it was the closest thing to closure we were likely to get. Some wounds never fully heal—they just become part of you, changing how you move through the world.

Ethan nodded, a ghost of relief passing across his features. He produced a thick envelope from under his jacket and dropped it on the end of the bed.

I reached for it, opened the flap, and stared at the thick stack of money.

My payment.

This meant I was officially done with Edge Ops.

Officially no longer Lyric's partner.

My gut clenched, and I tucked the envelope away in one of the pockets of my duffel.

"So where do you go from here?" Ethan asked. "Now that you're staging a jailbreak from the hospital. Another job?"

Before Monte Carlo, before Lyric, the answer would have been automatic. Get the job done, collect the payment, move on to the next contract. No attachments, no commitments, no team depending on me, or me depending on them. Clean. Simple. Safe.

But now?

I had a few more jobs lined up, but I wasn't sure I wanted them.

No, I knew I didn't want them.

I wanted Lyric.

But did she want me?

I busied myself with checking the contents of my duffel, buying time. "Haven't decided yet."

"No rush," Ethan said, though his tone suggested

otherwise. "I'm sure there are plenty of military contractors looking for someone with your skill set."

I glanced up. This wasn't just casual conversation. Ethan Voss didn't do casual.

"What are you getting at, E?"

He crossed his arms over his chest. "Edge Ops could use someone like you."

I stared at him, waiting for the punchline. When none came, I laughed, then immediately regretted it as pain lanced through my side. "Jesus, Voss. Did you hit your head during the extraction? Last I checked, you and I weren't exactly compatible colleagues."

"People change," he said simply. "Priorities shift."

"You want *me* on the team? Permanently?"

Ethan raised an eyebrow. "You're a good operator, Shepherd. One of the best I've worked with. Your tactical instincts are solid, and you think on your feet. The team respects you." A short pause. "I respect you."

Coming from Ethan, that last bit was practically a ringing endorsement with fireworks and a parade. I turned away, oddly unsettled by the sincerity in his voice.

"I work alone." The words were automatic. A defense mechanism I'd relied on for years. "Always have."

"And how's that working out for you?" Ethan's question was mild, but it hit like a sucker punch. "If the team hadn't been there—"

"I know." I didn't need the reminder of how close I'd come to dying on that helicopter, how Nolan's piloting skills and Alistair's medical expertise had pulled me back from the edge, how Lyric's voice had anchored me to this world when everything else was fading to black.

Lyric.

There it was—the real complication. The real reason I was hesitating instead of giving Ethan my usual speech on all the reasons I preferred to work alone. Because joining Edge Ops wouldn't just mean becoming part of a team again. It would mean seeing her every day, working alongside her. It would mean admitting that she'd changed something fundamental in me, something I'd thought was permanently broken after Yemen.

"Let me think about it," I said finally.

Ethan watched me for several seconds too long. As usual, his expression revealed nothing of his thoughts. "Fair enough."

I zipped the duffel closed with a finality that felt symbolic, though of what, I wasn't sure. Then I slung it over my shoulder, wincing at the pull on my stitches.

"I'm not saying no," I clarified, not sure why it mattered that he understand that. "Just... I need to sort some things out first."

"Things?" The question was pointed, his gaze even more so.

I thought of Lyric—her fierce competence in the field, the vulnerability she tried so hard to hide, the way she'd held my hand in the helicopter when I was slipping away.

The way she'd looked at me when I told her I loved

her, like she was seeing a ghost and a miracle simultaneously.

"Yeah," I said. "Things."

Ethan nodded once, accepting my non-answer. "The team's on stand-down for another week. After that, we're back in rotation." He straightened from his position by the window. "Don't take too long. Some opportunities don't wait around."

I knew he wasn't just talking about the job offer. The man never wasted words, and he certainly never stated the obvious. He was telling me, in his own way, that Lyric wouldn't wait forever, that what had started between us in Monte Carlo needed to be addressed directly, not left to wither in uncertainty.

"Message received," I said dryly.

A ghost of a smile touched Ethan's lips, there and gone so quickly I might have imagined it.

I nodded, shouldered my bag, and headed for the door. My hand hovered over the handle as I suddenly found myself balanced between two futures—the solitary path I'd walked for seven years, and a new one that offered connection, purpose, and complications I wasn't sure I was ready for.

But I wanted Lyric. I knew that without a shadow of a doubt. And Lyric came with nothing but complications. The biggest of which was this man I'd once called friend, then enemy, and now... something in between.

I glanced back at him. "Why the change of heart, Ethan? Really."

He considered the question for several seconds before answering. "Because I've seen the way you watch her." A pause, weighted with meaning. "It's how I used to look at Maya."

His expression gutted me. The great Grim Reaper—death incarnate, unshakable and cold-blooded in the field—looked… tired. A warrior who'd fought a thousand battles, but lost the one that mattered most. A man who'd run out of fight.

If I lost Lyric the way he'd lost Maya, I didn't know what would be left of me. Maybe nothing at all.

I swallowed hard. "Tell Lyric I'll be there as soon as I can."

Ethan didn't nod. Didn't smile. Just held my gaze like he was seeing all the pieces I didn't say out loud.

"Tell her yourself," he said quietly. "She's waiting."

CHAPTER 30
LYRIC

I'D SURVIVED A FIREFIGHT WITH KILLER DRONES, BEEN drugged and captured, killed an international arms dealer, and nearly lost Flynn to a knife wound, yet somehow, walking into Edge Ops headquarters felt more intimidating than any of it.

I'd stayed with Flynn for as long as I could at the hospital in France, but neither France nor Monaco was too happy about the chaos we'd caused off their coasts, so Ethan had insisted I return stateside with the team. The doctors had assured us he would make a full recovery, but he needed time to heal.

And I couldn't deny that I also needed the time and space to figure out what came next.

For me and my career.

For Flynn and this thing between us.

But Flynn left the hospital two weeks ago, and I hadn't heard a word from him. He'd gone off-grid, which was apparently typical Flynn behavior because when I complained about it, Alistair had shrugged and said, "Shepherd always disappears to lick his wounds. He'll turn up when he's ready."

I wasn't sure if that was reassuring or infuriating.

Edge Ops headquarters sat on the outskirts of Seattle, in the shadow of Mount Rainier, and looked more like a high-tech startup than a black ops base—all sleek glass and modern furniture, with state-of-the-art security that made the Pentagon's look like dollar-store padlocks.

I nodded at the security guards as I passed through the final checkpoint, my palm print and retinal scan confirming that I belonged here now. The thought still felt strange, like borrowed clothing that hadn't quite adjusted to my shape.

Rafe Castellanos was the first to spot me, looking up from where he was cleaning his rifle at one of the workstations. His leg was still in a cast from the op that killed Maya, but boredom had apparently overruled doctor's orders. Trent had him on light duty to keep him from climbing the walls.

Usually, his expression was as unreadable as a brick wall, but when he saw me, his dark eyes softened by a fraction, and his mouth tugged into the barest suggestion of a smile.

"Renard," he said in his thick Boston accent. He was a gruff man with a full, neatly trimmed beard and dark, intense eyes that missed nothing. His nod of acknowledgment might as well have been a bear hug and a fruit basket.

"Rafe," I replied, matching his tone. "How's the leg?"

He scowled at his cast. "Gonna cut the fucking thing off."

I looked down at the plaster and couldn't quite smother my laugh. Someone—probably Nolan—had drawn a big cartoon-style dynamite stick with a lit fuse, labeled "Sparky's Big Boom Stick." Under that was a gothic tombstone with "Here Lies Rafe's Social Life. Killed by Eye Contact" inscribed on it.

"Nolan got to you while you were sleeping, didn't he?"

Rafe grumbled.

"I mean, that tombstone's pretty good."

"Oh, that was my contribution," Leo Santiago said, appearing from the break room, two coffee mugs in hand. He deposited one in front of Rafe, then flashed a brilliant smile.

And, okay, yes, I was momentarily dazzled. He was the prettiest man I'd ever seen. Where Rafe was all hard edges and stoicism, Leo was charm personified.

Leo had suffered a bad concussion at the same time Rafe broke his leg, but you wouldn't know it to look at him. His dark hair was artfully tousled, his lean frame casually propped against the workstation as if he were posing for a magazine shoot rather than recovering from a traumatic brain injury.

"Welcome home, Siren," Leo said, his voice carrying the barest hint of a Spanish accent. "I hear you had an interesting first mission. Killed Moreau, saved the world, and broke Shepherd's heart all in one mission. Impressive efficiency."

I rolled my eyes. "I didn't break his heart."

"No?" Leo pulled himself up to sit on Rafe's desk, ignoring the other man's annoyed grunt. "Then how is our resident lone wolf?"

"I don't know," I admitted. "He disappeared."

And it still hurt. He'd told me—repeatedly—he loved me and wasn't going anywhere, but now he was gone without so much as a "see ya, it was fun."

Leo and Rafe exchanged a look, but I didn't know them well enough to interpret its meaning.

"That tracks," Rafe muttered.

A knot of emotion swelled in my throat. Oh, no. I had to go before I burst out crying in front of these guys.

I motioned vaguely toward the hallway. "I need to check in with Ethan."

"He's waiting for you," Leo confirmed, his magazine-worthy smile softening to something more genuine. "For what it's worth, I'm glad you're here, Lyric. The team needs you."

The unexpected sincerity caught me off guard, and I managed only a quick nod before heading down the corridor toward Ethan's office. The knot in my throat had grown, making it difficult to swallow. Flynn's absence was a hollow space beneath my ribs that shouldn't exist after such a short time together. We'd known each other for a matter of weeks, yet somehow he'd carved out a place inside me that now ached with emptiness.

I wasn't supposed to feel this way. Operatives didn't get attached. It was the first rule of survival in our line of work.

Nolan spotted me as I crossed the main operations floor, headed toward Ethan's office. He was sprawled in a chair at his usual station, feet propped on the desk, a protein shake in one hand and a tablet in the other. When he looked up, his perpetual smirk softened.

"Well, if it isn't our resident femme fatale," he called, loud enough to draw the attention of everyone within earshot. "Are you back for good or just here for more of Preacher's tender loving care? I hear his sponge baths are exceptional."

"I've been cleared for work." I rolled my eyes, but honestly, I was relieved for the distraction. Joking, I could do. The rest of it… I hadn't figured out yet. "You just love making poor Alistair uncomfortable, don't you?"

"Someone's gotta pull that stick out of his arse," Nolan replied, swinging his feet down and rising with an exaggerated stretch. "Besides, I'm Irish. Antagonizing clerics is practically a national pastime."

"I'm not a cleric," came Alistair's drawl as he emerged from the office I'd been aiming for.

Like Leo and Nolan, the doctor's expression softened when his gaze landed on me, and I suddenly wished they'd all stop doing that. I didn't want them to be soft and sensitive. I wanted them to treat me like one of the guys.

"Siren. Pleased to see you up and about. Your shoulder healing properly?"

I instinctively rolled the joint, feeling only the slightest twinge where a chunk of Sentinel's debris had sliced me open. "Good as new, Doc. Your handiwork holds up."

"Oh, that reminds me," Nolan said suddenly and reached into a drawer of his desk. He pulled out a fluffy porcupine toy and tossed it to Alistair.

Alistair caught the stuffed animal with a frown. "What on earth is this?"

"You said you'd rather spoon a rabid porcupine than me, so… there you go, mate. She's not rabid, but she's something soft to hold at night. Christ knows you need the practice. You might as well be a cleric with how often you get laid."

I choked on a laugh.

Alistair didn't even blink. "Just because I don't fuck everything with a pulse like you, Mav, doesn't mean I'm celibate."

I shook my head, half in disbelief. Two weeks ago, I'd been fighting to prove I belonged here. Now I was watching a trauma surgeon bicker with an Irish pilot over a stuffed animal. And somehow, it was starting to feel right. Maybe… even like I belonged.

"I'm going to set it on fire," Alistair said flatly, holding the toy between his fingers.

"Oh, you wouldn't!" I said. "She's adorable. Besides, how can you say no to that face?" I motioned to Nolan, who gave his best puppy eyes and pouty lips. And the man had really nice lips.

Alistair's gray eyes turned to me with a mock glare, but I saw the crinkles of amusement at their corners. "That's manipulative, Siren."

"No," Nolan chirped. "That's teamwork." He slung

an arm around Alistair's shoulders and grabbed the porcupine, holding it up. "Come on, mate. You know you love her. Her name is Prickles."

"Of course it is."

I laughed, genuinely laughed, as Alistair's expression shifted from long-suffering to reluctant amusement. It was these moments—the easy camaraderie, the teasing banter—that made me realize just how much had changed since I'd first walked through these doors.

"Some of us have actual work to do rather than tormenting colleagues." Alistair ducked out of Nolan's grasp but snatched the porcupine back and tucked it protectively under his arm rather than abandoning it.

"Aye, that's the spirit!" Nolan called as he retreated to the medical wing. He turned back to me with a wink. "Ten says he names it something poncy in Latin by the end of the week."

"No, twenty that he'll keep calling it Prickles," Leo called from across the room.

"I'll take that action," I said, smiling despite myself. "Fifty bucks says he'll name it after Nolan out of spite."

"Nah, I'm out. I'd never win that bet. Of course he'll name it after me. I'm magnificent." Nolan's grin was infectious, his blue eyes crinkling at the corners. "Speaking of bets, the pool on when Shepherd returns is still open if you're interested."

My smile faltered. "You're running a betting pool on Flynn?"

"Course we are. We're degenerates with too much downtime between missions." He shrugged unapologetically. "Current favorite is three more days. Trent's got money on tomorrow. Ethan refuses to participate but secretly told Kate to put fifty on 'already back and watching us.'"

I tried to keep my expression neutral, but something must have shown on my face because Nolan's teasing smile softened.

"He'll be back, Siren."

I nodded, not trusting myself to speak. The idea that Flynn might be somewhere nearby, watching, sent a shiver of awareness along my spine.

"You're back!"

I turned toward the voice that I usually only heard through static in my ear.

Kate.

I hadn't met her in person yet, and was surprised by how young she looked. Our comms specialist was very petite with a shock of purple-streaked hair that framed a face barely out of college. Yet those eyes behind geometric neon blue frames—sharp, assessing—belonged to someone who'd seen far more than her years suggested.

She bounced over, stopping just short of hugging me. "For good? These assholes haven't scared you off, have they?"

"For good," I replied, genuinely meaning it.

She exhaled. "Oh, thank God. This place sorely needs more estrogen to counteract all the testosterone poisoning." She gestured at the operations floor where Nolan was timing Leo with a stopwatch while he did push-ups on one arm, shouting something about "Edge Ops Olympic Trials."

I snorted and turned back to Kate. "I'll do my best, but we'll need a few more women to make a real dent in this level of machismo."

Kate sighed. "I know, right? I keep telling Ethan we need to recruit more women, but apparently 'qualified female operatives who can tolerate working with over-grown frat boys' is a surprisingly small talent pool." She adjusted her glasses and lowered her voice conspiratorially. "Between you and me, I think having you here might actually civilize them a little. Nolan's been using actual plates instead of eating over the sink, and Rafe said 'please' yesterday. Progress."

Warmth spread in my chest at the thought that my presence was making any difference. "Now, if we can just get them to remember to put the toilet seat down."

Kate's eyes lit up. "Toilet seats? Please, I have bigger plans for civilizing these savages." She leaned in and lowered her voice. "I set up dating profiles for them. It's called Operation: Soulmate."

I blinked. "Wait, what?"

"Dating profiles. Tinder, Bumble. Grindr for Nolan because he'll fuck anything with a pulse. The works. These men need to interact with humans who aren't carrying weapons or discussing tactical formations. Real people. Preferably ones who can teach them how to function in normal society."

"That's... diabolical," I said, genuinely impressed.

She grinned. "I'm just doing my part for world peace."

"Have any of them actually gone on dates?"

"Leo has. Obviously. I mean, you've seen him. He's

like catnip for women. Rafe deleted his profile and threatened to use my computer for target practice if I tried again. Alistair doesn't know his exists yet, and I'm saving that reveal for when he really pisses me off." She grinned. "As for Nolan... well, let's just say the Irish charm is working overtime. And he's enjoying every second of it."

"What about Ethan, Trent, and Oz?"

"Ethan, no. He's too..." She hesitated, searching for the right word. "Raw, I guess, right now. Maybe someday. And Trent is emotionally constipated, so I didn't even try. And Ozzy..." A flicker of annoyance crossed her face. "He's completely oblivious to anything that isn't code or quantum encryption. I swear I could strip naked and dance on his desk and he'd ask me to move so he could see his monitor better."

Something in her tone made me look at her more carefully. The way she fidgeted with her glasses, the slight flush creeping up her neck. "Kate... do you have a crush on Oz?"

"What? No! That's—I mean, he's a colleague, and I would never—" She stopped mid-protest, her shoulders sagging in defeat. "Fuck. Is it that obvious?"

"Only to another woman," I assured her. "The guys are completely clueless about this stuff."

"Great." She scowled and pushed her glasses up her nose. "So, yeah. I'm pining after a man who thinks social interaction is a form of malware. I created dating profiles for everyone else while I'm sitting here like some pathetic—"

"Hey, no." I caught her arm. "You're not pathetic. If

Oz doesn't notice how beautiful you are, he's the pathetic one, and you deserve better."

Kate gave me a watery smile. "Thanks. And you're probably right. Unless I suddenly develop a motherboard, he'll never notice me." She shook her head, sucked in a breath, and straightened her shoulders. "Anyway, Ethan's waiting for you." She nodded toward his door. "And, just so you know, he's been in a weirdly good mood today, which is frankly terrifying."

"Should I be worried?"

"With Ethan? Always." She grinned and gave me a little push toward his office. There was a crash from over by Nolan's desk, and she sighed. "Go on. I have to go make sure these idiots don't burn the place down."

"Right. Thanks." I squared my shoulders and moved toward Ethan's office, bracing myself for whatever came next. The familiar weight of uncertainty settled between my shoulder blades as I approached the frosted glass door with "E. Voss" etched in simple block letters.

I knocked once, heard a muffled "Come in," and pushed the door open.

My heart stopped. Then started again with a painful lurch.

CHAPTER 31
LYRIC

Flynn Shepherd sat perched on the edge of Ethan's desk, one leg swinging casually. His amber eyes locked onto mine the moment I appeared in the doorway. He wore dark jeans and a simple gray Henley that clung to his shoulders in a way that made my mouth go dry. A fresh scar bisected his left eyebrow, and he looked thinner than before, but otherwise whole.

Alive.

And here.

"Hey, princess," he said, his voice like gravel. "Miss me?"

I glanced back over my shoulder at my teammates. Kate bounced on her toes beside Leo, Nolan gave me an exaggerated thumbs-up, and—God help me—even Rafe's mouth twitched in what could almost be mistaken for a smile. Ethan and Trent stood just behind them, arms crossed, trying to pull off stern expressions and failing miserably.

"You all knew," I accused, my voice coming out steadier than I felt. "Every single one of you."

"Guilty," Nolan called cheerfully. "And, for the record, I won the pool. He came back yesterday."

My gaze returned to Flynn, who hadn't moved from his perch on Ethan's desk. His expression was carefully neutral, but I could see the tension in his shoulders, the way his fingers gripped the edge of the desk just a little too tightly.

"Can we have a minute?" I asked, not taking my eyes off Flynn.

"Take all the time you need," Ethan said, motioning for the others to clear out. "We'll be in the conference room when you're ready."

The team filed out, Nolan making kissy faces until Kate elbowed him sharply in the ribs. Ethan pulled the door closed behind him with a soft click, leaving Flynn and me alone in sudden, weighted silence.

For a long moment, neither of us spoke. I drank in the sight of him—alive, whole, here—while trying to sort through the tangle of emotions churning inside me. Relief warred with anger, joy with hurt. I wanted to throw my arms around him and also punch him in the face.

"Two weeks," I finally said, my voice low. "Two fucking weeks since you were released from the hospital and not a word."

Flynn pushed off the desk, wincing slightly as he put weight on his leg. "I know."

I took a step forward, then another, my anger growing with each. "You tell me you love me, nearly die in my arms, then disappear without so much as a text!"

He ran a hand through his hair, the gesture so achingly familiar it made my chest hurt. "I needed time."

"And I needed to know you were okay!" My voice cracked on the last word, betraying more emotion than I'd intended. "I thought we were partners."

"We are." He moved toward me, closing half the distance between us. "I'm so sorry, Lyric, but I had to go handle some things."

"Some things?" I echoed bitterly.

"Yes. I wasn't in a place with a cell signal and told Ethan to let you know I'd be back as soon as I could."

"Well, the bastard didn't say a word."

"Of course he didn't. Probably thought he was protecting you." Flynn sighed and rubbed at the space between his eyes like he had a headache. "Did Alistair at least tell you I'm healing and healthy?"

"He did," I admitted grudgingly. "But I still don't understand why you left. What *things?*"

"I had to go take care of final jobs after I got out of the hospital. Stuff I couldn't leave hanging if I plan to move here and join Edge."

I froze, the anger that had been building inside me suddenly stalling. "You're joining Edge Ops?"

Flynn's eyes never left mine. "If you'll have me."

The double meaning wasn't lost on me. My heart hammered against my ribs as I processed what he was saying. He hadn't abandoned me—he'd been tying up loose ends, preparing to commit to something permanent.

"Ethan offered me a position after Monaco," he continued when I didn't immediately respond. "Said the team needed someone with my particular skill set. Though I suspect it was just his way of keeping me where he could keep an eye on me."

I took another step closer, close enough now to catch the familiar scent of him—sandalwood and gunmetal and something uniquely Flynn. "And you accepted?"

"Not then." His voice softened. "I needed to be sure it was what I wanted. That I could actually be part of a team again."

"And is it? What you want?"

Flynn closed the remaining distance between us, his hand coming up to brush a strand of hair from my face. The touch was gentle, almost reverent. "I want you, and you want this team. So, yes, it's exactly what I want."

I opened my mouth to protest, but he silenced me with a soft kiss. "Don't deny it, princess. You're starting to love them."

"Okay, they're growing on me," I muttered and slid my hands up over his shoulders to tangle my fingers in the hair at the nape of his neck.

He grinned and brushed his nose against mine. "I know, right? Like mold."

"Infectious mold," I agreed, tugging him closer. "So you're really staying? Joining Edge Ops?"

"Already signed the paperwork." His hands settled at my waist, warm and solid. "Got an apartment lined up in Seattle. Ethan wants me to start training with the team next week."

Something unfurled in my chest, a tight knot loosening for the first time in two weeks. I searched his face, looking for any signs of hesitation or regret, but found only certainty in those amber eyes.

"What about your lone wolf thing?" I asked, my fingers absently tracing the new scar above his eyebrow. "The whole 'teams get people killed' philosophy you've been living by for years?"

Flynn's expression sobered. "Yemen was a long time ago. And Monaco..." His grip tightened slightly. "Monaco showed me that sometimes having people at your back is the difference between making it out alive and not making it out at all."

"So this is gratitude? For saving your life?"

"This is me choosing a future instead of running from the past." He leaned his forehead against mine. "And yes, choosing you."

The words sent a flutter through my stomach that I couldn't quite suppress. After Elodie died, I'd locked myself away from any real connections, convinced that loving people only led to pain. Yet here I was, heart racing at the simple admission that someone had chosen me.

"I don't know if I can say it back yet," I whispered, honesty seeming the only fair response. "What you want to hear."

Flynn's thumb traced my cheekbone, a tender gesture that belied the intensity in his gaze. "I'm not asking you to. I just want a chance to prove I'm not going anywhere this time."

"You'd better not," I said, trying for lightness but hearing the vulnerability beneath. "Because if you disappear on me again, I'll hunt you down myself."

His smile returned, slow and devastating. "I'd expect nothing less, princess."

I closed the remaining distance between us, pressing my lips to his in a kiss that started gentle but quickly deepened, weeks of worry and longing channeled into the contact. His arms wrapped around me, pulling me flush against him as he returned the kiss with equal fervor. My fingers curled into the fabric of his shirt, anchoring myself to him, to this moment.

When we finally broke apart, both slightly breathless, Flynn's eyes had darkened to burnt honey. "So, we're good?"

I pretended to consider, though we both knew my answer. "You're on probation."

"Fair enough." He tucked a strand of hair behind my ear, his expression turning playful. "Does probation include dinner tonight? I found this place near my new apartment that serves the best Thai food this side of Bangkok."

"Dinner sounds good," I admitted. "Though I'm not sure how I feel about you making plans before knowing if I'd forgive you."

"I'm an optimist."

I snorted. "Since when?"

"Since I met you." The sincerity in his voice caught me off guard, stealing the witty retort from my lips.

Flynn took advantage of my momentary silence to steal another quick kiss before stepping back. "Ready to face the team? They're probably placing bets on whether we're killing each other or making up."

"Both, technically." I straightened my shirt where his hands had rumpled it. "And Nolan's definitely listening at the door."

On cue, there was a shuffling sound from the hallway, followed by a muffled curse that sounded distinctly Irish. Flynn grinned, shaking his head. "Some things never change."

He moved toward the door, but I caught his hand, stopping him. There was one more thing I needed to say before we rejoined the others.

"Flynn," I began, my voice dropping to ensure it wouldn't carry beyond us. "I may not be ready to say... that. But I'm glad you're here. With me. With the team."

His expression softened, understanding in his eyes as he squeezed my hand. "One day at a time, Lyric. That's all I'm asking for."

One day at a time. I could manage that. And maybe, with enough days strung together, I could finally learn to trust this fragile, unexpected thing growing between us.

"Let's go," I said, nodding toward the door. "Before they send in a rescue team."

Flynn's laugh was warm as he pushed the door open, revealing Nolan and Leo attempting to look casual in the hallway, while Kate rolled her eyes behind them. Rafe stood a few feet away, arms crossed, his scowl firmly in place, but a glint in his dark eyes.

"Pay up," Leo said immediately, holding out his hand to Nolan. "Told you they wouldn't kill each other."

"She could still change her mind," Nolan grumbled, reaching for his wallet.

I met Flynn's gaze and found him already watching me, amusement dancing in his eyes. He winked, a silent acknowledgment of our shared secret—that whatever lay ahead, we'd face it together.

For the first time since Elodie died, the future didn't look like something to survive. It looked like something to embrace.

"Conference room," Ethan called from down the hall, his voice carrying the authority that had earned him command of Edge Ops. "Debrief in five. That means all of you."

As the team began moving toward the conference room, Flynn's hand found mine, his fingers intertwining with my own in a gesture that felt both possessive and protective. It should have made me uncomfortable—this public display, this acknowledgment of attachment. Instead, it felt right. Natural. As if all the broken, jagged pieces of my life were finally beginning to fit together into something whole.

"Ready, Siren?" Flynn asked.

I squeezed his hand, meeting his gaze with newfound certainty. "Ready, Outlaw."

Whatever came next—whatever mission, whatever danger—we would face it as partners. As a team. And for now, that was enough.

CHAPTER 32
FLYNN

The Thai place had been everything I'd promised, authentic enough to make Lyric close her eyes in pleasure at the first bite of green curry. But as good as dinner had been, I was more interested in showing her my new place. Not because it was impressive—just the opposite. I needed her to see how little I owned, how easily I could have disappeared again. I needed her to understand that choosing to stay was the biggest commitment I'd made in thirteen years.

"Home sweet home," I said, unlocking the door to my twelfth-floor apartment. "Such as it is."

Lyric stepped past me into the open-concept living area, her eyes taking in the sparse furnishings—a leather couch I'd picked up two days ago, a coffee table still bearing the assembly instructions, and not much else. The kitchen gleamed with unused appliances, and the dining area hosted a small table with exactly two chairs. No art on the walls, no photos, no personal touches at all. Just the essentials and the spectacular view of Puget Sound through floor-to-ceiling windows.

"It's very..." Lyric paused, searching for a diplomatic word.

"Empty?" I supplied, closing the door behind us. "Yeah, I know."

She turned to me with a smile that didn't quite reach her eyes. "I was going to say 'minimalist,' but empty works too."

I shrugged, tossing my keys on the kitchen counter. "Never saw much point in accumulating stuff when I might need to bug out at a moment's notice."

"And now?" She moved to the windows, silhouetted against the city lights that reflected off the dark waters of Puget Sound below.

I came up behind her, close enough to feel her warmth, but I didn't touch her. Not yet. Not until she was ready. "Now I'm thinking maybe a bookshelf. Some actual dishes instead of takeout containers."

"Wild," she teased, but I could hear the underlying question. Was I really staying? Could she trust that I wouldn't disappear again?

Damn Ethan for not telling her I hadn't abandoned her; I was just off the grid. And damn myself for not taking the time to tell her myself.

"I picked this place for the view," I told her, deflecting slightly. "And the security. Reinforced door, keycard elevator access, digital locks, and clear sight-lines to all approach vectors."

"The real estate agent must have loved that particular request."

I laughed. "She thought I was paranoid. Showed me some ground-floor units with 'charming garden access' until I explained I preferred not to be murdered in my sleep."

Lyric's smile was more genuine this time. "You're ridiculous."

"But alive," I countered. "Want the tour? It's pretty quick—living room, kitchen, bathroom, bedroom. End of tour."

She followed me through the apartment, her fingers trailing over surfaces as if testing their solidity. In the bedroom, a king-sized mattress sat on a simple frame, still unmade from where I'd rolled out of it this morning. A duffel bag rested in one corner, half-unpacked, and a gun safe was bolted to the closet wall—the only thing I'd installed permanently so far.

"I see the priorities," Lyric said, nodding toward the safe.

"I'm setting down roots, not going soft."

She snorted and continued exploring the space. She paused by the floor-to-ceiling windows and stared out over downtown Seattle. I waited, watching, trying to read her expression. Something was off. There was a tightness around her eyes, a tension in her shoulders that hadn't been there during dinner.

I crossed to her and turned her gently by the shoulders to face me. "Lyric, I know words don't mean much after I disappeared on you. But I need you to understand something." I gestured at the empty apartment. "This isn't just a place to crash between missions. This is me putting down roots for the first time since Yemen."

Her green eyes searched mine, and I hated that look of guarded suspicion. Hated that she had every right to doubt me.

If I had to spend every second of the rest of my life earning her trust back, I would.

"Roots," I added softly, tucking a loose strand of hair behind her ear, "for you. I want you to live here with me."

Her eyes widened slightly at that, and I watched her throat work as she swallowed. The defensive wall she'd maintained all evening faltered, just for a moment.

"Flynn," she breathed. "You can't just say things like that."

"Yes, I can." I stepped closer and curled my hand around the back of her neck, drawing her closer. "Because it's true."

Her eyes dropped to the floor between us, and I felt her shiver beneath my touch. "What if it doesn't work? What if this—us—falls apart? Then what?"

"Princess, we survived Sentinel together. We can survive anything."

"I don't know," she whispered, and the vulnerability in her voice cut through me. "Surviving drones and arms dealers is one thing. This—" she gestured between us, "—is something else entirely."

I traced my thumb along her jawline, feeling her pulse flutter beneath my touch. "I know it scares you. It scares me, too."

Her eyes met mine, surprise flashing across her face. "You? Scared?"

"Terrified," I admitted. "I've spent thirteen years making sure I never needed anyone. Then you walked into my life on those dagger-sharp heels and glared at me, and everything changed."

"After Elodie died," she said quietly, "I promised myself I'd never be vulnerable again. That I'd never give anyone the power to devastate me like that. And then you—" Her voice caught. "You nearly died in my arms, Flynn. Your heart stopped."

"It didn't stop. It just... wasn't beating right for a few minutes."

She shot me the same glare that made me fall head-over-heels in love with her in Monte Carlo. "You're not helping yourself here, buddy."

"You're right." I let my hands fall away from her face and took a step back, giving her room to breathe, to think. "I did almost die, and it scared the hell out of me, too. I cope with that by being glib. I'm sorry."

The space between us felt suddenly vast. My heart hammered against my ribs as I watched her struggle with whatever was going on inside her head.

"You okay?" I asked finally.

She nodded too quickly. "Fine."

"Lyric." I kept my voice soft. "It's me."

Her composure cracked, just a hairline fracture, but I saw it—the slight tremble of her lower lip before she caught it between her teeth. She turned toward the window again, arms wrapped around herself like armor.

"I lied," she said so quietly I had to strain to hear. "I'm not fine."

I moved to stand beside her, but didn't touch her again. "Want to talk about it?"

She was silent for so long I thought she might not answer. When she finally spoke, her voice had a brittle quality that made my chest ache.

"I can't stop feeling his hands."

I didn't need to ask whose hands. Moreau. The memory of him touching her while she was paralyzed, helpless, made rage coil in my gut like a venomous snake. I'd killed men for less, but Moreau was already dead. There was no one left to punish.

"Every night," she continued, her gaze fixed on some distant point beyond the window, "I wake up feeling them. His fingers on my face, in my hair… everywhere." She shuddered. "He touched me like he owned me, Flynn. And I couldn't move. Couldn't fight back. Couldn't even tell him to go to hell."

I clenched my jaw so hard my teeth ached, fighting to keep my expression neutral. She didn't need my anger right now; she needed my support.

"I'm sorry," I said, knowing the words were woefully inadequate. "I wish I could've stopped him."

She shook her head, finally turning to face me. In the low light, her green eyes were dark with memory. "You were right beside me, just as helpless. That's not why I'm telling you this."

"Then why?"

Her gaze dropped to my chest, then back to my face,

her eyes huge and glassy. "I need you to help me forget his hands."

Fuck. The lump rose up hard and fast in my throat, nearly strangling me. My Lyric was not fragile, but right now, she might shatter if I touched her wrong. I'd seen her face down arms dealers and killer drones without flinching, but this—this raw vulnerability—was something else entirely.

I understood what she was asking. Not just sex—we'd had that already. She was asking me to overwrite a violation with something healing. To replace the memory of Moreau's unwanted touch with something chosen. Something safe.

I had to clear my throat twice before I could respond, but my voice still sounded like gravel. "Are you sure?"

She nodded, closing the distance between us until I could feel her breath warm against my neck. "Please. You're the only one who can. The only one I trust enough." Her fingers curled into the fabric of my shirt. "I need this, Flynn. I need you."

I raised my hands slowly, telegraphing each movement, and cradled her face between my palms. Her skin felt like warm silk beneath my calloused fingers. "If anything feels wrong—anything at all—you tell me to stop. Promise?"

"I promise." She closed her eyes and leaned into my touch, a shuddering breath escaping her as I cupped her cheek. I brushed away a wayward tear with my thumb, my heart breaking and healing all at once as she pressed against my hand.

"Okay?" I asked.

"More than okay," she murmured.

I bent my head and brushed my lips against hers in the barest whisper of a kiss. She leaned into me, her hands coming up to grip my biceps, anchoring herself. I kept the kiss achingly tender, fighting against the desire to deepen it, to claim her mouth the way my body was screaming to do.

This wasn't about me. This was about Lyric reclaiming herself, her body, her choice.

When she parted her lips, inviting me deeper, I followed her lead, letting her set the pace. Her fingers slid up my arms to my shoulders, then around my neck, pulling me closer with growing confidence. The kiss deepened, her tongue brushing mine, sending heat spiraling through me.

I kept my hands where they were, framing her face, resisting the urge to explore further until she showed me she wanted more. This had to be her choice, every step of the way.

She broke the kiss, her breathing uneven, and rested her forehead against mine. "You can touch me, Flynn," she whispered. "I want you to."

Slowly, I let my hands drift down her neck, over her shoulders, tracing the elegant line of her collarbone with my thumbs. She shivered, but her eyes remained locked on mine, the haunted look replaced by heat.

"Still okay?" I asked.

She nodded, reaching for the hem of my shirt. "Take this off."

I complied, pulling the Henley over my head and

letting it drop to the floor. Her gaze traveled over my chest, lingering on the pink, freshly healed scars. Her fingertips traced the jagged line where Moreau's blade had nearly ended me, her touch feather-light and reverent. I fought to keep my breathing steady as her hand drifted lower, mapping the constellation of old scars and fresh wounds that told the story of my life.

"Does it hurt?" she asked.

"Not anymore," I lied. It still twinged when I moved too quickly, but that was nothing compared to seeing the shadow in her eyes when she looked at it.

Her eyes lifted to mine, something raw and aching flickering behind the green.

"You shouldn't have had to take that hit for me," she murmured.

I caught her hand before she could pull it back, pressed it flat against the scar.

"I would've taken worse," I said quietly. "Gladly."

Her throat worked like she was swallowing words she couldn't quite say.

Instead, she curled her fingers over my heart and held on.

I leaned in, my voice barely above a whisper. "Tell me what you want, Lyric. Tell me what you need."

"I want to feel only you. Your hands. Your touch." Her voice dropped lower, and her hands slid up my chest to link behind my neck, drawing me closer. "What I need is to feel safe again. And I feel safe with you, Flynn."

A single sentence, and it leveled me. Trust from Lyric Renard wasn't given easily—I'd learned that much in the short time I'd known her. The fact that she felt safe with me, that she was choosing to be vulnerable with me, was more significant than any declaration of love could have been.

I brushed my thumb across her cheekbone, tracing the spot where a faint bruise still discolored her skin. "Then I'll keep you safe."

This time, when our lips met, the kiss deepened. Her body relaxed against mine, degree by degree, tension melting away as her mouth opened under mine. My hands stayed carefully in neutral territory, framing her face, until her fingers closed around my wrists, guiding them to her waist.

"Touch me," she murmured against my lips. "Make me forget."

"Whatever you need, princess," I said, my voice rough with emotion. "However you need it."

CHAPTER 33
LYRIC

Flynn's hands trembled slightly as they framed my face, his touch so gentle it almost undid me. In the shadows of his bedroom, his amber eyes were dark with an emotion I couldn't quite name. Desire, yes, but also promise. I guided his hands to the buttons of my blouse, my fingers steady despite the storm of feelings inside me. This wasn't like our other times together—the frantic, adrenaline-fueled sex after a mission, or the demanding, desperate claiming that happened at Moreau's estate. This was deliberate, careful, tender. Tonight was all about healing.

"We can stop anytime," he whispered, his fingers hovering at the top button.

I shook my head. "I don't want to stop."

He undid each button with painful slowness, his eyes never leaving mine. When the last one slipped free, he parted the fabric but didn't push it off my shoulders. Instead, he skimmed his hands down my ribs, cupping my waist and pulling me closer. Such a simple touch, yet it sent shivers across my body that had nothing to do with cold.

But then a flash of memory intruded—Moreau's fingers on my ribs while I couldn't move—and I tensed. Of course Flynn noticed, and his hands stilled.

"Where did you go?" he asked softly.

"Just a memory." I swallowed hard. "Keep going. Please."

Flynn nodded, understanding without needing more explanation. He slid his hands under the open blouse, his palms warm against my shoulders as he eased the fabric down my arms. The air in the apartment was cool against my skin, raising goosebumps along my arms.

"You're beautiful."

His rough, whispered words helped anchor me to this moment, to him. I dragged my hands down his chest, needing to feel his skin against mine. I paused at the fresh scar slicing across his ribs, then bent to kiss it. "Thank you for staying alive."

His laugh was more breath than sound. "I'm pretty fond of being alive right now." He slid a hand around to my back, fingertips grazing the clasp of my bra. "May I?"

I nodded, unable to find my voice as his fingers made quick work of the hooks. The straps slipped down my shoulders, and I let the garment fall between us. Flynn's eyes darkened, but his touch remained reverent, almost worshipful as his palms skimmed my sides, never rushing, giving me time to adjust to each new sensation.

"Still with me?" he asked, his voice a low rumble that vibrated through me.

"Yes," I breathed, stepping closer until our bodies touched.

Flynn's lips found my neck, trailing soft kisses down to my collarbone. Where Moreau had taken, Flynn asked. Where Moreau had claimed, Flynn offered.

But then his fingers grazed my ribs again, and suddenly I was back in that room, paralyzed, with unwanted hands on my body. I stiffened, my breath catching.

"Lyric?" Flynn's voice pulled me back.

"I'm okay." I placed my hand over his, guiding it to my hip instead. "Just don't touch me there. Not tonight."

He nodded, accepting the redirection without question. "Your pace, your rules. Tell me what you need."

I laced our fingers together and led him toward the bed. "Touch me like I matter."

Something broke open in his expression as I pulled him down on top of me. "You matter more to me than anything in this world, Lyric."

His hand moved then, caressing every inch of exposed skin—except my ribs—with a tenderness that made my throat tight. When his fingers skimmed the waistband of my pants, he paused, waiting for permission.

"Yes," I said, helping him with the button and zipper.

He slid the fabric down my legs with the same careful attention he'd shown my blouse, his eyes taking in every newly revealed part of me with appreciation rather than possession.

But when his fingers brushed against my inner thigh, I tensed again, a flash of panic rising unbidden.

"Not ready?" he asked, already moving his hand away.

"No, wait." I caught his wrist. "I want this. I'm just —" I didn't know. I wasn't scared of him, but at the same time, I was also terrified that one wrong touch would send me hurtling into memories I didn't want to remember.

"It's okay." His understanding nearly broke me. I'd spent so many years being strong, never showing fear, never admitting vulnerability. And here was Flynn, seeing my fear and accepting it without judgment.

"Try something for me?" he asked.

I nodded.

"Close your eyes and focus on my voice. On my touch. If another memory comes, tell me, and we'll chase it away together."

I did as he suggested, letting my eyes drift closed as his hands resumed their gentle exploration, touching me everywhere while his deep, sexy voice rumbled dirty nothings in my ear.

When the unwelcome memory of Moreau surfaced again, I whispered, "He's here."

"No," Flynn said firmly. "He's not. He's dead. You killed him. There's only you and me here."

He was right. I had killed Moreau. I had taken back my power in the most final way possible. That realization washed through me like a cleansing wave, and I felt myself relax more fully.

"Kiss me," I whispered, opening my eyes to find Flynn watching me with such tenderness it made my chest ache.

He lowered his mouth to mine, the kiss deep and unhurried. His hands framed my face again, thumbs stroking my cheekbones as if I were something precious. When we broke apart, I felt steadier, more present in my own skin.

"Better?" he asked.

I nodded, reaching for the button on his jeans. "Your turn."

Flynn stood to remove them, and I allowed myself to really look at him—the lean muscle, the scars both old and new that mapped his survival, the unmistakable evidence of his desire for me. His cock sprang free, thick and ready, jutting proudly from his body as he rejoined me on the bed. Warmth pooled between my thighs at the sight of him, my body responding despite the shadows still lurking in my mind.

He settled between my thighs, the weight of him above me feeling like shelter rather than confinement.

"How do you want this?" he asked, his voice a low rumble against my neck.

I traced the planes of his face with my fingertips, memorizing every line, every angle. "I want to see you," I whispered. "I need to know it's you."

"Tell me if anything feels wrong," he murmured, lips brushing my shoulder.

"Everything about this feels right." I guided his hand between my legs. "Touch me."

His fingers moved with exquisite care, stroking me through the thin fabric. I thought I would freeze, would flash back to that horrible moment Moreau violated me, but I didn't. All I felt was Flynn touching me. All I saw were his worried eyes as he watched me.

"Flynn," I groaned, arching into his barely there touch. "Please. I won't break."

The tightness in his expression eased a fraction. "I just want to get this right. For you."

"You are." I pulled him closer, needing the weight of him now, the solid reality of his body against mine. "You're exactly what I need."

He groaned softly, and I felt a tremor go through him. His control was hanging on by a thread. "I'm trying to be gentle."

"I don't want gentle," I whispered against his lips, curling my fingers around his wrist and grinding my hips against his hand. "I want *you*."

His breathing hitched as I guided his hand beneath the fabric of my underwear, both of us groaning when his fingers slid through my wetness. The feeling was electric. His touch ignited something deep inside me that had nothing to do with the physical sensations and everything to do with choice—my choice to be here, with him, like this.

"Christ, Lyric," he murmured, his voice strained as he circled that sensitive bundle of nerves. "You're so wet."

I arched into his touch, my body responding with an

urgency that surprised me. There were no shadows here, no unwelcome memories—just Flynn and me, tangled together in the half-light of his bedroom. I slipped my hand between us, wrapping my fingers around his cock, feeling him pulse against my palm as I stroked him slowly. His sharp intake of breath made me smile.

"Need you," I whispered, guiding him closer. "Now."

His eyes darkened to burnt amber. "Do you want me to put on a condom?"

"We didn't use one last time."

"I know, and that was reckless of me," he said, brushing his thumb across my lower lip. "But I'm clean. I get tested regularly."

"Me too. Standard protocol. And I have a birth control implant."

"I need to be sure you're comfortable with everything tonight."

The concern in his voice made something warm bloom in my chest. I tightened my grip on his cock, enjoying the throb of him against my palm.

"I'm sure," I whispered. "Just you. Nothing between us."

He nodded, his throat working as he swallowed hard. The vulnerability in his eyes matched my own as he positioned himself at my entrance, the blunt head of his cock pressing against me without pushing in.

"Look at me," he whispered.

I did, our gazes locking as he slowly, carefully entered me. The stretch and fullness made me gasp, my body accommodating him inch by inch until he was seated fully inside me. We both stilled, breathing heavily, adjusting to the sensation of being joined so intimately.

"You okay?" he asked, his voice strained with the effort of holding back.

"More than okay," I assured him, wrapping my legs around his waist to draw him even deeper. "Move, Flynn. Please."

He began to rock into me with slow, deliberate strokes, his eyes never leaving mine. Each thrust felt like reclamation—of my body, my choice, my power. Flynn watched me with an intensity that should have been unnerving but instead felt like an anchor, keeping me present in the moment rather than lost in the shadows of memory.

"You're incredible," he murmured, his voice rough with emotion. "So strong. So brave."

I shook my head, unable to accept the praise when I still felt so broken inside. "I'm not—"

"You are," he insisted, punctuating each word with a deep, measured thrust that sent sparks of pleasure racing up my spine. "The bravest person I've ever known."

My chest tightened, eyes burning with unexpected tears. I turned my face away, not wanting him to see how deeply his words affected me, but Flynn gently turned me back to face him.

"Don't hide from me," he whispered, brushing away a tear that had escaped despite my efforts. "Not tonight."

The tenderness in his touch undid me. I surged up to capture his mouth, pouring everything I couldn't say into the kiss—my fear, my gratitude, my desperate need for connection. Flynn responded, kissing me back like he was desperate for a taste of me, his hips never faltering in their steady rhythm as he drove me higher.

"Flynn," I gasped against his lips as heat began to build low in my belly. "I need—"

"Tell me," he urged, shifting slightly to change the angle of his thrusts. "Whatever you need, it's yours."

"More," I pleaded, digging my fingers into his shoulders. "Harder."

"Like this?" He scooped one of my legs onto his shoulder, his hips snapping forward with a primal intensity that made me gasp. The cheap metal bed frame creaked beneath us as he drove deeper into me.

"Yes!" The new angle hit something exquisite, and I cried out, my back arching off the bed. "God, yes!"

My body sang under his touch, pleasure building with each stroke. This wasn't just sex—this was reclamation, validation, healing. Each place he touched erased Moreau's violation, replacing unwanted memories with new ones I'd chosen. With Flynn, I wasn't a victim or even a survivor. I was just a woman wanting—and being wanted.

"Flynn," I gasped as the tension coiled tighter, my body trembling on the precipice. "I'm close."

His hand slid between our bodies, his fingers unerringly finding my clit, circling with just the right pressure. The dual sensation—his cock deep inside me, his fingers working their magic—sent me spiraling over the edge. I cried out his name as pleasure crashed through me, my body clenching around him in rhythmic pulses.

Flynn groaned, his control slipping as my release triggered his own. His movements became more urgent, more primal, as he chased his pleasure. I wrapped my legs tighter around him, urging him deeper, wanting to feel every moment of his surrender.

"Lyric," he gasped, his voice breaking on my name as he shuddered above me. The warmth of his release filled me, his body tensing then gradually relaxing as he came down from his high.

For several heartbeats, we lay tangled together, our breathing gradually slowing. Flynn's weight pressed me into the mattress, and I traced idle patterns across his back, marveling at how different this felt from every other time we'd been together. The urgency was gone, replaced by something quieter but infinitely more powerful. I felt anchored, present in a way I hadn't been in years—maybe ever.

When he finally moved to roll off me, I tightened my arms around him.

"Not yet," I whispered.

He settled back against me, careful to brace some of his weight on his forearms. "I don't want to crush you."

"You're not. I like feeling you."

"How about this?" He rolled, dragging me onto his chest.

I nuzzled in closer. "This is perfect."

"Yes, it is." His hand moved to my shoulder, fingers finding the jagged scar that ran from my collarbone to just below my shoulder blade, a souvenir from a mission gone wrong in Caracas. He traced its outline with a gentleness that made my throat tight. "Does it have a story?"

"Machete. I zigged when I should have zagged."

His chuckle vibrated under my ear. "Rookie mistake."

"I was green." I smiled against his skin. "Thought I was invincible."

"And you don't now?"

"Oh, I'm still invincible," I said, lifting my head to grin at him. "Especially since I've learned when to zag instead of zig."

He laughed again, captured my hand, and brought it to his lips. Against my knuckles, he whispered, "Jesus, I love you so much," the words a warm breath across my skin.

It wasn't the first time he'd said it. Each time before, I'd deflected, or flinched, or changed the subject, or simply let the words hang in the air without acknowledgment. Each time, I'd seen the flash of resignation in his eyes, the acceptance that I might never say it back. Yet he'd kept saying it anyway, offering the words like a gift that required nothing in return.

But something had shifted tonight. The walls I'd built after Elodie died, the barriers I'd reinforced through years of loss and betrayal, had finally begun to crumble. Not all at once—not completely—but enough that I could see beyond them to what waited on the other side.

I thought of all the reasons I'd held back. Fear of

loss. Fear of vulnerability. Fear that loving someone meant eventually losing them. But hadn't I already learned the hard way that walls didn't protect you from pain? They just kept you from fully living.

Flynn had started to trace patterns on my back again, giving me the space he always did, expecting nothing. He'd whispered those three words against my skin so many times, never demanding them in return. He'd wait forever, I realized. He'd keep loving me even if I never said it back.

But I didn't want that anymore.

"Flynn." I shifted in his arms, moving up so our faces were level, our noses almost touching.

"I think—" I stopped and shook my head.

No, dammit. No qualifiers. No half-measures. Not with him.

"No, I know—" Again, the words caught in my throat.

"It's okay, princess," he murmured, pushing a wayward strand of hair back from my face. "You don't have to say it."

God, who would've thought there was so much sweet patience under all that swagger when we first met?

I was under no illusions—he wasn't perfect. Far from it. He was still cocky as hell and sometimes infuriatingly stubborn. He'd make me crazy with his recklessness and his habit of charging into danger and his alpha male possessiveness. But he was also loyal and brave and kind in all ways that mattered. He'd been patient with me in a way no one else had ever been, taking the time to peel away all my other identities to find the real me. And, in the process, he had become the person I trusted most in this world.

No, he wasn't perfect.

But he was perfect for me, and I would be an idiot to let him go.

I cupped his face between my palms, enjoying the feel of his rough stubble against my skin.

"I love you," I said, the words finally breaking free.

Flynn went still, his breathing suspended as if he were afraid the slightest movement might shatter the moment. I watched the emotions play across his face. Surprise, disbelief, and then a cautious, dawning joy.

"Say that again," he whispered.

"I love you, Flynn Shepherd." I smiled, feeling something unravel inside my chest, a tightness I'd carried for so long I'd forgotten it was there. "I'm in love with you, and I'm done pretending I'm not. I don't want to do this without you. Any of it. The missions, the team, this life—I want you there beside me for all of it, making me crazy, making me laugh… making me come when our team is standing right on the other side of the door."

A slow smile spread over his face. "Really like that last one."

"I figured you would."

"Are you sure?" he asked, his voice rough with emotion. "Because if you let me love you, if you love me back—that's it for me. There's no reset button."

"I've never been more sure of anything." And it was true. For someone who calculated risks for a living, who weighed every variable before making a decision, this felt strangely simple. Loving Flynn wasn't a choice anymore. It was as inevitable as gravity.

His smile widened into that cocky grin I'd grown to love, but there was something vulnerable beneath it—a brightness in his eyes that looked suspiciously like tears. It was the most unguarded I'd ever seen him, all his usual defenses down. His hands came up to cover mine where they rested against his face.

"I told myself I'd wait however long it took. That loving you without hearing it back was better than not having you at all." His thumb traced my lower lip. "But hearing you say it... Christ, Lyric."

He pulled me to him, kissing me with a rawness that took my breath away. This wasn't like the careful, healing touches we'd shared earlier. This was hunger and joy and relief all at once, his fingers tangling in my hair as he held me against him like he was afraid I might disappear.

When we finally broke apart, both breathless, he pressed his forehead to mine. "I thought I'd have to wait years to hear that."

"I'm not exactly known for my emotional transparency," I admitted with a soft laugh.

"No kidding." His fingers traced idle patterns on my bare shoulder. "You know what this means, right?"

"That we're going to scandalize the entire Edge Ops team with excessive PDA?"

"Well, that's a given." The corner of his mouth quirked up. "But I meant that I'm going to need a bigger closet. Your wardrobe alone could fill this entire apartment."

I blinked at him, not quite processing his words. "Are you asking me to move in with you?"

"I thought that was implied by showing you the apartment I bought for you." His expression turned serious. "Unless it's too soon. I know we're doing this backward—life-threatening situations first, then sex, then actual dating..."

I pressed my fingers to his lips. "It's not too soon. But this place is..."

"Empty," he supplied. "I know. That's the point. I want us to fill it together. Make it ours, not just mine."

The thought of building something permanent, something real, with Flynn sent a strange mix of terror and exhilaration through me. I'd spent so long living in temporary spaces—temporary identities, clothes, homes —never allowing myself to just... be myself. Never letting myself believe I could have anything that might last.

"I don't know how to do this," I admitted, my voice small. "The whole domestic thing. I've never..."

"Me neither. But we figured out how to disarm a killer drone together. I think we can handle furniture shopping."

I laughed, the sound bubbling up unexpectedly. "When you put it that way..."

"Is that a yes?" His amber eyes searched mine, that rare vulnerability still there beneath the surface.

"Yes," I whispered. "But I'm warning you now, I have strong opinions about throw pillows."

He groaned dramatically and flopped back on the bed. "I knew there'd be a catch."

I curled against him, my head finding that perfect spot on his shoulder again.

"What happens tomorrow?" I asked quietly.

His arm tightened around me. "Tomorrow we go to work, pretend we're professional adults who don't make out in supply closets, and try not to give Ethan an aneurysm."

"And after that?"

"After that..." His fingers trailed lazily up my spine. "We come home."

Home.

With Flynn.

A man who loved me for me.

It was mind-boggling.

For so long, I'd believed that love was a liability— that caring too much made you vulnerable, made you weak. I'd watched my mother wither after Elodie disappeared, had seen operatives compromise missions for loved ones, had witnessed how attachment could be leveraged as a weapon.

But lying here in Flynn's arms, I understood something I'd missed before: love wasn't the liability. Fear was. Fear of loss, fear of pain, fear of the very connection that made life worth living.

"Flynn," I whispered against his neck.

"Hmm?"

"Thank you."

He didn't ask what for. He just pressed a kiss to my forehead and held me tighter, as if he understood everything I wasn't saying. And maybe he did. Maybe that was part of what made us work—this ability to read between each other's lines, to understand the silence as clearly as the words.

Outside, rain began to patter against the windows, a gentle percussion that only enhanced the cocoon of warmth we'd created. In Flynn's arms, with his heartbeat steady beneath my ear, I felt something I hadn't experienced since Elodie's death: peace.

I was home.

CHAPTER 34
TRENT

I'VE SEEN A LOT OF FUCKED-UP TECH IN MY YEARS WITH Edge Ops, but nothing made my skin crawl quite like the tech Moreau had for sale on that goddamn island.

Sentinel was the headliner, sure, but the catalog of horrors went deeper than autonomous killer drones. Stealth suits that scrambled thermal and facial recognition. Biometric spoofs that let you walk through any secure door like you owned the place. Neural compliance implants disguised as wearable health tech. And worst of all—disposable soldiers. Gene-hacked embryos preloaded with combat aggression, grown in underground labs and programmed to die young.

Weaponized child soldiers.

Jesus fucking Christ.

My gut twisted as I leaned against the back wall of our war room, arms crossed, watching Kate and Ozzy dissect the digital remains of Moreau's auction like forensic surgeons. The room glowed with blue light from five massive monitors—each displaying another horrific piece of intel: weapons, buyers, transaction logs, surveillance footage.

"Tracking a transaction to Saudi Arabia," Kate said, her fingers flying over her keyboard.

"Saw that, too." Ozzy glanced over, face bathed in scrolling code. "Looks like our Saudi prince wasn't just in it for the scenery."

"Emilio Benítez was there, too," I said, nodding to El General's profile on screen.

"Yeah, that man's a piece of work," Decker said, lounging back in his chair and flipping a knife from blade to hilt to blade again. "Sick fuck wanted the embryos. Kept bragging about it all night."

Ethan stepped closer. "Did he get them?"

Kate shook her head. "They hadn't gone up for bidding yet. If he got them, he stole them in the chaos."

"Alright. Cross-reference his name with the transaction logs. I want to know what he did walk out with."

Ozzy pulled it up. "Nanovirus with geographic targeting."

Kate exhaled hard. "Jesus, this thing could wipe out a block while leaving the building next door untouched."

I pushed off the wall. If Benítez unleashed that in Caracas, he could take out all of his dissenters and plunge the country into even deeper chaos.

Ethan nodded. "Flag it. Ozzy, track all chatter around Benítez's network. If he plans to use that for a coup, I want to know."

"Already listening in," Oz said. "His passwords are tragic."

"Huh," Kate said and highlighted another series of transactions. "Northern Koreans were there too and they got…" She paused, frowning. "That's interesting."

"Define interesting," Decker said.

"They purchased agricultural nanotech. Drought-resistant seed enhancers." She glanced up at Ethan and then me. "Not exactly a weapon."

"Famine is a weapon." I'd seen starvation used as a control mechanism too many times to view this purchase as benign. "They're not planning to feed their people. They're strengthening their hold over them."

The room fell silent, the only sound the soft hum of cooling fans and fingers on keyboards. This was the reality of our work—seeing beyond the transactions to the human cost. Every piece of technology sold or stolen at that auction would impact lives, and rarely for the better.

The door opened, drawing everyone's attention away from the screens. Well. Everyone's attention except Ozzy's. If that man could implant a screen in his eyes, I had no doubt he would.

Leo hurried in, looking like he'd just stepped out of the shower. His dark hair was still dripping. "Sorry I'm late."

"Hot date last night?" Nolan asked.

Leo flipped him off, settled into a chair, and scanned the group. "Ah, c'mon. I'm not even the last to arrive."

"Flynn and Lyric aren't coming in," Ethan said and returned his attention to the screens.

"Aye," Nolan said with an eyebrow wiggle. "They're definitely fucking like bunnies right now."

Alistair shook his head. "Jesus, Nolan."

"What? We all know they are. I'm just stating facts."

Despite myself, I smirked. Truthfully, I hoped they were. They'd both been through hell and deserved a break. I turned my attention back to the screens, where a new set of data had just populated.

"What's this?" I asked, nodding toward a list of buyer IDs that Kate had just pulled up.

"Secondary purchases," Kate replied, highlighting a section. "Smaller tech that didn't hit the main auction block." She scrolled down, her brow furrowing. "These were handled through a separate system. Lower profile, but still dangerous as hell."

I scanned the list of names and purchases. Most were unfamiliar, likely shell companies or proxies for the real buyers. Standard operating procedure in the black market tech world.

"Wait." My blood ran cold as a familiar name jumped out at me and I pushed off the wall, stepping closer to the screen. "Stop. Go back."

"What did you see?" Kate's fingers paused over her keyboard as the entire room shifted focus to the transaction record displayed on the main screen.

I had to be wrong. Maybe I just saw it because she's been on my mind—

"There." I pointed to a line midway down the screen. "Buyer ID 45721. NeuroLink-II system."

"Neural interface technology," Ozzy said without looking up. "Military-grade mind-machine interface. Nasty piece of work. Military applications for enhanced soldier performance. Welcome to the future, where mind control isn't just science fiction anymore."

"Mind control?" Decker echoed.

"Yep. Not the crude kind, either. This would allow the controller to make suggestions that feel like the subject's own thoughts. The perfect sleeper agent delivery system. Your target wouldn't even know they were compromised."

But I wasn't listening to Ozzy's explanation. My focus had narrowed to the name listed beside the purchase.

Evelyn Phillips.

Impossible.

"Something wrong, Dalton?" Ethan asked, his tone casual but his eyes razor-sharp as they studied my reaction. He knew me like nobody else. He knew I didn't panic. He also knew I was panicking inside now.

I forced myself to breathe, to maintain the composure that had kept me alive through thirteen years of wetwork and black ops. But inside, alarm bells were screaming.

This couldn't be happening.

"Trent?" Ethan's voice sounded distant. "You recognize the buyer?"

I reached past Kate and froze the screen, enlarging the section. There was no mistake. Evelyn Phillips. The same Evelyn Phillips I'd extracted from a cult compound in California just over a month ago. The woman I'd personally escorted to a safe house in rural Montana, thirty miles from the nearest town, with a new identity so complete that even our own intelligence agencies couldn't trace it.

The woman who should be completely off-grid, invisible, safe.

"Trent." Ethan's voice was sharper now. "Talk to me."

"She didn't buy this," I said, my voice dangerously calm despite the adrenaline flooding my system. "Evelyn Phillips is a protected asset."

"Fuck," Decker muttered and sat up straighter in his chair. "That's the cult woman, isn't it? And now she has fucking mind control tech?"

"She's not—" I bit off the words and rubbed a hand over my head. "She was a single mother in a bad situation, who ended up in a worse one." I stared across the room at Ethan, waiting until he met my gaze. "She didn't buy this."

"Okay, are we sure it's the same person?" Kate asked, already typing. "Could be a coincidence. Evelyn Phillips is a common enough name."

Which was exactly why I'd chosen it for her new identity.

"It's not a coincidence." I was certain. She'd been completely off-grid since her extraction from the Hope's Embrace cult. New identity, new location, no digital footprint. Invisible. I made damn sure of it because Evelyn had a young daughter to protect.

Emma. Five years old with her mother's eyes and unshakable trust in me.

The memory of carrying that child through the chaos of the compound's collapse was still vivid. Her tiny arms around my neck, her mother stumbling beside us, half-blinded by the cult leader's final act of violence against her.

I'd promised them they'd be safe.

I'd *promised*.

And I don't break promises.

Ozzy finally looked up from his screen, his expression grave. "Then someone's sending a message."

Someone knew who Evelyn really was. And they knew I had hidden her.

"Or it's a trap," Ethan said, voicing what we were all thinking. "Someone's trying to flush her out."

I was already moving toward the door, grabbing my go-bag from where I'd stashed it beneath the conference table. My mind shifted into operational mode, cataloging what I'd need: weapons, cash, comms, medical supplies.

"Where is she, Trent?" Ethan asked.

"Classified," I replied automatically. The fewer people who knew, the safer she would be. That had been the protocol from the beginning.

"Not anymore," Ethan countered. "If someone's compromised her location—"

"Then I need to move her immediately." I checked my sidearm, confirming a round in the chamber. "Alone."

Ethan stepped in front of me, blocking my path to the door. "That's not how we operate. If one of our protected assets is compromised, we move as a team."

"With all due respect," I kept my voice steady despite the urgency pounding through my veins, "this is my responsibility. My extraction, my protection detail."

"Your emotions clouding your judgment," Ethan said quietly, for my ears only.

I stared him down. He was one to talk. "I'm the only one she trusts. If I show up with a team, she'll run."

A tense silence filled the room as the rest of the team watched our standoff. Ethan searched my face, looking for something—weakness, maybe, or deception. He wouldn't find either. What he would find was determination and the absolute certainty that I needed to handle this alone.

After what felt like an eternity, he stepped aside. "Twenty-four hours. Then you check in, or I send the team."

"Understood." I shouldered my bag and headed for the door.

"Take this," Ozzy called, tossing me a secure satellite phone. "It's untraceable. Call when you have her."

I caught the phone and nodded my thanks.

"And Trent," Ethan added as I reached the doorway. "Watch your six."

"Always do, boss." I didn't look back as I strode out the door, my mind already calculating routes, contingencies, extraction points.

Whoever had used Evelyn's name at that auction had made a fatal mistake. They'd revealed they knew about her, but they didn't know about me. They didn't know what I was capable of when someone I'd sworn to protect was threatened.

If they were coming for Evelyn... they'd have to go through me first.

———

Trent made a promise. Now it's time to keep it.

If you're ready for a fiercely protective operative, a mother with everything to lose, and a high-stakes rescue that could tear them apart—or bind them together forever—don't miss the next explosive Edge Ops novel.

Preorder Edge of Control now.

Want exclusive bonus scenes and sneak peeks? <u>Sign up for my newsletter</u> and get behind-the-scenes access before anyone else.

ALSO BY TONYA BURROWS

Loved this book? There's more where that came from!

My world is filled with explosive tension, swoony chaos, and emotionally messy heroes who'll risk everything for the ones they love.

Edge Ops

Edge of Control

Valor Ridge

Finding His Redemption

Redwood Coast Rescue

Searching for Rescue

Searching for Risk

Searching for Justice

Searching for Redemption

Searching for Shadows

Searching for Hope

Searching Blind

Searching for Secrets

Searching for Valor

<u>Northern Rescue</u>

Northern Escape

Northern Deception

Northern Salvation

<u>HORNET</u>

SEAL of Honor

Honor Reclaimed

Broken Honor

Code of Honor

Reckless Honor

Honor Avenged

<u>HORNET: Class Alpha</u>

Fragmented Loyalty

<u>Wilde Security</u>

Wilde Nights in Paradise

Wilde for Her

Wilde at Heart

Running Wilde

Too Wilde to Tame

Wilde Security Worldwide

A Wilde Christmas

Wilde & Deadly

Wilde & Untamed

Your next book boyfriend is waiting

(broodingly, probably shirtless)

at www.tonyaburrows.com